Travel in time writer. . . .

FORWARD

. . . . to the era when bodysnatching and graverobbing have been legalized by the government.

. . . . to the time when a flying saucer actually visits the earth with the most unpredictable results.

BACKWARD

. . . . to the day when a hypnotist keeps an appointment with a mad King of England.

. . . . to the moment when an early model camera takes on the terrifying power of destroying whatever it photographs.

Avram Davidson, recently appointed editor of *The Magazine of Science-Fiction and Fantasy*, winner of S-F's Hugo Award, and the Mystery Writers' of America Award for the best short story of 1961, is a writer like no other, a completely original voice—and this is his first published book.

OR ALL THE SEAS WITH OYSTERS

Avram Davidson

A BERKLEY MEDALLION BOOK
published by
BERKLEY PUBLISHING CORPORATION

ACKNOWLEDGMENTS

The following stories are reprinted from *The Magazine of Fantasy and Science Fiction*, copyright © 1954, 1955, 1956, 1957, 1958, 1959, 1960, by Mercury Press, Inc.: "Up the Close and Doun the Stair," "The Grantha Sighting," "The Sixth Season," "Negra Sum," "Or the Grasses Grow," "My Boy Friend's Name is Jello," "The Golem," "Summerland," "King's Evil," "Great is Diana," "I Do Not Hear You, Sir," "Author, Author," "Dagon," "The Montavarde Camera," and "The Woman Who Thought She Could Read."

The story "Let Us Sleep" is reprinted from *Venture*, copyright © 1957, by Mercury Press, Inc.

The following stories are reprinted from *Galaxy*, copyright © 1957, 1958, by Galaxy Publishing Corporation: "Or All the Seas with Oysters" and "Help!"

BERKLEY MEDALLION BOOKS are published by
Berkley Publishing Corporation
15 East 26th Street, New York 10, New York

Printed in the United States of America

CONTENTS

OR ALL THE SEAS WITH OYSTERS

WHEN THE MAN CAME IN TO THE F & O BIKE SHOP, OSCAR greeted him with a hearty "Hi, there!" Then, as he looked closer at the middle-aged visitor with the eyeglasses and business suit, his forehead creased and he began to snap his thick fingers.

"Oh, say, I know you," he muttered. "Mr.—um—name's on the tip of my tongue, doggone it . . ." Oscar was a barrel-chested fellow. He had orange hair.

"Why, sure you do," the man said. There was a Lion's emblem in his lapel. "Remember, you sold me a girl's bicycle with gears, for my daughter? We got to talking about that red French racing bike your partner was working on . . ."

Oscar slapped his big hand down on the cash register. He raised his head and rolled his eyes up. "Mr. Whatney!" Mr. Whatney beamed. "Oh, *sure*. Gee, how could I forget? And we went across the street afterward and had a couple a beers. Well, how you *been*, Mr. Whatney? I guess the bike—it was an English model, wasn't it? Yeah. It must of given satisfaction or you would of been back, huh?"

Mr. Whatney said the bicycle was fine, just fine. Then he said, "I understand there's been a change, though. You're all by yourself now. Your partner . . ."

Oscar looked down, pushed his lower lip out, nodded. "You heard, huh? Ee-up. I'm all by myself now. Over three months now."

The partnership had come to an end three months ago, but it had been faltering long before then. Ferd liked books, long-playing records and high-level conversation, Oscar liked beer, bowling and women. Any women. Any time.

The shop was located near the park; it did a big trade in renting bicycles to picnickers. If a woman was barely old enough to be *called* a woman, and not quite old enough to be called an *old* woman, or if she was anywhere in between, and if she was alone, Oscar would ask, "How does that machine feel to you? All right?"

"Why . . . I guess so."

Taking another bicycle, Oscar would say, "Well, I'll just ride along a little bit with you, to make sure. Be right back, Ferd." Ferd always nodded gloomily. He knew that Oscar would not be right back. Later, Oscar would say, "Hope you made out in the shop as good as I did in the park."

"Leaving me all alone here all that time," Ferd grumbled.

And Oscar usually flared up. "Okay, then, next time *you* go and leave *me* stay here. See if I begrudge you a little fun." But he knew, of course, that Ferd—tall, thin, pop-eyed Ferd—would never go. "Do you good," Oscar said, slapping his sternum. "Put hair on your chest."

Ferd muttered that he had all the hair on his chest that he needed. He would glance down covertly at his lower arms; they were thick with long black hair, though his upper arms were slick and white. It was already like that when he was in high school, and some of the others would laugh at him—call him "Ferdie the Birdie." They knew it bothered him, but they did it anyway. How was it possible—he wondered then; he still did now—for people deliberately to hurt someone else who hadn't hurt them? How was it possible?

He worried over other things. All the time.

"The Communists—" He shook his head over the newspaper. Oscar offered an advice about the Communists in two short words. Or it might be capital punishment. "Oh, what a terrible thing if an innocent man was to be executed," Ferd moaned. Oscar said that was the guy's tough luck.

"Hand me that tire-iron," Oscar said.

And Ferd worried even about other people's minor concerns. Like the time the couple came in with the tandem and the baby-basket on it. Free air was all they took; then the woman decided to change the diaper and one of the safety pins broke.

"Why are there never any safety pins?" the woman fretted, rummaging here and rummaging there. "There are *never* any safety pins."

Ferd made sympathetic noises, went to see if he had any; but, though he was sure there'd been some in the office, he couldn't find them. So they drove off with one side of the diaper tied in a clumsy knot.

At lunch, Ferd said it was too bad about the safety pins. Oscar dug his teeth into a sandwich, tugged, tore, chewed, swallowed. Ferd liked to experiment with sandwich spreads

—the one he liked most was cream-cheese, olives, anchovy and avocado, mashed up with a little mayonnaise—but Oscar always had the same pink luncheon-meat.

"It must be difficult with a baby." Ferd nibbled. "Not just traveling, but raising it."

Oscar said, "Jeez, there's drugstores in every block, and if you can't read, you can at least reckernize them."

"Drugstores? Oh, to buy safety pins, you mean."

"Yeah. Safety pins."

"But . . . you know . . . it's true . . . there's never any safety pins when you look."

Oscar uncapped his beer, rinsed the first mouthful around. "Aha! Always plenny of clothes hangers, though. Throw 'em out every month, next month same closet's full of 'm again. Now whatcha wanna do in your spare time, you invent a device which it'll make safety pins outa clothes hangers."

Ferd nodded abstractedly. "But in my spare time I'm working on the French racer . . ." It was a beautiful machine, light, low-slung, swift, red and shining. You felt like a bird when you rode it. But, good as it was, Ferd knew he could make it better. He showed it to everybody who came in the place until his interest slackened.

Nature was his latest hobby, or, rather, reading about Nature. Some kids had wandered by from the park one day with tin cans in which they had put salamanders and toads, and they proudly showed them to Ferd. After that, the work on the red racer slowed down and he spent his spare time on natural history books.

"Mimicry!" he cried to Oscar. "A wonderful thing!"

Oscar looked up interestedly from the bowling scores in the paper. "I seen Edie Adams on TV the other night, doing her imitation of Marilyn Monroe. Boy, oh, boy."

Ferd was irritated, shook his head. "Not that kind of mimicry. I mean how insects and arachnids will mimic the shapes of leaves and twigs and so on, to escape being eaten by birds or other insects and arachnids."

A scowl of disbelief passed over Oscar's heavy face. "You mean they change their *shapes?* What you giving me?"

"Oh, it's true. Sometimes the mimicry is for aggressive purposes, though—like a South African turtle that looks like a rock and so the fish swim up to it and then it catches them. Or that spider in Sumatra. When it lies on its back, it looks like a bird dropping. Catches butterflies that way."

Oscar laughed, a disgusted and incredulous noise. It died away as he turned back to the bowling scores. One hand groped at his pocket, came away, scratched absently at the orange thicket under the shirt, then went patting his hip pocket.

"Where's that pencil?" he muttered, got up, stomped into the office, pulled open drawers. His loud cry of "Hey!" brought Ferd into the tiny room.

"What's the matter?" Ferd asked.

Oscar pointed to a drawer. "Remember that time you claimed there were no safety pins here? Look—whole gah-damn drawer is full of 'em."

Ferd stared, scratched his head, said feebly that he was certain he'd looked there before . . .

A contralto voice from outside asked, "Anybody here?"

Oscar at once forgot the desk and its contents, called, "Be right with you," and was gone. Ferd followed him slowly.

There was a young woman in the shop, a rather massively built young woman, with muscular calves and a deep chest. She was pointing out the seat of her bicycle to Oscar, who was saying "Uh-huh" and looking more at her than at anything else. "It's just a little too far forward ("Uh-huh"), as you can see. A wrench is all I need ("Uh-huh"). It was silly of me to forget my tools."

Oscar repeated, "Uh-huh" automatically, then snapped to. "Fix it in a jiffy," he said, and—despite her insistence that she could do it herself—he did fix it. Though not quite in a jiffy. He refused money. He prolonged the conversation as long as he could.

"Well, thank *you,*" the young woman said. "And now I've got to go."

"That machine feel all right to you now?"

"Perfectly. Thanks—"

"Tell you what, I'll just ride along with you a little bit, just—"

Pear-shaped notes of laughter lifted the young woman's bosom. "Oh, you couldn't keep up with me! My machine is a *racer!*"

The moment he saw Oscar's eye flit to the corner, Ferd knew what he had in mind. He stepped forward. His cry of "No" was drowned out by his partner's loud, "Well, I guess this racer here can keep up with yours!"

The young woman giggled richly, said, well, they would see about that, and was off. Oscar, ignoring Ferd's outstretched hand, jumped on the French bike and was gone. Ferd stood in the doorway, watching the two figures, hunched over their handlebars, vanish down the road into the park. He went slowly back inside.

It was almost evening before Oscar returned, sweaty but smiling. Smiling broadly. "Hey, what a babe!" he cried. He wagged his head, he whistled, he made gestures, noises like escaping steam. "Boy, oh, boy, what an afternoon!"

"Give me the bike," Ferd demanded.

Oscar said, yeah, sure; turned it over to him and went to wash. Ferd looked at the machine. The red enamel was covered with dust; there was mud spattered and dirt and bits of dried grass. It seemed soiled—degraded. He had felt like a swift bird when he rode it . . .

Oscar came out wet and beaming. He gave a cry of dismay, ran over.

"Stand away," said Ferd, gesturing with the knife. He slashed the tires, the seat and seat cover, again and again.

"You crazy?" Oscar yelled. "You outa your mind? Ferd, no, don't, Ferd—"

Ferd cut the spokes, bent them, twisted them. He took the heaviest hammer and pounded the frame into shapelessness, and then he kept on pounding till his breath was gasping.

"You're not only crazy," Oscar said bitterly, "you're rotten jealous. You can go to hell." He stomped away.

Ferd, feeling sick and stiff, locked up, went slowly home. He had no taste for reading, turned out the light and fell into bed, where he lay awake for hours, listening to the rustling noises of the night and thinking hot, twisted thoughts.

They didn't speak to each other for days after that, except for the necessities of the work. The wreckage of the French racer lay behind the shop. For about two weeks, neither wanted to go out back where he'd have to see it.

One morning Ferd arrived to be greeted by his partner, who began to shake his head in astonishment even before he started speaking. "How did you *do* it, how did you *do* it, Ferd? Jeez, what a beautiful job—I gotta hand it to you—no more hard feelings, huh, Ferd?"

Ferd took his hand. "Sure, sure. But what are you talking about?"

Oscar led him out back. There was the red racer, all in one piece, not a mark or scratch on it, its enamel bright as ever. Ferd gaped. He squatted down and examined it. It *was* his machine. Every change, every improvement he had made, was there.

He straightened up slowly. "Regeneration . . ."

"Huh? What say?" Oscar asked. Then, "Hey, kiddo, you're all white. Whad you do, stay up all night and didn't get no sleep? Come on in and siddown. But I still don't see how you done it."

Inside, Ferd sat down. He wet his lips. He said, "Oscar —listen—"

"Yeah?"

"Oscar. You know what regeneration is? No? Listen. Some kinds of lizards, you grab them by the tail, the tail breaks off and they grow a new one. If a lobster loses a claw, it regenerates another one. Some kinds of worms—and hydras and starfish—you cut them into pieces, each piece will grow back the missing parts. Salamanders can regenerate lost hands, and frogs can grow legs back."

"No kidding, Ferd. But, uh, I mean: Nature. Very interesting. But to get back to the bike now—how'd you manage to fix it so good?"

"I never touched it. It regenerated. Like a newt. Or a lobster."

Oscar considered this. He lowered his head, looked up at Ferd from under his eyebrows. "Well, now, Ferd . . . Look . . . How come all broke bikes don't do that?"

"This isn't an ordinary bike. I mean it isn't a real bike." Catching Oscar's look, he shouted, "Well, it's *true!*"

The shout changed Oscar's attitude from bafflement to incredulity. He got up. "So for the sake of argument, let's say all that stuff about the bugs and the eels or whatever the hell you were talking about is true. But they're alive. A bike ain't." He looked down triumphantly.

Ferd shook his leg from side to side, looked at it. "A crystal isn't, either, but a broken crystal can regenerate itself if the conditions are right. Oscar, go see if the safety pins are still in the desk. Please, Oscar?"

He listened as Oscar, muttering, pulled the desk drawers out, rummaged in them, slammed them shut, tramped back.

"Naa," he said. "All gone. Like that lady said that time, and you said, there never are any safety pins when you want 'em. They disap—Ferd? What're—"

Ferd jerked open the closet door, jumped back as a shoal of clothes hangers clattered out.

"And like *you* say," Ferd said with a twist of his mouth, "on the other hand, there are always plenty of clothes hangers. There weren't any here before."

Oscar shrugged. "I don't see what you're getting at. But anybody could of got in here and took the pins and left the hangers. *I* could of—but I didn't. Or *you* could of. Maybe—" He narrowed his eyes. "Maybe you walked in your sleep and done it. You better see a doctor. Jeez, you look rotten."

Ferd went back and sat down, put his head in his hands. "I feel rotten. I'm scared, Oscar. Scared of what?" He breathed noisily. "I'll tell you. Like I explained before, about how things that live in the wild places, they mimic other things there. Twigs, leaves . . . toads that look like rocks. Well, suppose there are . . . things . . . that live in people places. Cities. Houses. These things could imitate—well, other kinds of things you find in people places—"

"*People* places, for crise sake!"

"Maybe they're a different kind of life-form. Maybe they get their nourishment out of the elements in the air. You know what safety pins *are*—these other kinds of them? Oscar, the safety pins are the pupa-forms and then they, like, *hatch*. Into the larval-forms. Which look just like coat hangers. They feel like them, even, but they're not. Oscar, they're not, not really, not really, not . . ."

He began to cry into his hands. Oscar looked at him. He shook his head.

After a minute, Ferd controlled himself somewhat. He snuffled. "All these bicycles the cops find, and they hold them waiting for owners to show up, and then we buy them at the sale because no owners show up because there aren't any, and the same with the ones the kids are always trying to sell us, and they say they just found them, and they really did because they were never made in a factory. They grew. They grow. You smash them and throw them away, they regenerate."

Oscar turned to someone who wasn't there and waggled his head. "Hoo, boy," he said. Then, to Ferd: "You mean one day there's a safety pin and the next day instead there's a coat hanger?"

Ferd said, "One day there's a cocoon; the next day there's a moth. One day there's an egg; the next day there's a chicken. But with . . . these it doesn't happen in the open daytime where you can see it. But at night, Oscar—at night you can *hear* it happening. All the little noises in the night-time, Oscar—"

Oscar said, "Then how come we ain't up to our belly-button in bikes? If I had a bike for every coat hanger—"

But Ferd had considered that, too. If every codfish egg, he explained, or every oyster spawn grew to maturity, a man could walk across the ocean on the backs of all the codfish or oysters there'd be. So many died, so many were eaten by predatory creatures, that Nature had to produce a maximum in order to allow a minimum to arrive at maturity. And Oscar's question was: then who, uh, eats the, uh, coat hangers?

Ferd's eyes focused through wall, buildings, park, more buildings, to the horizon. "You got to get the picture. I'm not talking about real pins or hangers. I got a name for the others—'false friends,' I call them. In high school French, we had to watch out for French words that looked like English words, but really were different. *'Faux amis,'* they call them. False friends. Pseudo-pins. Pseudo-hangers . . . Who eats them? I don't know for sure. Pseudo-vacuum cleaners, maybe?"

His partner, with a loud groan, slapped his hands against his thighs. He said, "Ferd, Ferd, for crise sake. You know what's the trouble with you? You talk about oysters, but you forgot what they're good for. You forgot there's two kinds of people in the world. Close up them books, them bug books and French books. Get out, mingle, meet people. Soak up some brew. You know what? The next time Norma—that's this broad's name with the racing bike—the next time she comes here, *you* take the red racer and *you* go out in the woods with her. I won't mind. And I don't think she will, either. Not *too* much."

But Ferd said no. "I never want to touch the red racer again. I'm afraid of it."

At this, Oscar pulled him to his feet, dragged him protestingly out to the back and forced him to get on the French machine. "Only way to conquer your fear of it!"

Ferd started off, white-faced, wobbling. And in a moment was on the ground, rolling and thrashing, screaming.

Oscar pulled him away from the machine.

"It threw me!" Ferd yelled. "It tried to kill me! Look—blood!"

His partner said it was a bump that threw him—it was his own fear. The blood? A broken spoke. Grazed his cheek. And he insisted Ferd get on the bicycle again, to conquer his fear.

But Ferd had grown hysterical. He shouted that no man was safe—that mankind had to be warned. It took Oscar a long time to pacify him and to get him to go home and into bed.

He didn't tell all this to Mr. Whatney, of course. He

merely said that his partner had gotten fed up with the bicycle business.

"It don't pay to worry and try to change the world," he pointed out. "I always say take things the way they are. If you can't lick 'em, join 'em."

Mr. Whatney said that was his philosophy, exactly. He asked how things were, since.

"Well . . . not *too* bad. I'm engaged, you know. Name's Norma. Crazy about bicycles. Everything considered, things aren't bad at all. More work, yes, but I can do things all my own way, so . . .

Mr. Whatney nodded. He glanced around the shop. "I see they're still making drop-frame bikes," he said, "though, with so many women wearing slacks, I wonder they bother."

Oscar said, "Well, I dunno. I kinda like it that way. Ever stop to think that bicycles are like people? I mean, of all the machines in the world, only bikes come male and female."

Mr. Whatney gave a little giggle, said that was *right*, he had never thought of it like that before. Then Oscar asked if Mr. Whatney had anything in particular in mind—not that he wasn't always welcome.

"Well, I wanted to look over what you've got. My boy's birthday is coming up—"

Oscar nodded sagely. "Now here's a job," he said, "which you can't get it in any other place but here. Specialty of the house. Combines the best features of the French racer and the American standard, but it's made right here, and it comes in three models—Junior, Intermediate and Regular. Beautiful, ain't it?"

Mr. Whatney observed that, say, that might be just the ticket. "By the way," he asked, "what's become of the French racer, the red one, used to be here?"

Oscar's face twitched. Then it grew bland and innocent and he leaned over and nudged his customer. "Oh, *that* one. Old Frenchy? Why, I put *him* out to stud!"

And they laughed and they laughed, and after they told a few more stories they concluded the sale, and they had a few beers and they laughed some more. And then they said what a shame it was about poor Ferd, poor old Ferd, who had been found in his own closet with an unraveled coat hanger coiled tightly around his neck.

UP THE CLOSE AND DOUN THE STAIR

Up the close and doun the stair,
But and ben wi' Burke and Hare.
Burke's the butcher, Hare's the thief,
Knox the boy that buys the beef.
—Edinburgh folk rime, 1828

THE INCIDENT AT HAVEN OF REST MEMORIAL PARK HIT THE papers with a bang.

That is, it hit the *Tribune-American* first, and the other papers picked it up from there. The *Trib* was one of the Greiss Chain and it was right up their alley—old Gregory Perkins Greiss was still alive when the M. R. Act was passed, and the chain continued to stir up trouble at every opportunity, prodded from time to time by lavender-scented, lavender-colored notes from Lavinia Griess, the Old Man's widow. *G. P. used to say*—and, *G. P. would have wished*—or, *"This horror-Bill," as G. P. used to call it*—so the notes began. But when the *Trib* got wind of this story it didn't require any prompting from the Dowager Publisher to break it.

Dr. Loren Winslow told the reporters, quite truthfully, that he hadn't had anything to do with Mrs. Hotaling's having signed the contract with the IAM. "*I* signed the death certificate: that was all," he told them. Pressed to make any comments he cared to on the situation in particular or in general, he said that the only comment he cared to make was "No comment."

Big Blue Hotaling was still alive—but just barely—when the neighbors broke down the door. He died while Dr. Winslow was just beginning to examine him. But that preliminary examination was enough. He turned to the widow and the neighbor woman who was comforting her, and said—rather without any attempt at sympathy, for he knew the Hotalings well—"Well I'll be darned. Pneumonia. *Nobody* dies of pneumonia anymore. . . . Leave it to Blue to be different."

There was, however, nothing different about the period just before his unusual death. He came home with a case of booze, kicked Dolly out of the apartment, locked the door and started drinking. He did this about every six weeks. *This* time, however, he got crocked so fast and so thoroughly that he didn't even notice when the oil-burner quit working. Dolly, coming back cautiously on the fourth day of the binge, heard no noise in the apartment—no usual noise, that is, no singing or cursing. Only a curious sort of something or other. She didn't realize at the moment it was the noise Blue made while he was drowning in his own lung-fluid, but it worried her enough to call the neighbors, and so—

"I don't remember the last time I've heard of anyone dying of pneumonia," the physician said.

Dolly looked dry-eyed at the body of her husband (he didn't make a very pretty corpse, but then, he wasn't very pretty when alive, either—now, at least, he was quiet) and tried to cry.

The neighbor (her name was Linny Hart) felt no such obligation. "Well, he went painlessly, dear," she pointed out. Then her eyes narrowed. "Say—doc. If it's so unusual, uh, wouldn't the IAM be interested? Huh, Doc?"

Winslow threw her a quick glance. "I suppose so," he said. "But that's not for me to say."

Linny nodded. "I don't suppose he left you no insurance or anything like that, Dolly? No, I thought not," as Dolly shook her head, silently. "Catch him doing someone else a favor! Well, he done one now, want to or not. *Sure*—I betchu the IAM will be *very* interested."

Dolly protested feebly, "Oh, Linny, I could-int! What Would People *Say?*"

"People don't have ta know," Linny pointed out. "Anyway, it's for their own good. Leave me see if the number is in this phone book here. . . . Unless the Dear Departed let his bill run on too long."

Blue's working companions were by no means as numerous as his drinking companions, but between the two groups, plus neighbors, there were quite a lot of people at the funeral, most of whom had turned in for a few prophylactic drinks before braving the raw cold en route to the crematorium. The minister made his departure as soon as he had shaken hands and murmured to the widow. The coffin slid out of sight. They waited for the flames. There were no flames. One or two of the men started to mutter. They looked at the mortician while the organ played. Then they looked toward the back of the room and growled. Dolly, by this time finally enabled to forget what Life With Big Blue had really been like, was snuffling into a handkerchief just large enough to cover the end of her nose. And the organ music went a note lower and the mortician opened the doors and indicated, with a glance at the people in the front row and a slight lift of his eyebrows, that the show was over and would they please file out and go away.

Fat Sol Feinstein stalked over and faced up to him.

"What's going on?" he asked, trying to reduce his hoarse rumble to a whisper.

"Why, ah, the services are over, sir," the mortician said, unhappily.

"Listen!" Sol twisted around, looked apologetically towards Dolly, swiveled back to the embalmer's flunkey. "Whaddaya mean: Over? Hah? How come no cremation, hah? Whaddaya tryin a pull?" He was joined by Fingers Feeney, Ugly Urquhart, and a few others.

"Gentlemen, gentlemen, *please.* I thought you knew, for Heaven's sake," the undertaker wound up. "This is a Reversion case. The actual cremation will take place—ah—'afterward' . . . No scene, please, gentlemen?"

The men turned red. "See? Whad I tell ya?" Sol demanded. "Whad I tell ya?" He took the attendant mortician's lapels in his large hands. "Listen: *We* knew the Deceased. See? And we *know* he never signed no——Reversion. *He* told us plenty often what he thought of it. So don't try and pull no—" He turned again, as the unhappy undertaker's eyes went past him, and he glared at the man who had come up from the back of the room. The man was as large and tough-looking as any of them, but it was a smooth toughness. His clothes were conservative—solid reds and purples, instead of the gay figured designs most of the men had on—closer to the fashions of the late '70s than to the present.

He spoke in a low, patient voice, as if this was an everyday matter with him—as, indeed, it probably was. "The Right of Reversion Contract was signed by the widow," the man said.

Feeney swore. "I tole ya the minute I walked in, dinn I?" he yelled. "I can smell 'em, I can smell 'em a mile away! He's one a them lousy Burke and Hares!"

The IAM man took a piece of paper from his pocket, ignoring the growls and oaths. "This is a photostat of the contract, signed by Mrs. Dora Hotaling . . ." Dolly shrank down in the chair as she heard her name. She glanced at Linny Hart, who sat next to her. Linny said, in a low, swift whisper, "Don't panic. Leave it to me." Linny jumped up, bustled over. "Leave me see that," she demanded. The IAM man held it out to her. Linny put on a fine performance. Her mouth dropped lower and lower, her eyebrows crept higher and higher, as she scanned the photostat. Then she put her palms to the sides of her face and screamed.

"Oh, please," begged the attendant. "Please, my dear madam—" Urquhart dragged him back.

"So *that's* what it was!" Linny shrieked. "Ooo, you bunch of rotten liars! Oh, you terrible—She thought it was for the insurance! I was there! The man came up and said it was for Blue's insurance. She *never* would of—she'd rather cut off her right hand than—*Oh,* what an awful thing! Oh, poor Dolly!"

As Dolly, really scared now, began to cry, Ugly Urquhart grabbed the mortician. "Where's the body?" he demanded. The others took up the cry, elbowing closer.

It was the IAM man who answered. "It's been removed," he said, "according to the terms of the contract. Following research—"

Fat Sol cried, "You gahdamn *ghoul!*" swung at him, missed.

"—the remains will be cremated and properly interred. I have to remind you"—he raised his voice over the shouts—"that interference with the fulfillment of this contract constitutes a Federal offense under the Medical Research Act of—" Sol swung again. This time he didn't miss. Dolly began to scream. The attendant, unnoticed, scuttled away. Linny pressed her lips together, looked on with satisfaction.

The *Tribune-American* put it on page one, and within an hour it was unfolding from the press-slot of every 3-D set in the greater metropolitan area (a triangle reaching from Atlantic City to Poughkeepsie to Hartford).

> THE SHAME OF AMERICA
> Bluford Hotaling (or "Big Blue" as his many friends affectionately called him) was not a rich man. He wasn't a very healthy man, either. If he had lived in a house heated by a fission-pile (as does Dr. Theodore Treyer) he would never have died of pneumonia brought on by cold when the old-fashioned oil-burner in his own house broke down. And because he was neither healthy nor wealthy, the shameless agents of the Institute for American Medicine, headed by Dr. Theodore Treyer, had little difficulty in conning his grief-stricken widow into signing the infamous Reversion Contract. "It's only a form," these carrion-crows assured her. "Just to see you get your insurance money." Oh, she received money, all right—

Ted Treyer threw down the paper with a sigh. He looked up at his companion and, seeing the expression on her face, smiled.

But Beety Lowndas didn't smile back. "Ted," she asked, her tone troubled as her face. "Ted, is there any chance that the IAM agent who went to see this Mrs. Hotaling . . . I mean, there are so many agents that—the law of averages—"

Ted's smile faded. Beety was wearing the two-tone hair-do currently modish, blond one side, raven-black the other. Full figures were in fashion now once more, after the Maypole Madness (as sociologists were already beginning to call it) had gone out—completely out. Women who were naturally thin wore moldafoam padding. Beety (as Ted was in exceptional position to testify) neither wore nor needed any padding.

"Beety, sweety . . . Sometimes I wonder if you don't disbelieve everything I've ever told you. In which case it's a waste of time to do it again. But I'll try. First: No one can be an IAM agent unless he or she has a graduate degree in law, social work, or science. We don't hire unfrocked house-coppers. Secondly: no agent ever calls unless he's been asked. Thirdly—you haven't mentioned this, but I will, since it's part of the American mythology: there is no quota. Not for the agent, not for the district supervisor, not for anybody. The only thing even faintly resembling a quota is the allotment. And it's been a long, long time since any college has failed to receive its allotment. Fourth: *you* ask it."

By now he had recovered his usual high level of spirit. He was dark and his gold-flecked suit showed off his athletic build to advantage. His doctorate was in science, but not in medicine—in fact, he was one of the first to receive a D.Sc. from his university which was not a merely honorary one, and the university was taking good care that the new D.Sc. didn't go the way of the Ph.D.; but there was hardly an M.D. in the country who didn't defer to him. The Director of the IAM was, in theory, outranked by the President of the AMA, but the latter kept changing. And Treyer was only the second man to hold his office. He'd had it for five years now. He liked it.

Beety suddenly smiled. It was a warm, sweet smile. She was a warm, sweet person. They had been lovers for over a year now, and though Treyer was modern enough to acknowledge her and to see to it that she was invited wherever his wife (if he'd had one) would have been, he wasn't modern enough to accede to her request for a "free-born" child—as the current, sociologically-approved phrase was. He had, of course, shared her pleasure when Justice Blakeney's famous decision was issued recently.

"The concept of illegitimacy of children belongs," the Justice had said, *"to the days of slavery and the killing of witches, not to a society supposedly modern and enlightened. If the free-born child can inherit from the mother, there is no reason why that same child cannot inherit from the father."*

Thinking aloud, Treyer said, "Good man, Blakeney."

Beety leaned over and kissed his forehead—the gesture, by its deliberate avoidance of the conventionally-erotic kiss, indicated nowadays in all sophisticated circles that love was being enjoyed to its fullest extent whenever desired: so why bother with a pale proxy?

"Then how about it, Ted?" she asked. Her hair and skin were like honey.

He grinned. "Unnatural female! Would you have a child by a ghoul?"

"I'm sorry," she said, contritely. "I know you're right. About there being nothing improper in IAM methods, I mean. I know that . . ." her voice ebbed.

Treyer asked, "What is it, then? Michael and Kevin been sneering?" She nodded. "Oh, why the Hell d'you let those poor sapless twigs bother you? I know you can't help meeting them—and others like them—in the interior decorating business. But surely you can see that the wretched fellows will sneer at anyone who is capable of a love which they're denied?"

Her bright dark eyes ceased wandering around the office—it had been decorated before she'd even *met* Ted Treyer, let alone become his mistress, but it was such a perfectly-appointed room she'd never wanted to change it—and rested on him. "It isn't just Michael and Kevin," she said, slowly. "It's everybody. I want everybody to give you the respect and the honor you deserve. I want papers like the *Tribune-American* to stop sniping at you. I want the cheap comedians to stop being able to get a laugh just by asking, 'Is Dr. Treyer in the house?' I want . . . oh—" She made a gesture of despair.

Ted didn't smile. "I'll get it, someday—everything you want. I'm young and healthy and expect to live a long time. And I will certainly live to see all our critics dead or converted." He gestured to the left wall, the gold-plashed sleeve falling back from his golden-brown arm. "Have you ever wondered why I have a picture of—of all *possible* people—the Reverend Cotton Mather? You know what a terrible old man he was, a devil-in-robes. When he said the witches in Salem should be put to death, he was cheered. And when he—somehow, from somewhere—got a correct idea in his hard old head, and urged inoculation against smallpox, why, the ones who'd cheered him a little while before, they threw rocks at his manse and smashed all the windows.

"I keep it as a lesson. If I were to go out this minute and preach that . . . oh"—he groped for words—"that all red-headed Swedes, let's say, have inferior genes, and shouldn't be allowed to marry, or should be interned, every yahoo and gutter gorilla who curses me now would stand up and cheer."

She nodded, rather sadly. The recorded peal of bells, which had replaced the harsh ring on all but the most old-fashioned phones, sounded their silvery tones. With a swift "Excuse me," Treyer switched on. A fat, furious face filled the screen.

"*Doc*-tor Treyer!" The face lit up with enraged glee, the voice grated out its heavy sarcasm. "Or should I say Doctor Knox? Or Mister Boik? Or Mister Hare?"

Treyer clicked his tongue. "What the devil—" He diddled the switch. No calls like this were supposed to get through to him, but there was a new girl at the Intake, and—the face flickered, but remained. Treyer gave up. "All right. What do you want?"

"We want Blue Hotaling's body—that's what we want. We're gunna swear out a injunction, see. You better not move him to none of your gahdamn vet schools in the meanwhile, see? He wasn't rich"—the face had evidently read the frontpage *Trib* editorial—"but he's got lotsa friends. So—" Treyer diddled the switch again, this time the face and voice vanished, were replaced by the apologetic Intake operator. Treyer muttered that it was all right, switched off.

He walked over and put his arms on Beety's shoulders. "You see? You and I can take it. But suppose we *did* have a child? Everytime some other child would quarrel with him, they'd throw it in his face: 'Your old man is a grave-robber.' Don't you *know* that?" She said not a word, but looked at him with sorrow deep in her eyes. He leaned closer, pressed his lips to her forehead.

In the kaleidoscope of colors the black robes of Judge Mountree drew every eye. There was talk, from time to time —shop talk, never making the public media—that the American judiciary was going to abandon black for scarlet. But if this imitaton of judgely garb in other countries was planned, it had yet to take place. Aside from the robe there was nothing unusual about Mountree's appearance. He listened attentively—or, at any rate, with every appearance of attention—to the lawyers.

MacKenna, for the IAM, wearing the blue with golden sunbursts which was almost his trademark, said that he was going to trace the background of the case before them. "Although it is the same background which I have traced for several hundred similar cases," he said, "the continued appearance of similar cases indicates that memory is short and requires continual refreshment. So—with your honor's indulgence . . ."

At the time the science of anatomy and of post-mortem section was first beginning its development [MacKenna said], the only source of bodies for the purpose of instruction was the gallows. The supply of executed criminals not being sufficient, a certain member of the medical profession in another country—Dr. Knox of Scotland, to be precise—prompted by a zeal which caused him to transgress the too-rigid laws of the time, contracted with a pair of ne'er-do-wells to purchase from them bodies taken clandestinely from graveyards. These two Resurrection Men, as they were then, with a rather grisly and irreverent humor, called, finding the physical labor of redigging graves and lifting out the heavy coffins . . .

(Dolly Hotaling, wearing a chic mourning-gown of pink and purple, gave a dying-fall groan and went stiff. Commotion in court. Dolly carried out. Order restored. MacKenna, still bland and benign and pink of face, continued.)

. . . began to murder such poor and friendless folk as fortune sent their way. They sold the bodies to Dr. Knox for his anatomy classes. Their discovery, the conviction and execution of one of them, the other having saved his life by giving evidence for the Crown—all these dreadful events produced a change in attitudes. Thereafter, both in Great Britain and the United States, the laws were altered so as to allow the bodies of those who died with none to claim their last remains—to allow these bodies to be assigned to medical schools for scientific purposes. This method sufficed for well over a century—for almost a century and a half.

But then it seemed that, in one way at least, science had outdistanced itself. It had drawn on the bodies of paupers, vagrants—people of that unfortunate class. The homeless, those without family or estate. We could well be proud that the advance of the American Economy—the American Way of Life—the progress of our social therapies on every front—had more or less completely eliminated this source. Source of—ah—*subjects*—for post-mortem sections. This posed a considerable problem. It affected not only the medical schools, but every living American—particularly if he wished to remain a *living* American. How could the science of anatomy—of surgery—be taught without proper subjects?

The various medical schools, together with the American Medical Association, met and, with admirable foresight, drew up the historical "Preliminary Agreement on Research Rights." The rest we all know. The only way that a person may now legally dispose of post humous rights in his or her own body is through the Institute for American Medicine, chartered by Congress for this very purpose. A very sizeable sum of money is paid—although the amount, of course, varies according to the age and general physical condition of the legator—and the fingerprints are recorded in the great central file in Washington. I may add, since it applies specifically to this case we are now considering, that it is also legally impossible for a next-of-kin to dispose of research rights in the body of a loved one, except to the IAM.

The Congress has supplied the necessary implimentive legislation, in the Medical Research Act. It is mandatory for the fingerprints of every person who dies to be checked via telephoto with the great central files. If Reversion in the body was sold, the body must be turned over to the IAM. No sale can ever be canceled or invalidated.

I think all right-thinking Americans will agree that the IAM performs its great public service with superb tact and efficiency. Funeral services according to all denominational usages are allowed before possession is taken of the body, and time is even allotted for additional ceremonies in case the legator had belonged to a fraternal organization with which funerary pomps are customary. Following the completion of the period of educational usefulness, the remains are then cremated—except in the case of Orthodox Jews and Roman Catholics, where burial is respectfully granted—and the ashes are returned for disposal according to the desires of the next-of-kin; or else they are placed without extra charge in the various regional columbaria.

The results are as follows: First, that medical science is enabled properly to educate its students. Second, that rivalry in purchase of bodies or of Reversional Research Rights in bodies has been completely eliminated. A fair allocation is made among all the medical schools of the country. Third, that the unsavory black market in post-mortem subjects, which flourished briefly before the passage of the Medical Research Act, has been completely eliminated. It is now several years since it was last found necessary to prosecute a so-called "Body Broker." It *is* still, alas, occasionally necessary to act to prevent clandestine burials, particularly on the part of certain obdurate religious groups, but we are confident that the passing of time and the inevitable spread of public enlightenment will see the end of this before very long.

Now, the facts in the case of the late Bluford Hotaling are quite clear. His widow, Mrs. Dora—or "Dolly"—Hotaling, or someone acting for her, called the regional office of the IAM and requested an agent. The agent was sent, you will hear his testimony, and will be able to satisfy yourself that neither guile nor duress was used in obtaining Mrs. Hotaling's signature. There is, therefore, no grounds at all for granting an injunction to interfere with a process sanctioned by law, and essential to the physical well-being of the great American people.

While Ted Treyer listened to MacKenna he kept rubbing the bruised place on his forehead. He felt almost no pain, having gotten medical care almost at once. But he continued to rub it. He scowled, thinking of what had happened.

It was only a block from the IAM Building. The moving-overhead was being repaired and it was necessary to hold up traffic to allow pedestrians to walk across the street. Three hulking men—housewreckers or piano-movers, by the looks of them—came clumping down the escalator from the m-o. Treyer had a few theories about people who *walked* on escalators—probably these three even walked on the m-o—they were unadjustable, they . . . but before he could consider the theories, they spotted him. One of them was the fellow who'd called him at the office. His eyes went wide with recognition.

"There's that sonofabitchbastard!" he yelled. "He's tryin a make a gedaway!"

And they swarmed up to his car, shouting, "Ya —— Boikenhare! Ya gahdamn ghoul! Graverobba!" Treyer tried simultaneously to roll up the shatterproof bubble and to dial Emergency on the dashboard, but in trying to do both he failed to do either well. The bubble went part way up and stopped, and the dial went red, showing he'd botched the call.

"Doctuh T'eadaw Body-snatchin Treyer!" the three gorillas howled, boosting one of their number up to climb over the stalled bubble. "You pulled ya last doidy trick—you ain't cheatin no maw gahdamn widows!"

They shrieked for his blood while other pedestrians called out their approval and those riding in the other stalled cars either sat scowling at him or joined the chorus.

"That's Treyer," he heard one well-groomed woman say. "You know—that awful person who—"

"Must've got some poor widow to sign when she didn't know what she was doing—drugged her, maybe—and I guess those are the dead woman's sons—"

"Go on—give it to him good! The dirty Burke and Hare!"

And the lead gorilla, standing on the shoulders of his sweating companions, leaned far forward and struck at Treyer with his huge fist. Ted fell back. He was fumbling in the compartment for his gun (thinking, all the while, *This will be a lovely scandal, if I shoot the sod!*) when the bubble suddenly sprang up, dumping the housewrecker and his friends into the street. Traffic cleared a split second later, and he sped away.

He'd been insulted before, of course, and once, in the slums of Madison Avenue (the advertising business had long since moved up to Pleasantville), he'd had a bag of garbage dropped on him from a window. But this was the first time a direct bodily attack had ever been made on him. He shivered, rubbed his forehead.

The lawyer for the Housewrecker's Union (or whatever organization it was which was fronting for Hotaling's friends) was a ruddy-faced man in eggshell-and-green. Treyer had never seen him before. He painted the domestic life of Big Blue and Dolly in such terms that the latter found herself (now that she was back in the courtroom, with a cup of water in one hand and a hankie in another) weeping steadily. It wasn't true, of course, but it ought to have been. She wept for the happy life Mr. Anger described, a life she'd never had.

There she sat, weeping then as she is weeping now [Anger chanted]—the body of her faithful, hardworking husband barely cold. There is a ring at the door—a harsh, old-fashioned ring, for the Hotalings, unlike Dr. Theodor Treyer, do not live in a luxurious modern apartment with a 3D screen to announce callers with its rich and melodious peal of bells. The poor widow, of course, is too broken with grief to answer it. This task is done for her by a neighbor, Mrs.

Linny Hart. In walks—or perhaps I *should* say, in *crawls*—a strange man. *We* know who it was. *She*—at that most dreadful moment—did not. How did he know that the Dark Angel had just been a-calling in this humble apartment? Doubtless he has his methods. Doubtless the vultures know when to swoop—and the hyenas—and the jackals.

From what loathsome bit of chicanery did this agent come? Had he gotten the trembling signature of some drink-sodden wretch on his wicked contract? Had he slipped gold into the hand of some callow college-boy? Had he found, had he smelled out, let us say, some unhappy young wife or husband who had lost the paycheck or the housekeeping money in a gambling den—the proprietor of which doubtless works hand-in-filthy-hand with such agents? No matter. The tale, whatever it was, cannot be any but an evil one.

Into the house of grief and sorrow comes the IAM man, his eyes quick to note the signs of honest poverty—for I say that poverty *does* still exist, despite my learned colleague's ingenuous disclaimer to the contrary. He notes the dazed and anguished expression on poor Dolly's care-worn face. *He even reads her mind!*—no hard task for him, he's done it before.

What *is* on her mind? Is she mourning the loss of a breadwinner? Is she worrying how to pay the next month's rent? Oh, no. Oh, no. It is not of her own concerns. *How will I bury him,* is what she thinks of. *How will I get the funds to give him a proper burial.* Instantly the IAM agent whips out his infamous document and presents it to the confused widow. *"Insurance,"* he says. *"Sign here. Cash payment."* And innocently, trustingly—she signs. Imagine, then, the scene at the Haven of Rest Memorial Park Chapel: imagine the widow's shock, her fright, her terror—on finding out that the so-called "Insurance" paper was in reality a Reversion Contract, and that [he half-turned towards the widow, and then ostentatiously lowered his voice] his body, before it can be committed to the clean fires, will be made the plaything of medical students.

Your Honor will recall the decision of New Jersey Chief Justice Arthur Vanderbilt in 1957 when a large corporation applied for the disinterment of a body. The corporation sought to perform an autopsy in order to question the decision in a workman's compensation case. The learned Chief Justice said: *"In the search for the truth we must not disregard the problems of religion, the wishes of the decedent, the sensitiveness of loved ones and friends or even the elements of public health and welfare. The law, then, will not reach into the grave in search of 'the facts' except in the rarest of cases, and not even then unless it is clearly necessary, and there is reasonable probability that such a violation of the sepulcher will establish what is sought."*

In a number of cases, decades later, this decision was cited to prevent the IAM from taking possession of bodies, and it was ruled that in such cases the IAM could sue for the return of whatever moneys it had paid for Rights of Research and Reversion in and of the bodies in question.

Later, of course, Mr. Justice Blakeney—who has lately gained more fame for another judicial opinion—overruled these decisions, ruled in favor of the IAM. He said, "the elements of public health and welfare" required that the IAM be upheld. He did *not* inquire—but we do now—why it is that not a single member of the medical profession has, in the last ten years, signed an IAM Contract. Why not? Is it because they know it is unnecessary? Or is it simply because they do not need the money? Is it only the bodies of the *poor* which are to be rifled from the tomb? This is "class legislation" at its wickedest!

Another aspect of the matter is the obdurate refusal of the IAM to permit the importation of cadavers. Unprejudiced experts have testified that enough such cadavers are and always will be available to make unnecessary the signing of an R. & R. Contract by a single American. But Dr. Treyer will not allow it. He sits pat on Article XXIII of his charter —the one known universally as the No Foreign Corpse Clause. One would have thought that chauvinism was absent from the scientific mind. Either one is wrong—or Dr. Treyer's is not a scientific mind.

We ask your honor to grant an injunction preventing the IAM from disposing of the body of the late Bluford Hotaling until a higher court shall decree otherwise. In the meanwhile, we intend to press for a decision from such a court declaring the Medical Research Act unconstitutional on the grounds that the right of contract cannot extend into the charnel house, that if there can be no right of property in a living man there can be none in a dead man, and that such contracts—like Restrictive Covenants—while not illegal, are legally unenforceable.

Let us have mercy on the dead. For—in the words of the poet—

Strength fails unto the grave.
Worms have fed on Hector brave.
Dust hath closéd Helen's eye.

I am sick. I must die.
Lord, have . . . mercy . . . upon
. . . us.

There was a long, long silence. Finally, as Judge Mountree cleared his throat, MacKenna leaned over and whispered to Treyer, "Anger has *talent!*"

Treyer whispered, "See if you can get him for *us*."

The Judge said, "Well, the court will take it under advisement. And, in the meanwhile: where is the deceased at present? In the mortuary of the Institute for American Medicine? He had better remain there." And he rustled out.

After that there was the hearing in connection with the scuffle at the funeral. Cases involving the slugging of IAM agents were common enough and usually attracted no particular attention from the communications media. But the Hotaling Case, thanks largely to the Greiss Chain's *Tribune-American*, was front-page, front screen news. The interview with the Associate President in connection with his meeting with the Assistant President on the proposed admission of Tannu-Tuva to the UN was switched to the side screens. Few viewers bothered to arrange their mirrors so as to be able to glance at both.

Treyer and MacKenna pressed their way slowly through the crowded corridor, Ted with his head low to avoid the 3D cameramen. A crew was interviewing someone just ahead of them—a sort of indoor version of the man-in-the-street.

"—guy was tellin me, an this guy he *knows*, see? he was tellin me that the Boikenhares got a quoda, see? they got this quoda an if it ain't filled so they loose their jobs. That's why they hang around the race tracks an the hawsrooms, see, they get these poor slobs which they're down on their luck, an ged um ta sign them lousy contracks."

Although Treyer had heard and read all this a thousand times, it was suddenly too much for him. He shoved forward and thrust his head in between the man and the camera-microphone.

"I want the people to know that this man is lying!" he cried.

"Now, *waida-min*-ute!" the man protested.

The 3D operator brightened. "This is Dr. Theodore Treyer, isn't it? The head of the IAM. Would you care to comment, Doctor—"

"Yes, I'd care to comment! This fellow should be down on his knees thanking me and all of us for the vital and necessary work which we are doing, instead of mouthing these lies. A generation ago he'd have been repeating the old slanders against the Red Cross—that they charged wounded soldiers for blood-transfussions, and so on." The crowd gathered around and began to mutter. Treyer raised his voice.

"In every generation there has to be at least one man who gets the dirty end of the stick, who has to bear the brunt of ignorance and fanaticism and reaction—and it looks like this time it's me. Well, I want you to know that I'm in good company! Men like Galileo—Semmelweiss—Pasteur—" Someone, with a muffled curse, gave him a low, swift punch. He turned and seized the man—or the one he thought was the man—and grappled with him. And then the mob was all around him, and then he went down.

That evening he lay on the divan in his apartment. Beety was across the room, making him a drink. The phone-screen was on and a man who looked like Warren G. Harding was speaking to him. On the floor lay a crumpled copy of the *Tribune-American*, the front page showing Treyer tussling with the man in the corridor. The caption: "GET DOWN ON YOUR KNEES TO ME," SAYS BURKE AND HARE CHIEF.

Dr. Lars P. Dana, the current President of the AMA, had been talking for ten minutes and had begun to repeat himself. "Tact, *tact*, TACT!" bellowed Dr. Dana. "You've got to keep your agents away from funerals. You've got to stop shooting off your mouth to reporters. You've got to stop brawling in public—twice in one day, well, I mean. And on *this* day, too, really."

"What else have I got to do?" Ted asked, softly, but not politely.

Dana's mouth worked. Then he turned red. "Listen here, young man—"

"My ears are ringing from all the listening I've been—"

"The honor and prestige of the medical profession may mean little to you, you're not a member of it, but—"

Ted sat up, wincing. Beety came over and handed him his drink. Dana scowled. "The IAM was headed, if you remember, by a member of the medical profession before I took it over. And a nice hash he made of it, too. Remember? If the AMA is willing to spend a few million on a campaign of public education—"

And so it went, back and forth, like a shuttlecock, until they both grew tired and switched off. Ted lay back and groaned. Then he reached out his arms to Beety. She didn't come. Instead, she asked, slowly, "Ted. Explain something to me."

"Can't I explain to you, *afterwards?*"

She shook her head. "*Why* won't you allow the importation of foreign subjects?"

He sighed. "Because dissecting dead coolies isn't the best possible training for a physician unless he's going to spend his life treating live coolies."

She nodded, but apparently there was something else on her mind. He didn't want to hear it. "It's been a long, weary day, love," he said. "I want you."

It was seldom that he even had to speak of his need or desire for her. She sensed it. But now she stayed where she was. "Ted—" she began again. He went limp, turned away. "Ted, today—this afternoon, I mean—I went with Edith Whitney to the Childs' Hospital Clinic. Her little baby has a clubfoot, and she's all broken up about it."

He said, coldly, still not looking at her, "No reason for emotion. The condition is completely operable."

"Yes, but still . . . Well, anyway, we were talking to a Dr. Kronengold—"

Ted said he knew him. "Trouble-maker," he said.

"Well, he was wonderful to Edith. And he said he was going to show us something, but we weren't to get frightened. A good thing he warned us . . . because I'd have sworn it was a baby's *foot!*"

Treyer muttered, " 'Don't bother to wrap it up: I'll eat it on the way home.' "

Beety smiled, briefly and uncertainly. "But Dr. Kronengold said it wasn't real—he said it was synthetic. Isn't it a funny thing—well, I mean, *curious*—that people will sign over their own bodies, but not those of children?" Treyer grunted. "So it's almost impossible to get subjects for dissection or even noncontractual autopsy—in pediatrics, I mean. But you surely know all that. Well, as a result, Kronengold and a few of his associates—"

"Ginzberg, Felberman, and Cohen," said Treyer, with a peculiar emphasis.

She stared at him. Then she went on, unhappy, but determined. "They've devised these simulacra to help them in their research on crippled children. He says they can duplicate any physical condition."

"At more than half the cost of natural subjects—and at a nice little profit to Drs. Kronengold, Ginzberg, Felberman and Cohen."

Doggedly, Beety went on. "The cost doesn't matter. What

I think *does* matter is that if the AMA will subsidize them in their work, you can get *out* of all this."

Painfully, Treyer swung himself to a sitting position. "The AMA has a fifty-year contract with the IAM," he said, "and I don't intend to release a single day of it. As for 'getting out of all this'—where do you think I could go? I'm notorious. I'm the nation's top ghoul. Mothers scare their children with me. I've stepped on too many toes and bloodied too many noses. There's no place for me except the place I've battled out for myself. Does an ex-whore, once she's gone respectable, hire her ex-pimp? I *can't* 'Get out of all this' —because if I do, the only way I can go is down."

She shook her head. After a minute she said, "But if you *lead* the movement . . . I mean, the public will forget . . ."

He smacked his hand into the divan. "Damn the public I spit on the public! You saw how they handled me today. What are they but oxen? And what is the natural fate of oxen, but the butcher? Who signs my contracts? Not the people who matter. Riffraff, scum, house-wreckers, beanpickers— nobody who matters."

She said, "Everybody matters. . . ." She said, "Then it is just the other way around, isn't it?"

He got to his feet, stretched his lithe, golden-brown body. He said, *"What's* just the other way around?" And he padded across the floor towards her, a crooked grin on his face.

"Don't—" She put out her hand, stiffly. He stopped, puzzled. "I mean, it's just the opposite from the way you've explained it. It isn't the newspapers or the 3D or the mobs who stand in the way of progress. It isn't the ignorant who want to hold the clock back. It's you: Theodore Treyer, Doctor of Science, Director of the Institute for American Medicine. You're the one who represents reaction. You're the king of the castle, with your huge salary and your army of agents who say 'Yes, chief' and your lawyers and your office and your three-level apartment. You'd go right on robbing graves? But you can't say it's for the sake of science any more. You can't hide behind that. . . ."

He took advantage of her engrossment in what she was saying to pad closer. He reached out now, and put his hands on her.

"It isn't so," he said, softly, "And I'll explain to you just how and why. But not now. Later." She relaxed, slowly, in his hands. He drew her to him, unprotesting but cold.

"We'll do it your way," he said.

Her face brightened. But they had different things in mind.

"I'll give you that baby you've been wanting," he said. "Free-born or in wedlock—whichever you prefer."

Suddenly she was standing away from him. Quite a distance away.

She said, "No."

His face grew dark. He swayed, began to move forward. "Why not?" he asked.

"You already said it. I won't have a child by a ghoul."

His head snapped back. She went on, "As long as I thought it was necessary, I could stand for anything. But now that I know it's not science—not medical necessity—but your own greed and ego only—I can't stand for any of it. I shuddered, just then, when you touched me. And whenever I think of the times before—how close I came to bearing your child—I'll shudder again. . . . I'll fight you, you know. You've *got* to lose."

He watched her in silence as she moved towards the door. Then he cried out her name. She turned. "Don't," he said. "Don't." But she said nothing as she went out.

The city, as he looked out from his window, was dark. It was full of people who hated him, feared him—but over whom he had power. "I'll fight!" he cried out to the silent city. "I'll fight! If I fall, I'll fall like Lucifer! If I can't be loved, then let me be hated. I can feed on that, if not on the other—" But then, far below, he heard a car start off. "It's her," he whispered. And he began to weep.

NOW LET US SLEEP

A PINK-SKINNED YOUNG CADET RAN PAST HARPER, LAUGHING and shouting and firing his stungun. The wind veered about, throwing the thick scent of the Yahoos into the faces of the men, who whooped loudly to show their revulsion.

"I got three!" the chicken cadet yelped at Harper. "Did you see me pop those two together? Boy, what a stink they have!"

Harper looked at the sweating kid, muttered, "You don't smell so sweet yourself," but the cadet didn't wait to hear. All the men were running now, running in a ragged semicircle with the intention of driving the Yahoos before them, to hold them at bay at the foot of the gaunt cliff a quarter-mile off.

The Yahoos loped awkwardly over the rough terrain, moaning and grunting grotesquely, their naked bodies bent low. A few hundred feet ahead one of them stumbled and fell, his arms and legs flying out as he hit the ground, twitched, and lay still.

A bald-headed passenger laughed triumphantly, paused to kick the Yahoo, and trotted on. Harper kneeled beside the fallen Primitive, felt for a pulse in the hairy wrist. It seemed slow and feeble, but then, no one actually knew what the normal pulse-beat should be. And—except for Harper—no one seemed to give a damn.

Maybe it was because he was the grandson of Barret Harper, the great naturalist—back on Earth, of course. It seemed as if man could be fond of nature only on the planet of man's origin, whose ways he knew so well. Elsewhere, it was too strange and alien—you subdued it, or you adjusted to it, or you were perhaps even content with it. But you almost never *cared* about the flora or fauna of the new planets. No one had the feeling for living things that an earth-born had.

The men were shouting more loudly now, but Harper didn't lift his head to see why. He put his hand to the shaggy grey chest. The heart was still beating, but very slowly and irregularly. Someone stood beside him.

"He'll come out of it in an hour or so," the voice of the purser said. "Come on—you'll miss all the fun—you should see how they act when they're cornered! They kick out and throw sand and—" he laughed at the thought—"they weep great big tears, and go, *'Oof! Oof!'* "

Harper said, "An ordinary man *would* come out of it in an hour or so. But I think their metabolism is different . . . Look at all the bones lying around."

The purser spat. "Well, don't that prove they're not human, when they won't even bury their dead? . . . *Oh,* oh!—look at that!" He swore.

Harper got to his feet. Cries of dismay and disappointment went up from the men.

"What's wrong?" Harper asked.

The purser pointed. The men had stopped running, were gathering together and gesturing. "Who's the damn fool who planned this drive?" the purser asked, angrily. "He picked the wrong cliff! The damned Yahoos *nest* in that one! Look at them climb, will you—" He took aim, fired the stungun. A figure scrabbling up the side of the rock threw up its arms and fell, bounding from rock to rock until it hit the ground. "*That* one will never come out of it!" the purser said, with satisfaction.

But this was the last casualty. The other Yahoos made their way to safety in the caves and crevices. No one followed them. In those narrow, stinking confines a Yahoo was as good as a man, there was no room to aim a stungun, and the Yahoos had rocks and clubs and their own sharp teeth. The men began straggling back.

"This one a she?" The purser pushed at the body with his foot, let it fall back with an annoyed grunt as soon as he determined its sex. "There'll be Hell to pay in the hold if there's more than two convicts to a she." He shook his head and swore.

Two lighters came skimming down from the big ship to load up.

"Coming back to the launch?" the purser asked. He had a red shiny face. Harper had always thought him a rather decent fellow—before. The purser had no way of knowing what was in Harper's mind; he smiled at him and said, "We might as well get on back, the fun's over now."

Harper came to a sudden decision. "What're the chances of my taking a souvenir back with me? This big fellow, here, for example?"

The purser seemed doubtful. "Well, I dunno, Mr. Harper. We're only supposed to take females aboard, and unload *them* as soon as the convicts are finished with their fun." He leered. Harper, suppressing a strong urge to hit him right in the middle of his apple-red face, put his hand in his pocket. The purser understood, looked away as Harper slipped a bill into the breast pocket of his uniform.

"I guess it can be arranged. See, the Commissioner-General on Selopé III wants one for his private zoo. Tell you what: We'll take one for him and one for you—I'll tell the supercargo it's a spare. But if one croaks, the C-G has to get the other. Okay?"

At Harper's nod the purser took a tag out of his pocket, tied it around the Yahoo's wrist, waved his cap to the lighter as it came near. "Although why anybody'd *want* one of these beats me," he said, cheerfully. "They're dirtier than animals. I mean, a pig or a horse'll use the same corner of the enclosure, but these things'll dirty anywhere. Still, if you *want* one—" He shrugged.

As soon as the lighter had picked up the limp form (the pulse was still fluttering feebly) Harper and the purser went back to the passenger launch. As they made a swift ascent to the big ship the purser gestured to the two lighters. "That's going to be a mighty slow trip *those* two craft will make back up," he remarked.

Harper innocently asked why. The purser chuckled. The coxswain laughed.

"The freight-crewmen want to make their points before the convicts. *That's* why."

The chicken cadet, his face flushed a deeper pink than usual, tried to sound knowing. "How about that, purser? Is it pretty good stuff?"

The other passengers wiped their perspiring faces, leaned forward eagerly. The purser said. "Well, rank has its privileges, but that's one I figure I can do without."

His listeners guffawed, but more than one looked down towards the lighters and then avoided other eyes when he looked back again.

Barnum's Planet (named, as was the custom then, after the skipper who'd first sighted it) was a total waste, economically speaking. It was almost all water and the water supported only a few repulsive-looking species of no discernible value. The only sizable piece of land—known, inevitably, as Barnumland, since no one else coveted the honor—was gaunt and bleak, devoid alike of useful minerals or arable soil. Its ecology seemed dependent on a sort of fly: A creature rather like a lizard ate the flies and the Yahoos ate the lizards. If something died at sea and washed ashore, the Yahoos ate that, too. What the flies ate no one knew, but their larvae ate the Yahoos, dead.

They were small, hairy, stunted creatures whose speech—if speech it was—seemed confined to moans and clicks and grunts. They wore no clothing, made no artifacts, did not know the use of fire. Taken away captive, they soon languished and died. Of all the Primitives discovered by man, they were the most primitive. They might have been left alone on their useless planet to kill lizards with tree branches forever—except for one thing.

Barnum's Planet lay equidistant between Coulter's System and the Selopés, and it was a long, long voyage either way. Passengers grew restless, crews grew mutinous, convicts rebellious. Gradually the practice developed of stopping on Barnum's Planet "to let off steam"—archaic expression, but although the nature of the machinery man used had changed since it was coined, man's nature hadn't.

And, of course, no one *owned* Barnum's Planet, so no one cared what happened there.

Which was just too bad for the Yahoos.

It took some time for Harper to settle the paperwork concerning his "souvenir," but finally he was given a baggage check for "One Yahoo, male, live," and hurried down to the freight deck. He hoped it would be still alive.

Pandemonium met his ears as he stepped out of the elevator. A rhythmical chanting shout came from the convict hold. "Hear that?" one of the duty officers asked him, taking the cargo chit. Harper asked what the men were yelling. "I wouldn't care to use the words," the officer said. He was a paunchy, gray-haired man, one who probably loved to tell his grandchildren about his "adventures." This was one he wouldn't tell them.

"I don't like this part of the detail," the officer went on. "Never did, never will. Those creatures *seem human* to me —stupid as they are. And if they're *not* human," he asked, "then how can we sink low enough to bring their females up for the convicts?"

The lighters grated on the landing. The noise must have penetrated to the convict hold, because all semblance of words vanished from the shouting. It became a mad cry, louder and louder.

"Here's your pet," the gray-haired officer said. "Still out, I see . . . I'll let you have a baggage-carrier. Just give it to a steward when you're done with it." He had to raise his voice to be heard over the frenzied howling from the hold.

The Ship's Surgeon was out having tea at the Captain's Table. The duty medical officer was annoyed. "What, another one? We're not veterinarians, you know . . . Well, wheel him in. My intern is working on the other one . . . *whew!*" He held his nose and hastily left.

The intern, a pale young man with close-cropped dark hair, looked up from the pressure-spray he had just used to give an injection to the specimen Yahoo selected for the Commissioner-General of Selopé III. He smiled faintly.

"Junior will have company, I see . . . Any others?"

Harper shook his head. The intern went on, "This should be interesting. The young one seems to be in shock. I gave him two cc's of anthidar sulfate, and I see I'd better do the same for yours. Then . . . Well, I guess there's still nothing like serum albumen, is there? But you'd better help me strap them down. If they come to, there's a cell back aft we can put them in, until I can get some cages rigged up." He shot the stimulant into the flaccid arm of Harper's Yahoo.

"Whoever named these beasties knew his Swift," the young

medico said. "You ever read that old book, 'Gulliver's Travels'?"

Harper nodded.

"Old Swift went mad, didn't he? He hated humanity, they all seemed like Yahoos to him . . . In a way I don't blame him. I think that's why everybody despises these Primitives: they seem like caricatures of ourselves. Personally, I look forward to finding out a lot about them, their metabolism and so on . . . What's *your* interest?"

He asked the question casually, but shot a keen look as he did so. Harper shrugged. "I hardly know, exactly. It's not a scientific one, because I'm a businessman." He hesitated. "You ever hear or read about the Tasmanians?"

The intern shook his head. He thrust a needle into a vein in the younger Yahoo's arm, prepared to let the serum flow in. "If they lived on Earth, I wouldn't know. Never was there. I'm a third generation Coulterboy, myself."

Harper said, "Tasmania is an island south of Australia. The natives were the most primitive people known on Earth. They were almost all wiped out by the settlers, but one of them succeeded in moving the survivors to a smaller island. And then a curious thing happened."

Looking up from the older Primitive, the intern asked what that was.

"The Tasmanians—the few that were left—decided that they'd had it. They refused to breed. And in a few more years they were all dead . . . I read about them when I was just a kid. Somehow, it moved me very much. Things like that *did* —the dodo, the great auk, the quagga, the Tasmanians. I've never been able to get it out of my mind. When I began hearing about the Yahoos, it seemed to me that they were like the old Tasmanians. Only there are no settlers on Barnumland."

The intern nodded. "But that won't help our hairy friends here a hell of a lot. Of course no one knows how many of them there are—or ever were. But I've been comparing the figures in the log as to how many females are caught and taken aboard." He looked directly at Harper. "And on every trip there are less by far."

Harper bowed his head. He nodded. The intern's voice went on: "The thing is, Barnum's Planet is no one's responsibility. If the Yahoos could be used for labor, they'd be exploited according to a careful system. But as it is, no one cares. If half of them die from being stungunned, no one cares. If the lighter crews don't bother to actually land the females—if any of the wretched creatures are still *alive* when the convicts are done—but just dump them out from twenty feet up, why, again: no one cares. Mr. Harper?"

Their eyes met. Harper said, "Yes?"

"Don't misunderstand me . . . I've got a career here. I'm not jeopardizing it to save the poor Yahoos—but if *you* are interested—if you think you've got any influence—and if you want to try to do anything—" He paused. "Why, now is the time to start. Because after another few stop-overs there aren't going to *be* any Yahoos. No more than there are any Tasmanians."

Selopé III was called "The Autumn Planet" by the poets. At least, the P.R. picture-tapes always referred to it as "Selopé III, The Autumn Planet of the poets," but no one knew who the poets were. It was true that the Commission Territory, at least, did have the climate of an almost-perpetual early New England November. Barnumland had been dry and warm. The Commissioner-General put the two Yahoos in a heated cage as large as the room Harper occupied at his company's Bachelor Executive Quarters.

"Here, boy," the C-G said, holding out a piece of fruit. He made a chirping noise. The two Yahoos huddled together in a far corner.

"They don't seem very bright," he said, sadly. "All my *other* animals eat out of my hand." He was very proud of his private zoo, the only one in the Territory. On Sundays he allowed the public to visit it.

Sighing, Harper repeated that the Yahoos were Primitives, not animals. But, seeing the C-G was still doubtful, he changed his tactics. He told the C-G about the great zoos on Earth, where the animals went loose in large enclosures rather than being caged up. The C-G nodded thoughtfully. Harper told him of the English dukes who—generation after ducal generation—preserved the last herd of wild White Cattle in a park on their estate.

The C-G stroked his chin. "Yes, yes," he said. "I see your point," he said. He sighed gustily. "Can't be done," he said.

"But why not, sir?" Harper cried.

It was simple. "No money. Who's to pay? The Exchequer-Commissioner is weeping blood trying to get the Budget through Council. If he adds a penny more— No, young fellow. I'll do what *I* can: I'll feed these two, here. But that's all I can do."

Trying to pull all the strings he could reach, Harper approached the Executive-Fiscal and the Procurator-General, the President-in-Council, the Territorial Advocate, the Chairman of the Board of Travel. But no one could do anything. Barnum's Planet, it was carefully explained to him, remained No Man's Land only because no man presumed to give any orders concerning it. If any government did, this would be a Presumption of Authority. And then every other government would feel obliged to deny that presumption and issue a claim of its own.

There was a peace on now—a rather tense, uneasy one. And it wasn't going to be disturbed for Harper's Yahoos. Human, were they? Perhaps. But who cared? As for Morality, Harper didn't even bother to mention the word. It would have meant as little as Chivalry.

Meanwhile, he was learning something of the Yahoos' language. Slowly and arduously, he gained their confidence. They would shyly take food from him. He persuaded the C-G to knock down a wall and enlarge their quarters. The official was a kindly old man, and he seemed to grow fond of the stooped, shaggy, splay-footed Primitives. And after a while he decided that they were smarter than animals.

"Put some clothes on 'em, Harper," he directed. "If they're people, let 'em start acting like people. They're too big to go around naked."

So, eventually, washed and dressed, Junior and Senior were introduced to Civilization via 3-D, and the program was taped and shown everywhere.

Would you like a cigarette, Junior? Here, let me light it for you. Give Junior a glass of water, Senior. Let's see you take off your slippers, fellows, and put them on again. And now do what I say in your own language . . .

But if Harper thought that might change public opinion, he thought wrong. Seals perform, too, don't they? And so do monkeys. They talk? Parrots talk better. And anyway, who cared to be bothered about animals *or* Primitives? They were okay for fun, but that was all.

And the reports from Barnumland showed fewer and fewer Yahoos each time.

Then one night two drunken crewmen climbed over the fence and went carousing in the C-G's zoo. Before they left, they broke the vapor-light tubes, and in the morning Junior and Senior were found dead from the poisonous fumes.

That was Sunday morning. By Sunday afternoon Harper was drunk, and getting drunker. The men who knocked on his door got no answer. They went in anyway. He was slouched, red-eyed, over the table.

"People," he muttered. "Tell you they were *human!*" he shouted.

"Yes, Mr. Harper, we know that," said a young man, pale, with close-cropped dark hair.

Harper peered at him, boozily. "Know you," he said. "Thir' gen'ration Coulterboy. Go 'way. Spoi' your c'reer. Whaffor. Smelly ol' Yahoo?" The young medico nodded to his companion, who took a small flask from his pocket, opened it. They held it under Harper's nose by main force. He gasped and struggled, but they held on, and in a few minutes he was sober.

"That's rough stuff," he said, coughing and shaking his head. "But—thanks, Dr. Hill. Your ship in? Or are you stopping over?"

The former intern shrugged. "I've left the ships," he said. "I don't have to worry about spoiling my new career. This is my superior, Dr. Anscomb."

Anscomb was also young, and, like most men from Coulter's System, pale. He said, "I understand you can speak the Yahoos' language."

Harper winced. "What good's that now? They're dead, poor little bastards."

Anscomb nodded. "I'm sorry about that, believe me. Those fumes are so quick . . . But there are still a few alive on Barnum's Planet who can be saved. The Joint Board for Research is interested. Are you?"

It had taken Harper fifteen years to work up to a room of this size and quality in Bachelor Executives' Quarters. He looked around it. He picked up the letter which had come yesterday. ". . . neglected your work and become a joke . . . unless you accept a transfer and reduction in grade . . ." He nodded slowly, putting down the letter. "I guess I've already made my choice. What are your plans. . . ?"

Harper, Hill, and Anscomb sat on a hummock on the north coast of Barnumland, just out of rock-throwing range of the gaunt escarpment of the cliff which rose before them. Behind them a tall fence had been erected. The only Yahoos still alive were "nesting" in the caves of the cliff. Harper spoke into the amplifier again. His voice was hoarse as he forced it into the clicks and moans of the Primitives' tongue.

Hill stirred restlessly. "Are you sure that means, *'Here is food. Here is water'*—and not, *'Come down and let us eat you'*? I think I can almost say it myself by now."

Shifting and stretching, Anscomb said, "It's been two days. Unless they've determined to commit race suicide a bit more abruptly than your ancient Tasmanians—" He stopped as Harper's fingers closed tightly on his arm.

There was a movement on the cliff. A shadow. A pebble clattered. Then a wrinkled face peered fearfully over a ledge. Slowly, and with many stops and hesitations, a figure came down the face of the cliff. It was an old she. Her withered and pendulous dugs flapped against her sagging belly as she made the final jump to the ground, and—her back to the wall of rock—faced them.

"Here is food," Harper repeated softly. "Here is water." The old woman sighed. She plodded wearily across the ground, paused, shaking with fear, and then flung herself down at the food and the water.

"The Joint Board for Research has just won the first round," Hill said. Anscomb nodded. He jerked his thumb upward. Hill looked.

Another head appeared at the cliff. Then another. And another. They watched. The crone got up, water dripping from her dewlaps. She turned to the cliff. "Come down," she cried. "Here is food and water. Do not die. Come down and eat and drink." Slowly, her tribes-people did so. There were thirty of them.

Harper asked, "Where are the others?"

The crone held out her dried and leathery breasts to him. "Where are those who have sucked? Where are those your brothers took away?" She uttered a single shrill wail; then was silent.

But she wept—and Harper wept with her.

"I'll guess we'll swing it all right," Hill said. Anscomb nodded. "Pity there's so few of them. I was afraid we'd have to use gas to get at them. Might have lost several that way."

Neither of them wept.

For the first time since ships had come to their world, Yahoos *walked* aboard one. They came hesitantly and fearfully, but Harper had told them that they were going to a new home and they believed him. He told them that they were going to a place of much food and water, where no one would hunt them down. He continued to talk until the ship was on its way, and the last Primitive had fallen asleep under the dimmed-out vapor-tube lights. Then he staggered to his cabin and fell asleep himself. He slept for thirty hours.

He had something to eat when he awoke, then strolled down to the hold where the Primitives were. He grimaced, remembered his trip to the hold of the other ship to collect Senior, and the frenzied howling of the convicts awaiting the females. At the entrance to the hold he met Dr. Hill, greeted him.

"I'm afraid some of the Yahoos are sick," Hill said. "But Dr. Anscomb is treating them. The others have been moved to this compartment here."

Harper stared. "Sick? How can they be sick? What from? And how many?"

Dr. Hill said, "It appears to be Virulent Plague . . . Fifteen of them are down with it. You've *had* all six shots, haven't you? Good. Nothing to worry—"

Harper felt the cold steal over him. He stared at the pale young physician. "No one can enter or leave any system or planet without having had all six shots for Virulent Plague," he said, slowly. "So if we are all immune, how could the Primitives have gotten it? And how is it that only fifteen have it? Exactly half of them. What about the other fifteen, Dr. Hill? *Are they the control group for your experiment?*"

Dr. Hill looked at him calmly. "As a matter of fact, yes. I hope you'll be reasonable. Those were the only terms the Joint Board for Research would agree to. After all, not even convicts will volunteer for experiments in Virulent Plague."

Harper nodded. He felt frozen. After a moment he asked, "Can Anscomb do anything to pull them through?"

Dr. Hill raised his eyebrows. "Perhaps. We've got something we wanted to try. And at any rate, the reports should provide additional data on the subject. We must take the long-range view."

Harper nodded. "I suppose you're right," he said.

By noon all fifteen were dead.

"Well, that means an uneven control group," Dr. Anscomb complained. "Seven against eight. Still, that's not *too* bad. And it can't be helped. We'll start tomorrow."

"Virulent Plague again?" Harper asked.

Anscomb and Hill shook their heads. "Dehydration," the latter said. "And after that, there's a new treatment for burns we're anxious to try . . . It's a shame, when you think of the Yahoos being killed off by the thousands, year after year, *uselessly*. Like the dodo. We came along just in time —thanks to you, Harper."

He gazed at them. *"Quis custodiet ipsos custodes?"* he asked. They looked at him, politely blank. "I'd forgotten. Doctors don't study Latin anymore, do they? An old proverb. It means: 'Who shall guard the guards themselves?' . . . Will you excuse me, Doctors?"

Harper let himself into the compartment. "I come," he greeted the fifteen.

"We see you," they responded. The old woman asked how their brothers and sisters were "in the other cave."

"They are well . . . Have you eaten, have you drunk? Yes? Then let us sleep," Harper said.

The old woman seemed doubtful. "Is it time? The light still shines." She pointed to it. Harper looked at her. She had been so afraid. But she had trusted him. Suddenly he bent over and kissed her. She gaped.

"Now the light goes out," Harper said. He slipped off a shoe and shattered the vapor tube. He groped in the dark for the air-switch, turned it off. Then he sat down. He had brought them here, and if they had to die, it was only fitting that he should share their fate. There no longer seemed any place for the helpless, or for those who cared about them.

"Now let us sleep," he said.

THE GRANTHA SIGHTING

THERE WERE VISITORS, OF COURSE—THERE WERE VISITORS pretty nearly every night nowadays. The side road had never had such traffic. Emma Towns threw the door open and welcomed them, beaming. Walt was there behind her, smiling in his usual shy way.

"Hello there, Emma," Joe Trobridge said. "Won't let me call her 'Mrs. Towns,' you know," he explained to his friends. They went into the warm kitchen of the farmhouse. "This is Si Haffner, this is Miss Anderson, this is Lou DelBello—all members of the Unexplained Aerial Phenomena Co-ordinators, too. And *this* gentleman," he added, when the other three had finished shaking hands, "is Mr. Tom Knuble."

"Just call me Long Tom," said Long Tom.

Emma said, "Oh, not the radio man? *Really?* Well, my goodness!"

"Tom would like to make some tape recordings from here," Joe explained. "To replay on his program. If you don't mind, that is?"

Why of *course* they didn't mind. And they made the visitors sit right down and they put hot coffee on the table, and tea and home-baked bread and some of Emma's preserves and some of Walt's scuppernong wine, and sandwiches, because they were sure their visitors must be tired and hungry after that long drive.

"This is mighty nice of you," Long Tom said. "*And* very

tasty." The Townses beamed, and urged him to take more. Joe cleared his throat.

"This must be at least the fifth or sixth time *I've* been up here," he said. "As well as people I've told they could come up—"

"Any time—" said Emma.

"Any friends—" said Walt.

Joe half-smiled, half-chuckled. A slight trace of what might have been embarrassment was in the sound. "Well, from what I hear, you always put out a spread like this no matter who comes, and I . . . we . . . well . . ."

Miss Anderson came to his rescue. "We talked it over coming up," she said. "And we feel and we are agreed that you are so helpful and accommodating and in every way," she floundered.

"So we want to pay for the refreshments which is the least we can do," Lou DelBello intervened. The visitors nodded and said, Absolutely. Only Right.

Walt and Emma looked at each other. Either the idea had never occurred to them or they were excellent actors. "Oh, *no!*" said Walt. "Oh, we wouldn't *think* of it," said Emma.

They were glad to, she said. It was their privilege. And nothing could induce them to take a cent.

Long Tom put down his cup. "I understand that you wouldn't take any payment for newspaper stories or posing for photographs, either," he said. The Townses shook their heads. "In short—wait a minute, let's get these tapes rolling . . .

"Now, Mr. and Mrs. Walter F. Towns up here in Paviour's Bridge, New York," he continued after a moment, having started the recording machine; "I understand that you have both refused to commercialize in any way your experiences on the third of October, is that right? Never taken any money—AP, UP, *Life* Magazine, *Journal-American*—wouldn't accept payment, is that right, Mr. and Mrs. Walter F. Towns up here in Paviour's Bridge, New York?"

Emma and Walt urged each other with nods of the head to speak first into the whizzing-rolling device, wound up saying together, "That's *No we* right *didn't.*"

"I would just like to say—oh excuse me Tom—" Lou began.

"No, go right ahead—"

"I would just like—"

"This is Lou DelBello, you folks out there on the party line: Lou. Del. Bello. Who is up here in Paviour's Bridge,

New York, at the Walter F. Townses', along with Miss Jo Anderson, Si Haffner, and Joe Trobridge—as well as myself, Long Tom—all members of that interesting organization you've heard of before on our five-hour conversations over Station WRO, sometimes called familiarly the Flying Saucer Club, but known officially as the Unexplained Aerial Phenomena Coordinating Corps. *Well.* Quite a mouthful. And we are up here accepting the very gracious hospitality of Walt and Emma who are going to tell us, in their own words just exactly. what. it was. that happened on the famous night of October third, known as the October Third Sighting or the Grantha Incident; go right ahead, Lou DelBello."

Still dogged and game, Lou went ahead. "I would just like to say that in speaking of that very gracious hospitality that Walt and Emma have refused to take one red cent for so much as a sandwich or a cup of coffee. To all the visitors up here, I mean. So that certainly should take care of in advance of any charges or even the mention of, ah, com*mer*cialism."

Long Tom paused with a piece of home-baked bread and apple butter half way into his mouth and gestured to Joe Trobridge.

"Yes, Lou," Joe leaped into the breach, "the same people who didn't believe Columbus and are now so scornful of all the various and innumerable U.A.P. sightings, well, the same *type* people, I mean—some certain individuals who shall be nameless who have been suggesting that the Grantha Incident is just a *trick,* or maybe the Townses and myself are in business together—"

Miss Anderson said, "The Cloth-Like Substance, you mean, Joe?"

Long Tom swallowed, wiped his mouth. "Well, I didn't know they *made* apple butter like that anymore, Emma," he said. "Yessir folks out there on the party line, the Townses up here in Paviour's Bridge, New York, are poultry farmers by profession but any time Emma wants to go into the preserves business she can sure count on me to—"

Joe interrupted. "I'd just like to clear up one point, Tom—"

"Why sure, Joe, go right ahead. This is the Long Tom Show, you folks out there on the party line. Five hours of talk and music on Station WRO . . ."

Si Haffner for the first time spoke up:

"I understand this Cloth-Like Substance is still refusing or rather I should say *defying* analysis in the laboratories; is that right Joe?"

Joe said it certainly was. This Cloth-Like Substance, he reminded the listeners-to-be, was left behind at the Townses after the October Third Sighting. It was soft, it was absorbent, it was non-inflammable; and it resembled nothing known to our terrestrial science. He had tried to analyze it in his own lab, but, failing to do so, he had turned it over to the General Chemical Company. So far even *they*, with their vastly superior facilities, were unable to say just what it was. And while in a way he was *flattered* that some people thought well maybe he was in cahoots with an outfit like GenChem, well—

"Yessir," said Long Tom; "just let me tell you folks out there on the party line that there is *noth*ing like this chicken-salad sandwich that Mrs. Emma F. Towns puts up out here in Paviour's Bridge, New York. *Won*derful. But I would like you to tell us in your own words, Emma, just what exactly *did* happen that certain night of October third, known to some as the Grantha Incident. Tell us in your own words."

Emma said, "Well."

"Tell us what kind of a day it was. What was the first thing you did?"

Emma said, "Well . . ."

The first thing she did was to get up and heat the mash for the chicks. Not that she minded getting up that early. Some people who'd lived in the city and talked of settling down on a little poultry farm, when it actually came *to* it, they found they didn't care for it too much. But not Emma. No; it wasn't the hours she minded.

And it wasn't the work. She *liked* work. The house was well-built, it was easy to keep warm, it had a lovely view. But it was so far away from everybody. Even the mailman left his deliveries way down at the bottom of the hill. There was the radio, there was the television, but—when you came right down to it—who came to the house? The man who delivered the feed. The man who collected the eggs. And that was all.

The day passed like every other day. Scatter cracked corn. Regular feeding. Scatter sawdust. Clean out from under the wiring. Mix the oats and the clarified buttermilk. Sardine oil. Collect the eggs. Wash them. Pack them. And, of course, while the chickens had to eat, so did the Townses.

No, there was nothing unusual about the day. Until about—

"—about five o'clock, I think it was," Emma said.

"*Nothing* unusual had happened previous to this?" Long Tom asked. "You had *no* warning?"

Emma said No, none.

"I would just like to say—" Joe Trobridge began.

"Well, now just a min—" Tom cut in.

"I just want to clear up one point," Joe said. "Now, prior to the time I arrived at your doorstep that night, had you ever seen or heard of me before, Emma?"

"No, never."

"That's all I wanted to say. I just wanted to clear up that point."

"You got that did you, all you folks out there on the party line?" inquired Long Tom. "They. had. never. seen, *or* heard. of each other. before. And then, Emma, you were about to say, about five o'clock?"

About five o'clock, when the dark was falling, Emma first noticed the cloud. She called it to Tom's attention. It was a funny-looking cloud. For a long time it didn't move, although the other clouds did. And then—as the bright reds of the sunset turned maroon, magenta, purple—the cloud slowly came down from the sky and hovered about ten feet over the Townses' front yard.

"Walt, there is something *very* funny about that cloud," said Emma.

"I don't believe it's no cloud," Walt declared. "Listen to that noise, would you." It came from the . . . cloud—thing—whatever it was: a rattling muffled sort of noise, and an angry barking sort of noise. The air grew very dark.

"Do you think we should put on the lights?" Emma said. Walt grunted. And the—whatever it was—came down with a lurching motion and hit the sod with a clonk. It was suddenly lit up by a ring of lights, which went out again almost at once, went on, went out. Then there was a long silence.

A clatter. A rattle. And again, the barking sound.

"Sounds like someone's cussing, almost. Somehow," Walt said.

"*I* am going to put on the *light*," said Emma. And she did. The noise stopped. Emma put on her sweater. "Come out on the porch with me," she said. They opened the door and stepped out on the porch. They looked over at the . . . thing. It sat on the ground about fifty feet away.

"Is anything *wrong?*" Emma called. "Yoo-hoo! Anything wrong?"

There was a slither and a clatter. The lights went on

again in the thing and there was now an opening in it and two figures in the opening. One of them started forward, the other reached out a—was that an *arm?* but the first figure barked angrily and it drew back. And there was another sound now, a sort of yelping noise, as the first figure walked towards the house and the second figure followed it.

"A man and his wife," said Emma. Walt observed they were dressed light, considering the time of year.

"That's really nothing but what you might call, well, bloomers, that they got on, though they *are* long and they *do* reach up high."

"Sssshh! Hello, there. My name is Mrs. Towns and this is my husband, Mr. Towns. You folks in any trouble?"

The folks halted some distance away. Even at that distance it was possible to see that they were much shorter and broader than the Townses.

"Why you'll catch your *death* out there with no coats on!" Emma exclaimed. "You're all *blue!*" Actually, it was a sort of blue-*green*, but she didn't want to embarrass them. "Come in, come on in," she gestured. They came on in. The yelping noise began again. "There. Now isn't it warmer?" Emma closed the door.

From the crook of her—*was* it an arm? It couldn't be anything else—one of the figures lifted up the source of the yelping. Emma peered at it.

"Well, my *goodness!*" Emma said. She and Walt exchanged glances. "Isn't it just the picture of its father!" she said. An expression which might have been a smile passed over the faces of the two figures.

The first figure reached into its garment and produced an oval container, offered it, withdrew it as a petulant yelp was heard. The figure looked at Emma, barked diffidently.

"Why, don't you *know* what she's saying, Walt?" Emma asked.

Walt squirmed. "It seems like I do, but I know I couldn't, hardly," he said.

Emma was half-indignant. "Why, you can, too. She's saying: 'The car broke down and I wonder if I might warm the baby's bottle?' *That's* what she's saying.—Of *course* you may. You just come along into the kitchen."

Walt scratched his ear, looked at the second figure. It looked at him.

"Why, I guess I'd better go along back with you," Walt said, "and take a look at your engine. That was a bad rattle you got there."

It was perhaps half an hour later that they returned. "Got it fixed all right now," Walt said. "Loose umpus on the hootenanny . . . baby OK?"

"Sshh . . . it's asleep. All it wanted was a warm bottle and a clean diaper."

There was a silence. Then everyone was talking (or barking) at once— of course, in low tones. "Oh, glad to do it, glad to be of help," said Emma. "Any time . . . and whenever you happen to be around this way, why just you drop in and see us. Sorry you can't stay."

"Sure thing," Walt seconded. "That's right."

Emma said, "It's so lonely up here. We hardly ever have any visitors at all. . . . Goodby! Goodby, now!" And finally the visitors closed the opening in their vehicle.

"Hope the umpus stays fixed in the hootenanny . . ." There was a burst of pyrotechnic colors, a rattling noise, and a volley of muffled barks. "It didn't," Walt said. *"Hear* him cussing!" The rattling ceased, the colors faded into a white mist. "Got it now . . . look at those lights go round and round . . . there they go. Wherever it is they're going," he concluded, uncertainly. They closed the door. Emma sighed.

"It *was* nice having someone to visit with," she said. "Heaven only knows how long it will be before anyone else comes here."

It was exactly three hours and five minutes. Two automobiles came tearing up the road and screamed to a stop. People got out, ran pounding up the path, knocked at the door. Walt answered.

At first they all talked at once, then all fell silent. Finally, one man said, "I'm Joe Trobridge of the U.A.P.C.C.—the Unexplained Aerial—listen, a *sighting* was reported in this vicinity! Did you see it? A flying saucer? Huh?"

Walt nodded slowly. "So *that's* what it was," he said. "I thought it was some kind of a airship."

Trobridge's face lit up. Everyone began to babble again. Then Trobridge said, "You *saw* it? Was it close? What? SHUT UP, EVERYBODY! On your front lawn? What'd they look like? What—?"

Walt pursed his mouth. "I'll tell ya," he began. "They were blue."

"Blue?" exclaimed Trobridge.

"Well . . ." Walt's tone was that of a man willing to stretch a point. "Maybe it was green."

"Green?"

"Well, which was it?" someone demanded. "Blue or green?"

Walt said, in the same live-and-let-live tone, "Bluish-green." Joe Trobridge opened his mouth. "Or, greenish-blue," Walt continued, cutting him off. The visitors milled around, noisily.

"How were they dressed?"

Walt pursed his mouth. "I'll tell ya," he said. "They were wearing what ya might call like bloomers . . ."

"Bloomers?"

Emma glanced around nervously. The visitors didn't seem to like what Walt was telling them. Not at all.

Joe Trobridge pressed close. "Did they say what their purpose was, in visiting the Earth?" he asked, eagerness restored somewhat—but only somewhat.

Walt nodded. "Oh, sure. Told us right away. Come to see if they could warm the baby's bottle." Someone in the crowd made a scornful noise. "That was it, y'see . . ." his voice trailed off uncertainly.

The man named Joe Trobridge looked at him, his mouth twisted. "Now, *wait* a minute," he said. "Just wait a *minute* . . ."

Emma took in the scene at a glance. No one would believe them. They'd all go away and never come back and no one would ever visit them again—except the man who delivered the feed and the man who collected the eggs. She looked at the disappointed faces around her, some beginning to show anger, and she got up.

"My husband is joking," she said, loudly and clearly. "Of *course* it wasn't like that."

Joe turned to her. "Did you see it, too, lady? What happened, then? I mean, *really* happened? Tell us in your own words. What did they look like?"

Emma considered for a moment. "They were very tall," she said. "And they had on spacesuits. And their leader spoke to us. He looked just like us only maybe his head was a bit bigger. He didn't have no hair. He didn't really speak English—it was more like telepathy—"

The people gathered around her closely, their eyes aglow, their faces eager. "Go on," they said; "go on—"

"His name was . . . Grantha—"

"Grantha," the people breathed.

"And he said we shouldn't be afraid, because he came in peace. 'Earth people,' he said, 'we have observed you for a long time and now we feel the time has come to make ourselves known to you. . . .' "

Long Tom nodded. "So that's the way it was."

"That's the way it was," she said. "More coffee, anybody?"

"You brew a mighty fine cup of coffee, Mrs. Emma Towns up here in Paviour's Bridge, New York, let me tell the folks on the party line," Long Tom said. "No sugar thanks, just cream. . . . Well, say, about this piece of Cloth-Like Substance. It's absorbent—it's soft—it doesn't burn—and it can't be analyzed. Now, about how big is this wonderful item which Grantha and his people left behind as a sample of their superior technicology and peaceful intentions and which continues to baffle scientists? About how big is it? Just tell [illegible] in your own words. . . ."

Emma considered. Joe pursed his lips.

Lou DelBello smiled. "Well, I've had the good fortune to see it," he said, "and—speaking as the father of three—the, uh, best comparison of its size which I could give you, I'd say it's just about as big as a diaper!"

He guffawed. Joe burst out laughing, as did Si Haffner. Miss Anderson giggled. Long Tom chuckled. Emma and Walt looked nervously at each other, looked anxiously at their oh, so very welcome guests—but only for a moment. Then, reassured, they leaned back and joined in the merriment.

HELP! I AM DR. MORRIS GOLDPEPPER

I

FOUR OF THE MEN, WEINROTH, MCALLISTER, DANBOURGE and Smith, sat at the table under the cold blue lighting tubes. One of them, Rorke, was in a corner speaking quietly into a telephone, and one, Fadderman, stood staring out the window at the lights of the city. One, Hansen, had yet to arrive.

Fadderman spoke without turning his head. He was the oldest of those present—the Big Seven, as they were often called.

"Lights," he said. "So many lights. Down here." He waved his hand toward the city. "Up there." He gestured toward the sky. "Even with our much-vaunted knowledge, what," he asked, "do we know?" He turned his head. "Perhaps this is too big for us. In the light of the problem, can we really hope to accomplish anything?"

Heavy-set Danbourge frowned grimly. "We have received the suffrage of our fellow-scientists, Doctor. We can but try."

Lithe, handsome McAllister, the youngest officer of the Association, nodded. "The problem is certainly not worse than that which faced our late, great colleague, the immortal Morton." He pointed to a picture on the panneled wall. "And we all know what *he* accomplished."

Fadderman went over and took his hand. "Your words fill me with courage."

McAllister flushed with pleasure.

"I am an old man," Fadderman added falteringly. "Forgive my lack of spirit, Doctor." He sat down, sighed, shook his head slowly. Weinroth, burly and red-haired, patted him gently on the back. Natty, silvery-haired little Smith smiled at him consolingly.

A buzzer sounded. Rorke hung up the telephone, flipped a switch on the wall intercom. "Headquarters here," he said crisply.

"Dr. Carl T. Hansen has arrived," a voice informed him.

"Bring him up at once," he directed. "And, Nickerson—"

"Yes, Dr. Rorke?"

"Let no one else into the building. *No* one."

They sat in silence. After a moment or two, they heard the approach of the elevator, heard the doors slide open, slide shut, heard the elevator descend. Heavy, steady footsteps approached; knuckles rapped on the opaque glass door.

Rorke went over to the door, said, "A conscientious and diligent scientist—"

"—must remain a continual student," a deep voice finished the quotation.

Rorke unlocked the door, peered out into the corridor, admitted Hansen, locked the door.

"I would have been here sooner, but another emergency interposed," Hansen said. "A certain political figure—ethics prevent my being more specific—suffered an oral hemorrhage following an altercation with a woman who shall be nameless, but, boy, did she pack a wallop! A so-called *Specialist*, gentlemen, with offices on Park Avenue, had been, as he called it, 'applying pressure' with a gauze pad. I merely used a little Gelfoam as a coagulant agent and the hemorrhage stopped almost at once. When will the public learn, eh, gentlemen?"

Faint smiles played upon the faces of the assembled scientists. Hansen took his seat. Rorke bent down and lifted two tape-recording devices to the table, set them both in motion. The faces of the men became serious, grim.

"This is an emergency session of the Steering Committee of the Executive Committee of the American Dental Association," Rorke said, "called to discuss measures of dealing with the case of Dr. Morris Goldpepper. One tape will be deposited in the vaults of the Chase Manhattan Bank in New York; the other will be similarly secured in the vaults of the Wells Fargo and Union Trust Company Bank in San Francisco. Present at this session are Doctors Rorke, Weinroth and Smith—President, First and Second Vice-presidents, respectively—Fadderman, Past President, McAllister, Public Information, Danbourge, Legal, and Hansen, Policy."

He looked around at the set, tense faces.

"Doctors," he went on, "I think I may well say that humanity is, as of this moment, face to face with a great danger, and it is a bitter jest that it is not to the engineers or the astronomers, not to medicine nor yet to nuclear nor any other kind of physics, that humanity must now look for salvation—but to the members of the dental profession!"

His voice rose. "Yes—to the practitioners of what has become perhaps the least regarded of all the learned sciences! It is indeed ironical. We may at this juncture consider the comments of the now deceased Professor Earnest Hooton, the Harvard anthropologist, who observed with a sorrow which did him credit that his famed University, instead of assisting its Dental School as it ought, treated it—and I quote his exact words—'Like a yellow dog.' " His voice trembled.

McAllister's clean-cut face flushed an angry red. Weinroth growled. Danbourge's fist hit the table and stayed there, clenched. Fadderman gave a soft, broken sigh.

"But enough of this. We are not jealous, nor are we vindictive," President Rorke went on. "We are confident that History, 'with its long tomorrow,' will show how, at this danger-fraught point, the humble and little thought-of followers of dental science recognized and sized up the situation and stood shoulder to shoulder on the ramparts!"

He wiped his brow with a paper tissue. "And now I will call upon our beloved Past President, Dr. Samuel I. Fadderman, to begin our review of the incredible circumstances which have brought us here tonight. Dr. Fadderman? If you please . . ."

The well-known Elder Statesman of the A.D.A. nodded

his head slowly. He made a little cage of his fingers and pursed and then unpursed his lips. At length he spoke in a soft and gentle voice.

"My first comment, brethren, is that I ask for compassion. *Morris Goldpepper is not to blame!*

"Let me tell you a few words about him. Goldpepper the Scientist needs no introduction. Who has not read, for instance, his 'The Bilateral Vertical Stroke and Its Influence on the Pattern of Occlusion' or his 'Treatment, Planning, Assemblage and Cementation of a 14-Unit Fixed Bridge'—to name only two? But I shall speak about Goldpepper the Man. He is forty-six years of age and served with honor in the United States Navy Dental Corps during the Second World War. He has been a widower since shortly after the conclusion of that conflict. Rae—the late Mrs. Goldpepper, may she rest in peace—often used to say, 'Morry, if I go first, promise me you'll marry again,' but he passed it off with a joke; and, as you know, he never did.

"They had one child, a daughter, Suzanne, a very sweet girl, now married to a Dr. Sheldon Fingerhut, D.D.S. I need not tell you, brethren, how proud our colleague was when his only child married this very fine young member of our profession. The Fingerhuts are now located on Unbalupi, one of the Micronesian islands forming part of the United States Trust Territory, where Dr. Sheldon is teaching dental hygiene, sanitation and prosthesis to the natives thereof."

Dr. Hansen asked, "Are they aware of—"

"The son-in-law knows something of the matter," the older man said. "He has not seen fit to inform his wife, who is in a delicate condition and expects shortly to be confined. At his suggestion, I have been writing—or, rather, typing—letters purporting to come from her father, on his stationery, with the excuse that he badly singed his fingers on a Bunsen burner whilst annealing a new-type hinge for dentures and consequently cannot hold his pen." He sipped from a glass of water.

"Despite his great scientific accomplishments," Dr. Fadderman went on, "Morry had an impractical streak in him. Often I used to call on him at his bachelor apartment in the Hotel Davenport on West End Avenue, where he moved following his daughter's marriage, and I would find him immersed in reading matter of an escapist kind—tales of crocodile hunters on the Malayan Peninsula, or magazines dealing with interplanetary warfare, or collections of short stories about vampires and werewolves and similar superstitious creations.

" 'Morry,' I said reproachfully, 'what a way to spend your off-hours. Is it worth it? Is it healthy? You would do much better, believe me, to frequent the pool or the handball court at the Y. Or,' I pointed out to him, 'if you want to read, why ignore the rich treasures of literature: Shakespeare, Ruskin, Elbert Hubbard, Edna Ferber, and so on? Why retreat to these immature-type fantasies?' At first he only smiled and quoted the saying, 'Each to his or her own taste.' "

The silence which followed was broken by young Dr. McAllister. "You say," he said, " 'at first.' "

Old Dr. Fadderman snapped out of his revery. "Yes, yes. But eventually he confessed the truth to me. He withheld nothing."

The assembled dental scientists then learned that the same Dr. Morris Goldpepper, who had been awarded not once but three successive times the unique honor of the Dr. Alexander Peabody Medal for New Achievements in Dental Prosthesis, was obsessed with the idea that *there was sentient life on other worlds—that it would shortly be possible to reach these other worlds—and that he himself desired to be among those who went.*

" 'Do you realize, Sam?' he asked me," reported Fadderman. " 'Do you realize that, in a very short time, it will no longer be a question of fuel or even of metallurgy? That submarines capable of cruising for weeks and months without surfacing foretell the possibility of traveling through airless space? The chief problem has now come down to finding how to build a take-off platform capable of withstanding a thrust of several million pounds.' And his eyes glowed."

Dr. Fadderman had inquired, with good-natured sarcasm, how the other man expected this would involve *him*. The answer was as follows: Any interplanetary expedition would find it just as necessary to take along a dentist as to take along a physician, and that he—Dr. Goldpepper—intended to be that dentist!

Dr. Weinroth's hand slapped the table with a bang. "By thunder, I say the man had courage!"

Dr. Rorke looked at him with icy reproof. "I should be obliged," he said stiffly, "if there would be no further emotional outbursts."

Dr. Weinroth's face fell. "I beg the Committee's pardon, Mr. President," he said.

Dr. Rorke nodded graciously, indicated by a gesture of his hand that Dr. Fadderman had permission to continue speaking. The old man took a letter from his pocket and placed it on the table.

"This came to me like a bolt from the blue beyond. It is dated November 8 of last year. Skipping the formal salutation, it reads: 'At last I stand silent upon the peak in Darien' —a literary reference, gentlemen, to Cortez's alleged discovery of the Pacific Ocean; actually it was Balboa—'my great dream is about to be realized. Before long, I shall be back to tell you about it, but just exactly when, I am not able to say. History is being made! Long live Science! Very sincerely yours, Morris Goldpepper, D.D.S.' "

He passed the letter around the table.

Dr. Smith asked, "What did you do on receiving this communication, Doctor?"

Dr. Fadderman had at once taken a taxi to West End Avenue. The desk clerk at the hotel courteously informed him that the man he sought had left on a vacation of short but not exactly specified duration. No further information was known. Dr. Fadderman's first thought was that his younger friend had gotten some sort of position with a Government project which he was not free to discuss, and his own patriotism and sense of duty naturally prevented him from making inquiries.

"But I began, for the first time," the Elder Statesman of American Dentistry said, "to read up on the subject of space travel. I wondered how a man 46 years of age could possibly hope to be selected over younger men."

Dr. Danbourge spoke for the first time. "Size," he said. "Every ounce would count in a spaceship and Morris was a pretty little guy."

"But with the heart of a lion," Dr. Weinroth said softly. "Miles and miles and miles of heart."

The other men nodded their agreement to this tribute.

But as time went on and the year drew to its close and he heard no word from his friend, Dr. Fadderman began to worry. Finally, when he received a letter from the Fingerhuts, saying that *they* had not been hearing either, he took action.

He realized it was not likely that the Government would have made plans to include a dentist in this supposed project without communicating with the A.D.A. and he inquired of the current President, Dr. Rorke, if he had any knowledge of such a project, or of the whereabouts of the missing man. The answer to both questions was no. But on learning the reasons for Dr. Fadderman's concern, he communicated with

Col. Lemnel Coggins, head of the USAF's Dental Corps.

Col. Coggins informed him that no one of Dr. Goldpepper's name or description was or had been affiliated with any such project, and that, in fact, any such project was still—as he put it—"still on the drawing-board."

Drs. Rorke and Fadderman, great as was their concern, hesitated to report Dr. Goldpepper missing. He had, after all, paid rent on apartment, office and laboratory, well in advance. He was a mature man, of very considerable intelligence, and one who presumably knew what he was doing.

"It is at this point," said Dr. Danbourge, "that I enter the picture. On the 11th of January, I had a call from a Dr. Milton Wilson, who has an office on East 19th Street, with a small laboratory adjoining, where he does prosthetic work. He told me, with a good deal of hesitation, that something exceedingly odd had come up, and he asked me if I knew where Dr. Morris Goldpepper was . . ."

The morning of the 11th of January, an elderly man with a curious foreign accent came into Dr. Wilson's office, gave the name of Smith and complained about an upper plate. It did not feel comfortable, Mr. Smith said, and it irritated the roof of his mouth. There was a certain reluctance on his part to allow Dr. Wilson to examine his mouth. This was understandable, because the interior of his mouth was blue. The gums were entirely edentulous, very hard, almost horny. The plate itself—

"Here is the plate," Dr. Danbourge said, placing it on the table. "Dr. Wilson supplied him with another. You will observe the perforations on the upper, or palatal, surface. They had been covered with a thin layer of gum arabic, which naturally soon wore almost entirely off, with the result that the roof of the mouth became irritated. Now this is so very unusual that Dr. Wilson—as soon as his patient, the so-called Mr. Smith, was gone—broke open the weirdly made plate to find why the perforations had been made. In my capacity as head of the Association's Legal Department," Dr. Danbourge stated, "I have come across some extraordinary occurrences, but nothing like *this*."

This was a small piece of a white, flexible substance, covered with tiny black lines. Danbourge picked up a large magnifying glass.

"You may examine these objects, Doctors," he said, "but it will save your eyesight if I read to you from an enlarged photostatic copy of this last onc. The nature of the material, the method of writing, or of reducing the writing to such size all are unknown to us. It may be something on the order of microfilm. But that is not important. The important thing is the *content* of the writing—the *portent* of the writing.

"Not since Dr. Morton, the young Boston dentist, realized the uses of sulphuric ether as an anesthetic has any member of our noble profession discovered anything of even remotely similar importance; and perhaps not before, either."

He drew his spectacles from their case and began to read aloud.

II

Despite the fact that our great profession lacks the glamour and public adulation of the practice of medicine, and even the druggists—not having a Hippocratic Oath—can preen themselves on their so-called Oath of Maimonides (though, believe me, the great Maimonides had no more to do with it than Morris Goldpepper, D.D.S.), no one can charge us with not having as high a standard of ethics and professional conduct as physicians and surgeons, M.D. Nor do I hesitate for one single moment to include prostheticians not holding the degree of Doctor of Dental Surgery or Doctor of Dental Medicine, whose work is so vital and essential.

When the records of our civilization are balanced, then —but perhaps not before—the real importance of dental science will be appreciated. Now it is merely valued at the moment of toothache.

It is only with a heavy heart that I undertake deliberately to produce inferior work, and with the confidence that all those to whom the standards of oral surgery and dental prosthetics are dear will understand the very unusual circumstances which have prompted me so to do. And, understanding, will forgive. No one can hold the standards of our profession higher or more sacred than I.

It must be admitted that I was not very amused on a certain occasion when my cousin, Nathaniel Pomerance, introduced me to an engineering contractor with these words, "You two should have a lot in common—you both build bridges," and uttered a foolish laugh. But I venture to say that this was one of the truest words ever spoken in questionable jest.

Humility is one thing, false pride another. Those who know anything of modern dentistry at all know of the Goldpepper Bridge and the Goldpepper Crown. It is I, Dr. Morris Goldpepper, inventor of both, and perfector of the Semi-retractable Clasp which bears my name, who writes these words you see before you. Nothing further should be needful by way of identification. And now to my report.

On the first of November, a day of evil import forever in the personal calendar of the unhappy wretch who writes these lines, not even knowing for sure if they will ever be read—but what else can I do?—shortly after 5:00 P.M., my laboratory door was knocked on. I found there a curious-looking man of shriveled and weazened appearance. He asked if I was Dr. Morris Goldpepper, "the famous perfector of the Semi-retractable Clasp," and I pleaded guilty to the flattering impeachment.

The man had a foreign-sounding accent, or—I thought—it may be that he had an impediment in his speech. Might he see me, was his next question. I hesitated.

It has happened to me before, and to most other practitioners—a stranger comes and, before you know it, he is slandering some perfectly respectable D.D.S. or D.M.D. The dentist pulled a healthy tooth—the dentist took such and such a huge sum of money for new plates—they don't fit him, he suffers great anguish—he's a poor man, the dentist won't do anything—*et cetera, ad infinitum nauseamque*. In short, a nut, a crank, a crackpot.

But while I was hesitating, the man yawned, did not courteously cover his mouth with his hand, and I observed to my astonishment that the interior of his mouth was an odd shade of blue!

Bemused by this singular departure from normalcy, I allowed him to enter. Then I wondered what to say, since he himself was saying nothing, but he looked around the lab with interest. "State your business" would be too brusque, and "Why is your mouth blue?" would be too gauche. An impasse.

Whilst holding up a large-scale model of the Goldpepper Cap (not yet perfected—will it ever be? Alas, who knows?) this curious individual said, "I know all about you, Dentist Goldpepper. A great scientist, you are. A man of powerful imagination, you are. One who rebels against narrow horizons and yearns to soar to wide and distant worlds, you are."

All I could think of to say was, "And what can I do for *you?*"

It was all so true; every single word he said was true. In my vanity was my downfall. I was tricked like the crow with the cheese in the ancient fable of Aesop.

The man proceeded to tell me, frankly enough, that he was a denizen of another planet. He had *two hearts,* would you believe it? And, consequently, two circulatory systems. Two pulses—one in each arm, one slow, the other fast.

It reminded me of the situation in Philadelphia some years ago when there were two telephone systems—if you had only a Bell phone, you couldn't call anyone who had only a Keystone phone.

The interior of his mouth was blue and so was the inside of his eyelids. He said his world had three moons.

You may imagine my emotions at hearing that my long-felt dream to communicate with otherworldly forms of sentient life was at last realized! And to think that they had singled out *not* the President of the United States, *not* the Director-General of the U.N., but *me,* Morris Goldpepper, D.D.S.! Could human happiness ask for more, was my unspoken question. I laughed softly to myself and I thought, What would my cousin Nathaniel Pomerance say *now?* I was like wax in this extraterrestrial person's hands (he had six distinct and articulate digits on each one), and I easily agreed to say nothing to anyone until the question of diplomatic recognition could be arranged on a higher echelon.

"Non-recognition *has* its advantages, Goldpepper Dental Surgeon," he said with a slight smile. "No passport for your visit, you will need."

Well! A personal invitation to visit Proxima Centauri Gamma, or whatever the planet's name is! But I felt constrained to look this gift-horse just a little closer in the mouth. How is it that they came inviting *me,* not, let us say, Oppenheimer? Well?

"Of his gifts not in need, we are, Surgical Goldpepper. We have passed as far beyond nuclear power as you have beyond wind power. We can span the Universe—*but in dentistry, like children still,* we are. Come and inspect our faculties of your science, Great Goldpepper. If you say, 'This: Yes,' then it will be yes. If you direct, 'This: No,' then it will be no. In respect to the science of dentistry, our Edison and our Columbus, you will be."

I asked when we would leave and he said in eight days. I asked how long the trip would take. For a moment, I was baffled when he said it would take no longer than to walk the equivalent of the length of the lab floor. Then he revealed his meaning to me: Teleportation! Of course. No spaceship needed.

My next emotion was a brief disappointment at not being able to see the blazing stars in black outer space. But, after all, one ought not be greedy at such a time.

I cannot point out too strongly that at no time did I accept or agree to accept any payment or gratuity for this trip. I looked upon it in the same light as the work I have done for various clinics.

"Should I take along books? Equipment? What?" I asked my (so-to-speak) guide.

He shook his head. Only my presence was desired on the first trip. A visit of inspection. Very well.

On the morning of Nov. 8th, I wrote a brief note to my old and dear friend, Dr. Samuel Fadderman, the senior mentor of American Dentistry [on hearing these words, the Elder Statesman sobbed softly into his cupped hands], and in the afternoon, so excited and enthralled that I noticed no more of my destination than that it was north of the Washington Market, I accompanied my guide to a business building in the aforesaid area.

He led me into a darkened room. He clicked a switch. There was a humming noise, a feeling first of heaviness, then of weightlessness, and then an odd sort of light came on.

I was no longer on the familiar planet of my birth! I was on an unknown world!

Over my head, the three moons of this far-off globe sailed majestically through a sky wherein I could note unfamiliar constellations. The thought occurred to me that poets on this planet would have to find another rhyme, inasmuch as *moons* (plural form) does not go with *June* (singular form). One satellite was a pale yellow, one was brown, and the third was a creamy pink. Not knowing the names of these lunary orbs in their native tongue, I decided to call them Vanilla, Chocolate and Strawberry.

Whilst my mind was filled with these droll fancies, I felt a tug at my sleeve, where my guide was holding it. He gestured and I followed.

"Now," I thought to myself, "he will bring me before the President of their Galactic Council, or whatever he is called," and I stood obediently within a circle marked on the surface of the platform whereon we stood.

In a moment, we were teleported to an inside room somewhere, and there I gazed about me in stupefaction, not to say astonishment. My eyes discerned the forms of Bunsen burners, Baldor lathes, casting machines and ovens, denture trays, dental stone, plaster, shellac trays, wires of teeth, and all the necessary equipment of a fully equipped dental prosthetic laboratory.

My surprise at the progress made by these people in the science at which they were allegedly still children was soon mitigated by the realization that all the items had been made on Earth.

As I was looking and examining, a door opened and several people entered. Their faces were a pale blue, and I realized suddenly that my guide must be wearing makeup to conceal his original complexion. They spoke together in their native dialect; then one of them, with a rod of some kind in his hand, turned to me. He opened his mouth. I perceived his gums were bare.

"Dentical person," he said, "make me teeth."

I turned in some perplexity to my guide. "I understood you to say my first visit would be one of inspection only."

Everyone laughed, and I observed that all were equally toothless.

The man in the chair poked me rudely with his rod or staff. "Talk not! Make teeth!"

Fuming with a well-justified degree of indignation, I protested at such a gross breach of the laws of common hospitality. Then, casting concealment to the winds, these people informed me as follows:

Their race is entirely toothless in the adult stage. They are an older race than ours and are born looking ancient and wrinkled. It is only comparatively recently that they have established contact with Earth, and in order that they should not appear conspicuous, and in order to be able to eat our food, they realized that they must be supplied with artificial teeth.

My so-called guide, false friend, my enticer and/or kidnaper, to give him his due, had gotten fitted at a dentist's in New York and cunningly enquired who was the leading man in the field. Alas for fame! The man answered without a second of hesitation, "That is no other one than Morris Goldpepper, D.D.S., perfector of the Semi-retractable Clasp."

First this unscrupulous extraterrestrial procured the equipment, then he procured *me*.

"Do I understand that you purport that I assist you in a plan to thwart and otherwise circumvent the immigration laws of the United States?" was my enquiry.

The man in the chair poked me with his rod again. "You understand! So now make teeth!"

What a proposition to make to a law-abiding, patriotic American citizen by birth! What a demand to exact of a war veteran, a taxpayer and one who has been three times on jury duty since 1946 alone (People vs. Garrity, People vs. Vanderdam, and Lipschutz vs. Krazy-Kut Kool Kaps, Inc.)! My whole being revolted. I spoke coldly to them, informing them that the situation was contrary to my conception of dental ethics. But to no avail.

My treacherous dragoman drew a revolver from his pocket. "Our weapons understand, you do not. Primitive Earth weapons, yes. So proceed with manufacture, Imprisoned Goldpepper."

I went hot and cold. Not, I beg of you to understand, with fear, but with humiliation. *Imprisoned Goldpepper!* The phrase, with all the connotations it implied, rang in my ears.

I bowed my head and a phrase from the literary work "Sampson Agonistes" (studied as a student in the College of the City of New York) rang through my mind: Eyeless in Gaza, grinding corn . . . Oh, blind, blind, blind, amidst the blaze of noon. . . .

But even in this hour of mental agony, an agony which has scarcely abated to speak of, I had the first glimmering of the idea which I hope will enable me to warn Earth.

Without a word, but only a scornful glance to show these blue-complected individuals how well I appreciated that their so-called advanced science was a mere veneer over the base metal of their boorishness, I set to work. I made the preliminary impressions and study casts, using an impression tray with oval floor form, the best suited for taking impressions of edentulous ridges.

And so began the days of my slavery.

Confined as I am here, there is neither day nor night, but an unremitting succession of frenum trims, post dams, boxing in, pouring up, festoon carving, fixing sprue channels, and all the innumerable details of dental prosthetic work. No one assists me. No one converses with me, save in brusque barks relevant to the work at hand. My food consists of liqueous and gelatinous substances such as might be expected would form the diet of a toothless race.

Oh, I am sick of the sight of their blue skins, bluer mouths and horny ridges! I am sick of my slavish serfdom!

I have been given material to keep records and am writing this in expectation of later reducing it in size by the method here employed, and of thereinafter inserting copies between the palatal and occlusual surfaces of the plates. It will be necessary to make such plates imperfect, so that the wearers will be obliged to go to dentists on Earth for repairs, because it is not always practical for them to teleport—in fact, I believe they can only do it on the 8th day of every third month. Naturally, I cannot do this to every plate, for they might become suspicious.

You may well imagine how it goes against my grain to produce defective work, but I have no other choice. Twice they have brought me fresh dental supplies, which is how I calculate their teleporting cycle. I have my wristwatch with me and thus I am enabled to reckon the passing of time.

What their exact purpose is in going to Earth, I do not know. My growing suspicion is that their much-vaunted superior science is a fraud and that their only superiority lies in the ability to teleport. One curious item may give a clue: They have questioned me regarding the Old Age Assistance programs of the several States. As I have said, they all *look* old.

Can it be that elsewhere on this planet there is imprisoned some poor devil of a terrestrial printer or engraver, toiling under duress to produce forged birth certificates and other means of identification, to the fell purpose of allowing these aliens to live at ease at the financial expense of the already overburdened U.S. taxpayer?

To whom shall I address my plea for help? To the Federal Government? But it has no official or even unofficial knowledge that this otherworldly race exists. The F.B.I.? But does teleporting under false pretenses to another planet constitute kidnaping across State lines?

It seems the only thing I can do is to implore whichever dental practitioner reads these lines to communicate at once with the American Dental Association. I throw myself upon the mercy of my fellow professional men.

Dentists and Dental Prostheticians! Beware of men with blue mouths and horny, edentulous ridges! Do not be deceived by flattery and false promises! Remember the fate of that most miserable of men, Morris Goldpepper, D.D.S., and, in his horrible predicament, help, oh, help him!

III

A long silence followed the reading of this document. At length it was broken by Dr. Hansen.

"That brave man," he said in a husky voice. "That brave little man."

"Poor Morris," said Dr. Danbourge. "Think of him imprisoned on a far-off planet, slaving like a convict in a salt mine, so to speak, making false teeth for these inhuman aliens, sending these messages to us across the trackless void. It's pitiful, and yet, Doctors, it is also a tribute to the indomitable spirit of Man!"

Dr. Weinroth moved his huge hands. "I'd like to get ahold of just one of those blue bastards," he growled.

Dr. Rorke cleared his throat. All present looked at their President respectfully and eagerly.

"I need hardly tell you, Doctors," he said crisply, "that the A.D.A. is a highly conservative organization. We do not go about things lightly. One such message we might ignore, but there have been eleven reported, all identical with the first. Even eleven such messages we might perhaps not consider, but when they come from a prominent scientist of the stature of Dr. Morris Goldpepper—

"Handwriting experts have pronounced this to be *his* handwriting beyond cavil of a doubt. Here"—he delved into a box—"are the eleven plates in question. Can any of you look at these clean lines and deny that they are the work of the incomparable Goldpepper?"

The six other men looked at the objects, shook their heads.

"Beautiful," murmured Dr. Smith, "even in their broken state. Poems in plastic! M.G. *couldn't* produce bad work if he tried!"

Dr. Rorke continued. "Each report confirmed that the person who brought in the plate had a blue mouth and edentulous ridges, just as the message states. Each blue-mouthed patient exhibited the outward appearance of old age. *And* gentlemen, of those eleven, no less than *eight* were reported from the State of California. Do you realize what that means? California offers the highest amount of financial assistance to the elderly! Goldpepper's surmise was right!"

Dr. Hansen leaned forward. "In addition, our reports show that five of those eight are leaders in the fight against fluoridation of drinking water! It is my carefully considered belief that there is something in their physical makeup, evolved on another planet, which cannot tolerate fluorine even in minute quantities, because they certainly—being already toothless—wouldn't be concerned with the prevention of decay."

Young Dr. McCallister took the floor. "We have checked with dental supply houses and detail men in the New York metropolitan area and we found that large quantities of prosthetic supplies have been delivered to an otherwise unknown outfit—called the Echs Export Company—located not far north of the Washington Market! There is every reason to believe that this is the place Dr. Goldpepper mentioned. One of our men went there, found present only one man in appearance an *old* man. Our representative feigned deafness, thus obliging this person to open his mouth and talk loudly. Doctors, he reports that this person *has a blue mouth!*"

There was a deep intake of breath around the table.

Dr. Rorke leaned forward and snapped off the tape recorders. "This next is off the record. It is obvious, Doctors, that no ordinary methods will suffice to settle this case, to ensure the return of our unfortunate colleague, or to secure the withdrawal of these extraterrestrial individuals from our nation and planet. I cannot, of course, officially endorse what might be termed 'strong-arm' methods. At the same time, I feel that our adversaries are not entitled to polite treatment. And obviously the usual channels of law enforcement are completely closed to us.

"Therefore—and remember, no word of this must pass outside our circle—therefore I have communicated something of this matter to Mr. Albert Annapollo, the well-known waterfront figure, who not long ago inaugurated the splendid Longshoremen's Dental Health Plan. Mr. Annapollo is a somewhat rough person, but he is nonetheless a *loyal* American. . . .

"We know now the Achilles heel of these alien creatures. It is fluorine. We know also how to identify them. And I think we may shortly be able to announce results. Meanwhile—" he drew a slip of paper from his pocket—"it is already the first of the month in that quarter when the dental supplies are due to be transported— or teleported, as Dr. Goldpepper terms it—to their distant destination. A large shipment is waiting to be delivered from the warehouses of a certain wholesaler to the premises of the Echs Exporting Company. I have had copies of this made and wrapped around each three-ounce bottle of Ellenbogen's Denture Stik-Phast. I presume it meets with your approval."

He handed it to Dr. Hansen, who, as the others present nodded in grimly emphatic approval, read it aloud.

"From The American Dental Association, representing over 45,000 registered dentists in the United States and its Territories, to Dr. Morris Goldpepper, wherever you may be: DO NOT DESPAIR! We are intent upon your rescue! We will bend every effort to this end! We shall fight the good fight!

"Have courage, Dr. Morris Goldpepper! You shall return!"

THE SIXTH SEASON

CARVILLE'S FLAGSHIP MUST HAVE GOTTEN CLEAR PAST THE last system before The Coalsack; that was obvious, for the small ten-jet flagship gig could never have gotten as far as it did otherwise.

("The *Marie Celeste,*" muttered the anitquarians. No one listened, disappearances were too common to spend much time on.)

They asked themselves what of the main vessels, but there was nothing in the gig itself—no living person, nor any dead one for that matter—to give any information about the fate of the *16-G*, the *18-G*, or the *32-L*. Except for the regulation stores and three small objects, the gig was empty.

The three items (three of the same sort, that is: the originals were on Earth, in a locked case) stood on the table in headquarters hut. Hyatt looked at them without favor. "If Carville had to vanish, why," he asked, "couldn't he do a clean job of it, at least?"

The calendar-clock gave a little ping, the *1* in the right-hand space in the slot trembled, slid up out of sight, was replaced by a *2*.

"Day 12," said Leiser, brightly. The hour-gauge stayed blank, numbers crawled around the spindle showing seconds. Leiser always made the obvious comment; when the photo-cells turned the tubes on, Leiser would remark, "Let there be light!" Always, always, *always*. Now, his duty done (for certainly no one would have noticed the end of another twenty-four hour period unless Leiser had pointed it out: no one, that is, except Hyatt, Koley, and Macklin, the other members of the expedition), the biochemist turned his attention to the sherry-colored fluid dripping slowly through the filter. Muttering something about viscosity, he made a minute adjustment to his equipment.

Once again Hyatt looked at the three things on the table, the things almost exactly like those found in the gig which had been found in The Coalsack—the bifurcated root, the lump of gummy brown sap, the bottle of (as it was promptly named) Carville's Fluid. The original liquid was darker, the Second Expedition having had only a regulation still with it. The one which Leiser now brooded over had been made especially for the purpose, and produced a fluid with fewer impurities. (Just what those impurities might be like—and be good for—was a matter which took much of his time.)

There was little doubt where the three things had come from: Carville had not been scheduled to stop at any new place, for one thing. And the root had the characteristic blonde nap which appeared on all the floral specimens the First Expedition had brought back from its brief visit ten years earlier.

"He either should have vanished completely—gig and all—or brought the fleet back intact," Hyatt went on. "In either case, we wouldn't be here, because it's a certainty a third trip would've been made up of his men."

Leiser paused, pipette in hand. "Whose men, George?" he asked.

Hyatt gave him a sour look. "The Panchen Lama's," he said. Leiser nodded, then he started to frown, then his face cleared.

"Oh, the *Panchen* Lama's!" he said. "For a minute I thought you'd said the *Dalai Lama's,* George." He emptied a drop from the pipette into a little dish, proceeded to do things to it.

Hyatt swore. Then he went into the next room, the center section of headquarters hut. Koley was cutting roots into three parts and adding each part to a different heap. Trunks went in one pile, the short legs in a second, the long ones in a third. Later, he would put each pile through the grinder, then the blender. Next step was the still, followed by a battery of tests designed to show up differences. The differences, if any, were minute—but Koley had a lot of tests—and a lot of time.

They all had a lot of time. Two hundred times twenty-four hours minus twelve times twenty-four hours.

"Hello, all you Gentlemen Adventurers," Hyatt said. The botanist looked up, smiled, looked down again. *K'ch'ch'k'ch't,* went the saw-edged knife. Macklin waved a hand, lazily. His book, perched on his stomach, rose and fell to the slow rhythm of his breathing.

"Studying irregular native verbs, Mack?" Hyatt asked.

Mack grunted. "Are there any other kinds?" he asked. "Or, for that matter—are there any verbs? It wouldn't surprise me if the natives communicate by wiggling their ears, and these noises they give out have no more meaning than those of deaf-mutes . . . What about you, George? You're tabbed for Languages, as well as Logistics and Records: Why don't you have a try at the local Volapük? Don't you feel the challenge of it?"

Hyatt stumbled over a box on the cluttered floor, said several words, of which only two—"the challenge"—were in English.

Koley paused in sweeping up a tiny heap of sawdust, which he would put in a tiny envelope with an identifying label on it. "Isn't that the Vegan version of 'son-of-a-bitch'?" he asked.

Macklin heaved himself up into a semi-sitting position.

"To be precise—or as precise as one can be, considering—it is the Vegan for 'hermaphrodite - illegitimately - begotten - during - its - mother's - moulting - period - by - a - slave-suffering - from - venereal - encephalitis.' "

The botanist whistled. "Seems comprehensive enough," he said, picking up a tiny envelope. "The more taboos a culture has, the richer its obscenity."

The linguist nodded. "Oh, Vegan is expressive, all right, though terse . . . No, George: this is one of my own books. Listen." He found his place, began to read. " 'So-called "magic" can say to so-called "science": "Where wast thou when I laid the foundations of the Earth? Declare it, if thou hast understanding!" And who art thou to say to Nature, "Thus far shalt come, and no farther, and here shall thy proud waves be stayed?' "

"I'll cap your book's quotation with another," Hyatt said. " 'Who do you have to be?' "

The door at the far end of the hut began to reverberate. Hyatt repeated his Vegan curse, yelled, "Okay—I'm coming—*T'lah-k'ch—oh'h'rr-um*—knock it off, gahdamn it—*t'lah* . . ." His voice subsided as he loped off towards the door, but the banging continued, as it always did, until he opened the door.

The door-kicking was followed, as usual, by the sound of stomping. It may have been social, but it also served the function of getting all the snow shaken off the robe between the door and the central room. One last *thump-thump* and the visitor entered, and flung his robe on the floor, seating himself on it. He was tall, dark and warty, and smelled like a roomful of ill-trained cats, but in his hand he held a bundle of Carville's Roots, so—

"He ain't no rose, don't smell him, trade with him," said Macklin, seeing a familiar expression settle on Hyatt's face; for local protocol seemed to require the purchaser's holding one end of the bundle while the seller held the other.

"Damn Carville, anyway," said Hyatt, opening the box of knives with his free hand.

" 'Thou shalt not curse the dead,' " murmured Koley, beginning to weigh the few whole roots left on his table. "Anyway, he came just in time, we're about fresh out."

Hyatt began to spread knives on the robe.

Macklin said, "And furthermore—as you seem to forget mighty often—the lives you are helping to prolong may include your own." And he saw, by the latest expression on Hyatt's face, that he *had* forgotten.

For there it was: Whatever else the second planet of

Fisher's Binary (called, by those in the know, "Fishbein Two") might produce, Earth and its colonies were interested only in Carville's Fluid. And in that, only because it seemed to offer a perfect medium for the administration and retention of gerontium. Rats, mice, guinea-pigs, Vegan tharses, and those curious creatures from the Cornwall System which British discoverers had named "Golliwogs"—all, without exception, had had their lives prolonged, in full vigor, by periods ranging up to 35% beyond the norm, by gerontium. It was not precisely a new discovery. But larger living things, beings with slower metabolisms—men, for instance—had been helped not at all by gerontium. The human body would not retain it long enough for it to be of use.

Until Carville's Fluid came on the scene.

A small escape gig, lying inert in the center of The Coalsack, its hull-lights on, its emergency signal still sending, and empty, absolutely empty, except for regulation stores—and three small objects: a bifurcated root with an odd blonde nap, a gummy lump of an unknown substance, and a small vial of brown fluid.

"You're right, Mack—of course you're right," Hyatt said. "Gentlemen Adventurers, I beg your pardons." He began to count the roots. "Hey, these are small," he said to the native. The native gestured towards the knives with his free hand, gurgled something. "Small—" Hyatt indicated with his fingers how small they were, measured off a distance, frowned, shook his head. "Hey, Koley, toss me one of those there. Thanks."

The native, after being shown repeatedly that his latest batch were visibly smaller than the others, blew out his lips and began to talk. He picked up a knife, gestured, gurgled.

"I *think*," said Macklin, "he may be saying, 'Small roots? So, small knives.' "

"We haven't *got* any small knives," Hyatt exclaimed. "The Fisher Expedition Reports just said they liked *knives*. How in the Hell—"

Softly, softly, Macklin said, "Take it easier, George. If I may coin a phrase, you'll live longer."

The rate of exchange was finally settled at two small roots for one knife. The knives fastened up with the same piece of braided grass that had bound the roots, the native took a leisurely look around the room, and then a large bite out of one of Macklin's blankets. He masticated it thoughtfully for a long, silent moment, then spat it out. The linguist sighed, relieved.

"Goodie, he doesn't like it. Insulation, heating, or not, with these blizzards raging outside, I don't feel I care to part with more than a mouthful of my blanket."

The native held up a moist scrap, emitted a liquid syllable.

"I should venture that means 'What?,' " Macklin said. "I'd write it down—if there existed a phonetic system capable . . . Well, since it seems to be time for the language lesson—" Grunting, he pushed himself up from his bed, took out the recorder, inserted a cartridge. "Then he repeated an approximation of the native's word. "Blanket," he said. "Blanket."

"Brrwahng-airw . . ."

Koley began to weigh the new batch of roots. "The fat cat sat on the mat," he murmured. Then, "I wonder how long the snow will last," he said. "It was only powdering the ground when we landed . . . Fisher's Notes don't say anything about any snow. He mentioned 'light rains.' Of course, he wasn't here very long."

"Damn Fisher," Hyatt said. "Damn Carville, too."

A little over two weeks later the blizzards stopped, gave way to light falls of snow like those they had seen when the flagship put them down with supplies and equipment for two hundred days, the length of a year on the second planet of Fisher's Binary. For two hundred days the four of them were to stay—

". . . or for such lesser or greater period as the Expedition Authorities may think proper or necessary, until relieved," said the Final Directives. ("As if we had a chance to go anywhere else," Hyatt growled.) There wasn't anything new in the FDs, there never was. It had been made clear to them from the start that they were to "secure as large a quantity of Carville's Roots as possible, similar amounts of the gum and/or sap of the plant if made available, and any specimens of the whole plant taken *in situ* if, on investigation, you are satisfied this may be done without any affront to local mores."

It was also repeated, in both General Instructions and Final Directives, that the Expedition "should endeavor to obtain specimens of the plant in each season, so that the stages of development may be observed." This was in order to find out at what stage of development it might be best suited for medical use. Whilst engaged in plucking the plants *in situ* (making damned sure this was not an offense against the moral code of Fishbein Two), they were to make a large number of standard tests of the *situ* "in order to ascertain the feasibility of cultivating the plant aforesaid in some region more closely proximate to the Settled Systems." And, in their spare time, to carry on the usual routines of meteorological, socio-anthropological, geological, ecological, and etceteralogical research and observation.

The blizzards had prevented most of this, of course. Now, with even the light falls of powdery snow ceased, two-man teams had started out scouting the place in the blower.

Fisher's Notes had stated that the largest land-mass (which appeared to be the only inhabited one) lay in the southern hemisphere of the second planet. The snows were melting slightly, the two suns glowed thinly in the misty sky. It was Day 37—as Leiser had, of course, pointed out the instant the cal-clock pinged the departure of Day 36—when he and Hyatt set off in the blower to make dimension shots of the western end of the mainland.

"Still no signs of anything like a settlement in this whole place," Hyatt said. "Guess they can't stand one another's conversation. Not that I blame—"

"I was wondering about my ladinos," said Leiser, giving no references as to when, where, why, or what.

"You were, huh?"

"Gosh, they probably won't know me when I get back."

"No, huh."

"But I'll stop, first, and get some little worms for them."

"Is that a forest fire ahead?" Hyatt pointed. "Look—and there, too!"

Dirty-colored columns rose, wavering, high into the air ahead of them at several points—then blended into a dun, diffused mass.

"Doesn't *look* like a forest fire, George. Or even a brush fire." They took the blower down to just above safety level and, turning at right angles, began to skim parallel to the lines of smoke—if it was smoke.

"Ladinos, you know, George, ladinos aren't easy to—George? *George, what—?*"

Later on he joked about it, comparing himself to the coal-miner's canary. But at that particular moment George Hyatt wasn't joking. His face blue and congested, he reached—lungs straining vainly—for the oxygen mask. It eluded his struggling fingers. It was Leiser who, even before adjusting his own, fixed Hyatt's mask on his face and turned on the oxygen. It was Leiser who piloted the blower back to the camp. And, of course, it was Leiser—it *would* be Leiser—who remarked, on entering the headquarters hut, "Gee, the funniest thing just happened: We had some trouble breathing out there—didn't we, George?"

Macklin and Koley, forewarned and foremasked, took the blower out to get a look. "It seems to come right out of the ground," Mack said, on his return. "Right up from rifts in the snow-banks. I thought at first it might be a subterranean fire—your coal-mine simile, George—but now I rather think it may be some sort of natural gas."

Koley, looking out the window, said, "Smokey gas drifting down from the northwest—mist and fog drifting up from the southeast—what will happen if they meet? Let's take a look at the barometer."

The glass was down, way down; and what happened when "they" met was the thickest, filthiest, foulest smog any of them had ever seen. The headquarters hut was insulated, but it wasn't pressurized (Fisher's Notes having said nothing about any smog), and the fumes crept in faster than they could be driven out. A perpetual ginger-colored haze hung in the air, the men peered at one another through burning, weeping eyes.

"Item," said Macklin, "my eyes feel like they'd rather not. Item, my head aches fit to burst. Item, my mouth tastes like a convict's shoe—"

Leiser rubbed the tears away, squinted at the still-gauges. "I don't seem to have any appetite, sort of," he mourned. "I'm hungry, but I can't *eat*. Isn't that a funny thing?"

"Remind me to laugh," said Hyatt.

The door started its familiar resounding. "Beware the Gooks," Hyatt croaked, "when they come bearing—oh, gahdamn it, all *right! T'lah-k'ch! Oh'h'rr-um!* And he always moves in so slowly, too—" He took an oxygen set with him, and no one gainsayed him. The usual stomping noises heralded the return of the native. Koley murmured that now, at least, they knew those must be social, as now there was no snow to knock off.

Wisps of the smog seemed to play about the visitor. He had nothing else on, certainly, except his warts, which went all the way down and all the way up.

"Hherrhwo," he gargled at them.

"Tippecanoe and Tyler, too," said Macklin. They had still no idea of his own name, if he had one, and all of them had long since passed through and out of the stage of giving aliens odd, arch, fancy or ridiculous names. So, reviving an ancient if short-lived fad of naming pets with common proper names, they had decided to call him Joseph.

"Hherrhwo. Dz'hosegh," said the alien, now. It was not at all certain he got the idea. He had a bundle of roots with him, as always—fine, jumbo ones this time, and he wanted two knives apiece. What he did with all the knives, was another question. Hyatt suggested he traded them for wives in the mating season.

"Ahoy, Joseph," Macklin said, tapping the cartridge and listening to it. It seemed to have enough use in it yet, so he fitted it into the recorder. "Listen, how long will this smog last?" And he tried, haltingly, to repeat the question in Joseph's language. Joseph thought it over, blowing out his lips and rubbing his warts. Then he said something which might have meant Soon, Tomorrow, By and By, or Presently.

It lasted, by actual count, thirty-three days from the onset. They arose (decidedly precipitously) from sleep on Day 34. Their eyes were clear, their heads didn't ache, there was no offensive taste in their mouths, and they all had fine appetites. . . . But the water reached up to their knees.

It rose slowly enough after that, the first day of the rising, so that they were able to convey most of their supplies and equipment to the nearest hill. And the waters kept on rising.

"I guess Fisher must have come either at the beginning or end of the rainy season," Macklin said, after they had—laboriously, and by dangerously overloading the blower—managed to save about half of their gear from the floods by moving to the highest point of land in the vicinity. " 'Light rains'—ha!"

Hyatt damned Fisher with the most lurid curses available to English, Hindi, Neo-Xosa, Intergal, and Vegan. Then he repeated them for Carville—"With knobs on," he said.

Koley, returning from his task of spraying a repellant circle around the camp to discourage such minor specimens (fortunately, there seemed no major ones) of local fauna as had decided to share the hill, had a question to ask.

"Well, we know how long the rains will last, anyway, don't we?"

"Forty days and forty nights," said Hyatt, huddling over the heating unit in the emergency shelter, and watching the rains come down—not so much in sheets as in blankets.

The botanist shook his head. "It was snowing lightly when we came," he said. "After about twenty-six days of blizzards it started slackening. The smog lasted just thirty three days. We can figure that we missed about three days of snow before we landed. And there were about three days between the end of it and the start of the smog. So, say, thirty-two days for the snow season. There ought to be a month of rain."

And there was, too, though after a week or so the waters stopped rising. Joseph came less frequently, but he came, none the less, banging lustily on the piece of tree-trunk (lighter than balsa) on which he paddled up. Since they had observed at their original meeting that he had only four digits on each hand, it had come as no surprise that he couldn't count past eight (and the inevitable argument among them: did the six-unit system of counting—dozens, sixty seconds, sixty degrees—imply the former existence of a six-fingered race?). It was equally expected that he was unable to tell exactly when the rains would stop, but answered Macklin's inquiries with a phrase which might have meant A Long Time, Never, or, After A While.

"Gee, isn't it a funny thing," Leiser mused, "that we never see any of the other natives, except from the blower. Is Joseph their chief, maybe?"

"Maybe he's cornered the supply of roots," Hyatt suggested. "He drives a hard bargain with the knives."

But Macklin rather thought that Joseph acted as agent or comprador for his brethren. "What comes after the rains, Joseph?" he asked. "After the Big Waters—what? Hey?"

"Khey? . . . After Big Waters—No Waters."

"What, none at all?"

He busied himself with binding up his bundle of newly-acquired knives, and made no answer. On the thirtieth day the waters began to subside rapidly and only scattered showers fell. On the thirty-third day these stopped.

And then the drought began.

All the springs dried up, the ponds vanished, the brooks retreated underground, and in a sky suddenly free of any haze the double suns blazed down. For a few days they were able to bring up small amounts of water by drilling in the creek-beds. After that the still was obliged to cease operations on Carville's Fluid and start refining sea-water brought in by the blower. It didn't produce enough, of course, for more than drinking, cooking, and a wipe with a damp cloth.

"This can't go on," said Hyatt, faintly, on the twentieth day.

" 'Thus far shalt thou come, and no farther—' Hey?" From Macklin.

"Only eighty-five more days before the relief comes," Koley pointed out in his soft voice. "And think of afterwards: When you're a hundred and fifty, in the prime of vigorous middle-age, you'll look back on this time and smile about it."

In just twelve days time Hyatt did smile. That was when the water returned to the springs, brooks and ponds. "Come on in," he yelled to Macklin. "The water's fine . . . What are you standing there brooding about?"

Macklin shrugged, began to take off his clothes. "I was wondering what's next," he said.

He found out the next day.

Leiser was the first one up. "Gee," he said, "look at all the flowers!" Then he sneezed.

Hyatt yawned, stretched, padded to the window. "What flowers?" he asked. Leiser gestured. As far as they could see, the ground was carpeted with a kaleidescope of colors. "You mean, for once—a *nice* season on this damned place? I can't believe it. They're probably poisonous."

In a way, he was right.

Evidently they were not all allergic to the same plants. Leiser sneezed continuously until his nose began to bleed. Then he went on sneezing again—deep, painful, convulsive sneezes. Hyatt's eyes turned yellow and began to exude a pussy discharge. The slightest light was agony to him. Koley broke out in blisters which burned like fire, inside and out. Macklin could keep no solid food down and had the dry heaves almost continuously.

And yet it was Macklin who went to the door to let Joseph in, Hyatt lying on his bed with his eyes tightly covered, silent for once.

"They're smaller than usual," Mack said, gagging and grimacing. "But I can't haggle . . . a knife apiece: take them and—"

After a long, quiet minute Koley asked, "What's the matter?" Macklin handed over the bundle of roots. "Sticky, aren't they?" Koley said. Then, "The sap! This is the first time we've seen them gummy." He looked up. Mack gestured towards Joseph. Lesicr began to sneeze again. Joseph was licking his fingers of the sap with a long, black tongue.

"There's nothing wrong with *him,*" the linguist said. " 'For every venom, nature hath her antidote . . .' " He scraped a dark blob off a root, tasted it, raised his eyebrows, began to nibble.

After eight hours he pronounced himself entirely cured, and ate a hearty meal. The others, whom he had urged to wait and see, fell upon the bundle of fresh roots, scraping, licking, chewing. It provided a perfect cure for all of them—or, more exactly, a relief which began to flag only the day Joseph arrived with another batch.

"The Expedition Authorities won't like it that we ate up the sap we're supposed to collect," Leiser pointed out. Hyatt suggested that the Expedition Authorities participate in a particularly complex Vegan perversion, and even Koley and Macklin seemed undisposed to worry.

"Look at what some of the ancient expeditions had to put up with," he said. "They even, on occasion, ate one another."

Koley looked up from his worktable. "Do you suppose that's what might have happened to Carville and his men?" he asked.

Hyatt wiggled. "I'd rather not think of Carville and his men," he said. "As the time gets close to our relief, I find myself getting rather nervous . . . Do you suppose they will get here before the snows?"

"Before the snows?"

Hyatt glared. "I assumed I spoke clearly. And I also assume that the seasons on this planet follow a definite cycle. Hence, as it was snowing when we arrived, it ought to be snowing again when we leave—if we leave exactly on time, that is. I trust I have made this clear, Koley."

Koley swung around and glared back. "Clear as mud," he said, in a loud voice. "Your assumptions are based on the further assumption that you can do simple arithmetic. Which you obviously can't. The year here is two hundred days long. We are to spend two hundred days here. Of these, one hundred seventy-odd have elapsed. Since each season lasts somewhat over thirty days, and since thirty days have passed since the flower season began, there is every reason to believe that we are scheduled to have one more season *before* the snows start. Or is this too complicated?"

Leiser said he wished to hell Koley would shut up. "Yell, yell, yell, that's all you do," he said. In a short time none of them were on speaking terms.

It was five days later that Hyatt, brooding from the corner in which he had taken to spending much of his time (it was safer that way: no one could sneak up on him from behind), saw Koley tip-toe across the room and brain Leiser with the hammer. Macklin laughed heartily.

"Should we eat him?" he asked, tears spilling down his cheeks.

Hyatt said, "It must be the gum of the roots. We took too much of it. We took too much of it. We took too much of it. We—"

Koley gave Leiser another smash for good measure. Then he looked up. "The trouble with you, George," he said, "is that you're out of your mind. So was Leiser out of his mind. So is Macklin out of his mind. You know who the only sane people are around here? Joseph and I, that's who. And Joseph's friends, I guess, too."

But Koley was wrong about Joseph, as they learned very

shortly. . . . Another thing they learned about Joseph—and his friends—when the natives broke the door down and poured into the room, screaming incoherently, was just exactly what all the knives had been wanted for.

NEGRA SUM

FOR MOST OF THE DAY AND OFTEN WELL INTO NIGHT, MR. Edwards sat in a little cubicle at the head of a narrow shabby-carpeted stairway. People ascended and descended, but there were no angels among them; there were, indeed, wrestlings, but they never ended in benediction. On the window of the downstairs door was a sign reading, in large letters: ROOMS $1.50. In a smaller lettering was the sentence: *And Up, on weekly rates.* No one, so it seemed to Mr. Edwards, ever read past the first line. When he was newly installed in his office he had carefully explained that rooms were *not* available at $1.50 for a single night, that it was necessary to pay for seven nights in advance in order to enjoy this rate; but he had gotten tired of it. . . .

Stumble or shuffle on the steps. "Gotta room fra dollena-haf?" A beery breath through the tiny window. Mr. Edwards shook his head.

"None left. Sorry. *Two* dollars? Two fifty, with bath?" It was surprising how little interest the guests, potential, showed in having a private bath, or even in splurging two dollars for a room and the privilege of using the public shower. When the bars closed at two in the morning the stumbling and shuffling on the stairs increased. Sometimes Mr. Edwards was able to hang up the NO VACANCY sign and go to sleep by half past two. If he was lucky he might be able to as early as twelve. Hang up the sign, that is, not sleep. Oh, he went to bed, but even with his eyes closed the procession continued . . . up and down, up and down, past his eyes . . . the red bristly beer-dewed faces that begrudged every copper not slid across a bar . . . the dough-like loose-lipped cunning faces that told—even without words—that all they wanted, Bud, was a room for two for just about twenny minutes, Bud . . . the uncertain roving-eyed oh-so-polite faces, "just starting in work and wouldn't get paid till tamorra night" or else "had gotten in town too late to cleck the check, just my doggone luck, Fella; but, uh, first thing in the morning, now—" . . . they passed and they repassed, creating their own light even in the darkness and bearing their own darkness even in the light.

Few of these faces, even if they stayed, ever put down fifty cents for a key deposit, so Mr. Edwards had no need to see them as they departed in the morning. He slept late and would gladly have slept later to put off the hour when he awoke, yawning and gummy-eyed. It is accounted one of the Eleusinian Mysteries that the sun rose at midnight, but for Mr. Edwards it rose at half past nine or half past ten in the morning, and the only mystery was that he was ever able to rise with it.

Last night's warmed-over coffee. Homogenized orange. The first cigarette, bearing Death on every puff. Something as bitter as the coffee in the dirty cup: the memory of a Mr. Edwards—not Mister then—who sat in a classroom with folded hands and sang, they all sang, children and teachers, a certain song.

> Father, we thank Thee for the night
> And for the shining morning bright. . . .

It *had* seemed shining and bright then. It really had.

> Help us to do the things we should,
> And be to others kind and good. . . .

Well, as soon as breakfast was over, the things we should do were as follows: Make a list of all guests delinquent in rent and lock them out by noon, if there was baggage to lock, or else have the maid make the room up to rent. . . . Wake up and escort out, no matter what language, any gin-weary old trulls whom the transients may have sneaked up the back stairs. . . . Count the laundry and bundle it before Louie got there with the clean linens, and have his blood if there was any shortage in the count. . . . Roust from their rooms the two or three old pensioners, turn off their dim electric lights, and send them out into the friendly streets—"Until the maid gets through"—the hotel having no lobby or lounge. *Kind and good?* Not in *this* business, brother.

But by twelve fifteen Mr. Edwards was back at his little window and—for the first and last time during the day—he was smiling. At twelve fifteen—no matter when he'd come in the night before—Jack Tristram went out, dressed for tennis or the beach, clean-garbed, clear-eyed, smooth-combed, always with a smile and a cheerful word for Mr. Edwards. The other guests were deadbeats, hasbeens, neverweres. What had Jack in common with them, indeed? with his long-limbed, smooth-skinned, beautifully built and handsome body and face, his youth, his charm? If he never worked, what of it? If he was now and then a few days due on his rent, Mr. Edwards covered up for him. It was a pleasure. When Jack showed those clean white teeth in a half-smile, half-grin that crinkled the golden-brown skin around his eyes (incredibly blue) and said, "Well, another swell day, and how's my pal?" Mr. Edwards knew it really was a swell day, that he really was Jack's pal. He felt the world, after all, was not completely rotten, if Jack could go happily off to tennis or swimming. He felt renewed in strength to put up with the vile-tempered MacIde in #20 who walked up and down on the thin carpet with heavy shoes, the stupid Miss Worth in #6 and her ridiculous never silent twittering voice, the sow-like Mrs. Roltt in #11 who dropped food all over the floor so that it swarmed with roaches, and the incompetence of Mary the chambermaid. . . .

"How's my buddy on this beautiful day?"

"Fine, Jack, and you? Going swimming?"

"Ee-yup. Goin to see whut the waves washed up fr me today." He would wink drolly. Mr. Edwards would chuckle. Officially, of course, he had to turn away his eyes when Jack came back, as he often did, with a girl as young and attractive as himself, their feet trotting nimbly and swiftly up the stairs, their hands joined and arms swinging, her eyes fixed upon his face, her breath swelling the proud promise of her young bosom; into his room together, the click of the night latch, the rattle of the chain-bolt, the single submissive squeak of the bed.

On this day Mr. Edwards was feeling worse than usual. He had made a mistake in calculating the fiscal status of one Sweeney, a port-soaked frycook in #5, who—after enjoying a night's free lodging—had broke bivouac and departed with all his gear. This was certain to affect for the worse the never very jolly manner of Mr. Brock, the owner of this and several other cheap hotels and "guest houses." Two downy-faced chicken Marines, failing to prove that rum and vodka were socially compatible, had vomited on the floor, and Mr. Edwards was obliged to clean up because Mary said such things kind of turned her stomach, like. And all night long, in the room next to his, the sullen feet of that damned MacIde had clumped back-and-forth, back-and-forth.

"How's m' cobber this lovely noontime?" Jack Tristram stood grinning at him. It seemed a vacuous grin to Mr. Edwards. He observed, only half-aware, that Jack was not wearing his silver chain as usual. He noted that Jack had failed to use any mouthwash and he was disturbed at having noticed it. Stupid grin . . .

"Your cobber'd feel better if he could see the color of your money for a change!" he said, snappishly.

"Huhhh? Oh. Well, yeah . . . sure." He backed away, uncertain, grinned emptily again, and galloped down the steps.

Mr. Edwards grunted. He locked the office and went out in the dingy hall, tracing down Mary by her invariable spoor of spilt scouring powder and dropped towels, traced her to the showers where the dirt was just moved from one corner to another and the polish left to dry to a gray crust on the brightwork. There she stood, mop in hand, staring dreamily at the scabrous wall and patting her dyed-red hair with its gray roots.

He had seen her six days a week for several years and never had she seemed any more to him than a necessary nuisance. Her mild good nature had merely annoyed him. Now, suddenly, he felt an overwhelming affection for her. She seemed charming. He seized her about the waist and planted a smacking kiss on her cheek.

"How is the most beautiful chambermaid on Southwest Third Street?" he sang out. Mary turned deep rose-pink.

"Why, Mis Ter Ed Wards! Ooohoohooheeyeeyeehee!"

"Why aren't you making some good man happy? Why aren't you making *me* happy? Hey, Mary?" He squeezed.

"OhohahahaNowstopPIT!" But she wasn't angry.

"Well, reluctant as I am to do so, I must tear myself away from this sweet vision. But I shall return." And he was off. Mary gazed after him, shook her head, said Well she never. She looked at the floormop, flicked its dirty coils aimlessly for a moment. "Now what did I want to tell him?" she asked herself. "Oh," she said, and rummaged in her packrat's nest of a pocket. Two tiny bars of soap, a half-broken stick of gum, three violated books of matches, a locket on a chain, a ticket to a TV show, a penny . . . A locket on a chain. She ran out into the hall.

"Hoo hoo! Mr. Edwards!" He came back, eyebrows raised in inquiry, took her right hand and kissed it.

"Yum yum," Mr. Edwards said. Mary tittered.

"Ooo, look what I found in the shower, now," she said. "A locket on a chain, silver it looks like, though I spose it could be that now german silver, like imitation."

"Why not keep it to grace the lovely contours of your throat?" He leaned over, mouth apout, as if he were about to—

"Now, you *stop.* No, uh-uh. It probly blongs to some now person. You better take it." And she dropped it in his hand.

"OK. See you later. Keep track of your towels." He was off again, swinging the locket. . . . *Was* it familiar to him, or did he only think so?

"Such a *nice* man," Mary said, looking at his retreating back.

Mr. Edwards rounded the corner and almost ran into the clump-footed MacIde. Who stood there, smiling shyly and awkwardly. "Oh," said Edwards.

"Hope I haven't bothered you by my nocturnal prowlings," MacIde began. Absently he caught the locket Edwards was swinging on its chain.

"Oh, that's all right," Mr. Edwards said. "I wish all the guests were as little trouble as you." *Very* nice fellow, MacIde.

The locket clicked open in MacIde's hand and both men bent over to look. Inside was a cameo, about the size of a thumbnail. Black on a pink background was the delicately carven head of a young woman, and black were the letters which rimmed it.

"Pretty, isn't it?" Mr. Edwards remarked. "What's it say?"

"I suppose I have enough Latin for that," MacIde said. *"Ex Africa aliquid semper novi*— 'Out of Africa always something new'—Plautus? Pliny? One of those lads. And as for this other: *Negra sum sed formosa*— that's the Vulgate for sure. 'Black am I, but beautiful'—well, she *is,* isn't she? But I must say, old Jerome, saint or not, shows himself unmistakably a white man, doesn't he?"

"Mmmm?"

"I mean, 'Black am I, *but* beautiful.' . . . Now, the original Hebrew, if you'll pardon that scholastic cliché, is *Sh'chorah ani, v'naavah:* 'Black am I, *and* beautiful'—true of all of us, in a way, isn't it? I mean, well, we all have our black aspect, and yet, really, we all have—"

"Our beautiful aspects, too, you mean?"

"Exactly." MacIde beamed. "How well you understand me . . . and yet, here we are, contrasting the two—still committed to that attitude—and it my well be that the two are one, or two aspects of the same thing . . . Whose is it?"

"Oh, mmm, what?" Mr. Edwards, who had been thinking what a pleasant fellow MacIde was, after all—couldn't remember when he'd met anyone he liked as well—said, "Oh, the locket . . . well, I'm not sure I know whose it is. I'll keep it for a while to see if it's claimed." And they parted with pleasant words, both holding on to the locket until the last moment.

The afternoon drew to a close. It was about time for Jack Tristram to be back, girl in hand; but no Jack. Instead, someone looking for Jack.

"You're *sure* he's not in?" the youngish man insisted. "You're not just *saying* that?" Mr. Edwards shook his head. The youngish man clicked his tongue and looked petulant. He smelled sweetly. "How long has he lived here?" was his next question.

"Oh, a while," Mr. Edwards said, vaguely.

The youngish man clicked his tongue again. There was silence.

Slouching up the steps came Miss Worth, a withered sagging virgin of sixty-odd, twittering to herself. She saw the two men and stopped, embarrassed. She smiled an uncertain smile, hesitated, and finally sidled by. Once past, she minced down the hallway, stopped a moment as if to pick up something—and looked back, but the men were not watching. She went on her way.

"He owe you any money? Jackie, I mean?" the youngish man asked, after a silent spell. Mr. Edwards looked at him, said nothing. "Well, he owes *me* money. And not *just* money. Oh, the help and assistance I gave that un*grate*ful—and *then*, just as calmly as you please, *out* he goes through the french windows. My *money*, my *clothes*, my *cuff* links . . ." He tightened his lips for a moment. "*And* a certain *objet d'art* of both financial and senti*ment*al value." A woebegone look settled on his smooth face. "Since he left, *ev*erything seems to have gone wrong."

A slow solid step on the stairs, and Tristram was there. He was in bathing trunks and carried his clothes on his arm. He was alone, there was no girl in sight, and he looked as woebegone as the youngish man. Who at once ceased looking woebegone and began to look waspish.

"*Well!*" he now said, and tapped his foot.

"Oh, hullo, Robbie," Tristram said, listlessly.

"Thank you for keeping in *touch* with me. It was very easy for *you* to find *me*." Tristram scratched the calf of his left leg with the big toe nail of his right foot, and looked at the rug. "*How*ever, never mind. There are a few things I *will* trouble you for. The clothes you may keep—if you can en*dure* to conceal that body beautiful. The cuff links, as I am *sure* you know, were a gift from my aunt and—"

"I haven't got 'em now. I'll get 'em to y'."

"*Pawned* them, I suppose? *And* the locket, the pride of my Sicilian souvenirs?"

Tristram's hand went up to his neck, groped without finding

anything, and finally occupied itself with scratching his broad smooth chest. "I haven't got it. I, uh, I suppose I must of lost it, Robbie."

Mr. Edwards remembered suddenly. His hand slipped in his pocket. It was empty . . . well, in that case, he would say nothing. Lost once, lost again: let it stay lost.

"You *what?*" Robbie's voice rose to a shriek. He put his hands to his temples. "Oh, damn the day I first saw you! What I ever saw *in* you, I don't know. Beef. Beef. That's all you are: Just so much *beeeefff!*"

Tristram scowled. Looking at him, Mr. Edwards was inclined to agree with Robbie. Wearing only his trunks, Tristram did remind him now of nothing so much as a well-trimmed side of beef. Edwards wondered why he had ever thought him charming.

Robbie shrilled, "Why, you're only a common, ordinary *thief!*"

And there was a noise that went *chunck*. Robbie staggered back against the wall, Tristram's arm dropped to his side. Then he moved a step forward, and Mr. Edwards opened his door and scurried out between them.

"All right, now, that's enough of that, you better stop that, I'm warning you, are you hurt?"

Robbie held his hand to the side of his face. He made a noise between a sob and a snuffle. Still clutching his cheek, he moved slowly down the steps. Tristram looked down. Then, when the door closed below, he spoke.

"I'll get you that money I owe you tonight. My uncle'll let me have it. I'm going to ask him for a job, too. Sick of this kind of a life. Sick of those damn tramps of girls, and of guys like Robbie . . ."

He walked off towards his room. En route he passed Miss Worth, coming from hers, fingers fiddling nervously with a silver chain around her neck. "Hi," he said, suddenly cheerful. Miss Worth blushed with delight and surprise.

"Been swimming?" she twittered, unable to keep looking at him, and unable to keep from looking at him.

"Ee-yup. . . . *Say!* How about you and me going out for a movie and an ice-cream cone or something, one of these days? Hmm?"

"*Silly!*" Miss Worth was scarlet. "Why, I'm old enough to be your mother."

"Well, I guess I can take my mother out if I want to. I'm serious, now. I'll be seeing you about it. G'bye now." And he gave her hand a shake.

Miss Worth knew what she had, and although she'd hardly dared hope it would work, it *was* working.

Black am I, but beautiful. . . . Oh yes, *she* knew Latin; Dear Pa*pa* had taught her—*he* had known she was beautiful, but not the others—dogs, all of them, rogues, beasts—how shamefully they had treated her; but no longer: now they would come crawling—*crawling, groveling* . . . Miss Worth laughed aloud as she came up to Mr. Edwards' desk.

He had watched in amazement. What was Tristram bothering with *her* for? But now he found himself smiling back at her, leaning across so as to speak to her when she came to the desk. She wasn't young, she wasn't handsome . . . but still . . . there was *something* about her that was certainly mighty attractive. He just wondered how it was he'd never noticed it before.

OR THE GRASSES GROW

ABOUT HALFWAY ALONG THE NARROW AND ILL-PAVED COUNTY road between Crosby and Spanish Flats (all dips and hollows shimmering falsely like water in the heat till you get right up close to them), the road to Tickisall Agency branches off. No pretense of concrete or macadam—or even grading—deceives the chance or rare purposeful traveler. Federal, State, and County governments have better things to do with their money: Tickisall pays no taxes, and its handful of residents have only recently (and most grudgingly) been accorded the vote.

The sunbaked earth is cracked and riven. A few dirty sheep and a handful of scrub cows share its scanty herbage with an occasional swaybacked horse or stunted burro. Here and there a gaunt automobile rests in the thin shadow of a board shack, and a child, startled doubtless by the smooth sound of a strange motor, runs like a lizard through the dusty wastes to hide, and then to peer. Melon vines dried past all hope of fruit lie in patches next to whispery, tindery cornstalks.

And in the midst of all this, next to the only spring which never goes dry, are the only painted buildings, the only decent buildings in the area. In the middle of the green lawn is a pole with the flag, and right behind the pole, over the front door, the sign:

U. S. BUREAU OF INDIAN AFFAIRS
TICKISALL AGENCY
OFFICE OF THE SUPERINTENDENT

There were already a few Indians gathering around that afternoon, the women in cotton-print dresses, the men in overalls. There would soon be more. This was scheduled as the last day for the Tickisall Agency and Reservation. Congress had passed the bill, the President had signed it, the Director of the Bureau of Indian Affairs had issued the order. It was supposed to be a great day for the Tickisall Nation—only the Tickisalls, what was left of them, didn't seem to think so. Not a man or woman of them spoke. Not a child whimpered. Not a dog barked.

Before Uncle Fox-head sat a basket with four different kinds of clay, and next to the basket was a medicine gourd full of water. The old man rolled the clay between his moistened palms, singing in a low voice. Then he washed his hands and sprinkled them with pollen. Then he took up the prayer-sticks, made of juniper—(once there had been juniper trees on the reservation, once there had been many trees)—and painted with the signs of Thunder, Sun, Moon, Rain, Lightning. There were feathers tied to the sticks—once there had been birds, too . . .

Oh, People-of-The-Hidden Places,
Oh, take our message to The Hidden Places,
Swiftly, swiftly, now . . .

the old man chanted, shaking the medicine-sticks.

Oh, you, Swift Ones, People-with-no-legs,
Take our message to The-People-with-no-bodies,
Swiftly, swiftly, now . . .

The old man's skin was like a cracked, worn moccasin. With his turkey-claw hand he took up the gourd rattle, shook it: West, South, Up, Down, East, North.

Oh, People-of-the-hollow Earth,
Take our message to the hollow Earth,
Take our song to our Fathers and Mothers,
Take our cry to the Spirit People,
Take and go, take and go,
Swiftly, swiftly, now . . .

The snakes rippled across the ground and were gone, one by one. The old man's sister's son helped him back to his sheepskin, spread in the shade, where he half-sat, half-lay, panting.

His great-nephews, Billy Cottonwood and Sam Quarterhorse, were talking together in English. "There was a fellow in my outfit," Cottonwood said, "a fellow from West Virginia, name of Corrothers. Said his grandmother claimed she could charm away warts. So I said my great-uncle claimed he could make snakes. And they all laughed fit to kill, and said, 'Chief, when you try a snow-job, it turns into a blizzard!' . . . Old Corrothers," he reflected. "We were pretty good buddies. Maybe I'll go to West Virginia and look him up. I could hitch, maybe."

Quarterhorse said, "Yeah, you can go to West Virginia, and I can go to L.A.—but what about the others? Where *they* going to go if Washington refuses to act?"

The fond smile of recollection left his cousin's lean, brown face. "I don't know," he said. "I be damned and go to Hell, if I know." And then the old pick-up came rattling and coughing up to the house, and Sam said, "Here's Newton."

Newton Quarterhorse, his brother Sam, and Billy Cottonwood, were the only three Tickisalls who had passed the physical and gone into the Army. There weren't a lot of others who were of conscripting age (or any other age, for that matter), and those whom TB didn't keep out, other ailments active or passive did. Once there had been trees on the Reservation, and birds, and deer, and healthy men.

The wash-faded Army suntans had been clean and fresh as always when Newt set out for Crosby, but they were dusty and sweaty now. He took a piece of wet burlap out and removed a few bottles from it. "Open these, Sam, will you, while I wash," he said. "Cokes for us, strawberry pop for the old people . . . How's Uncle Fox-head?"

Billy grunted. "Playing at making medicine snakes again. Do you suppose if we believed he could, he could?"

Newt shrugged. "So. Well, maybe if the telegrams don't do any good, the snakes will. And I'm damned sure they won't do no worse. That son of a bitch at the Western Union office," he said, looking out over the drought-bitten land. " 'Sending a smoke-signal to the Great White Father again, Sitting Bull?' he says, smirking and sneering. I told him; 'You just take the money and send the wire.' They looked at me like coyotes looking at a sick calf." Abruptly, he turned away and went to dip his handkerchief in the bucket. Water was hard come by.

The lip of the bottle clicked against one of Uncle Fox-head's few teeth. He drank noisily, then licked his lips. "Today we drink the white man's sweet water," he said. "What will we drink tomorrow?" No one said anything. "I will tell you, then," he continued. "Unless the white man relent, we will drink the bitter waters of The Hollow Places. They are bitter, but they are strong and good." He waved his withered hand in a semi-circle. "All this will go," he said, "and the Fathers and mothers of The People will return and lead us to our old home inside the Earth." His sister's son, who had never learned English nor gone to school, moaned. "Unless the white men relent," said the old man.

"They never have," said Cottonwood, in Tickisall. In English, he said, "What will he do when he sees that nothing happens tomorrow except that we get kicked the Hell out of here?"

Newt said, "Die, I suppose . . . which might not be a bad idea. For all of us."

His brother turned and looked at him. "If you're planning Quarterhorse's Last Stand, forget about it. There aren't twenty rounds of ammunition on the whole reservation."

Billy Cottonwood raised his head. "We could maybe move in with the Apahoya," he suggested. "They're just as dirt-poor as we are, but there's more of them, and I guess they'll hold on to their land a while yet." His cousins shook their heads. "Well, not for us. But the others . . . Look, I spoke to Joe Feather Cloud that last time I was at the Apahoya Agency. If we give him the truck and the sheep, he'll take care of Uncle Fox-head."

Sam Quarterhorse said he supposed that was the best thing. "For the old man, I mean. I made up *my* mind. I'm going to L.A. and pass for Colored." He stopped.

They waited till the new shiny automobile had gone by towards the Agency in a cloud of dust. Newt said, "The buzzards are gathering." Then he asked, "How come, Sam?"

"Because I'm tired of being an Indian. It has no present and no future. I can't be a white, they won't have me—the best I could hope for would be that they laugh: 'How, Big Chief'—'Hi, Blanket-bottom.' Yeah, I *could* pass for a Mexican as far as my looks go, only the Mexes won't have me, either. But the Colored will. And there's millions and millions of them—whatever price they pay for it, they never have to feel lonely. And they've got a fine, bitter contempt for the whites that I can use a lot of. 'Pecks,' they call them.

I don't know where they got the name from, but, Damn! it sure fits them. They've been pecking away at us for over a hundred years."

They talked on some more, and all the while the dust never settled in the road. They watched the whole tribe, what there was of it, go by towards the Agency—in old trucks, in buckboards, on horses, on foot. And after some time, they loaded up the pick-up and followed.

The Indians sat all over the grass in front of the Agency, and for once no one bothered to chase them off. They just sat, silent, waiting. A group of men from Crosby and Spanish Flats were talking to the Superintendent; there were maps in their hands. The cousins went up to them; the white men looked out of the corners of their eyes, confidence still tempered—but only a bit—by wariness.

"Mr. Jenkins," Newt said to one, "most of this is your doing and you know how I feel about it—"

"You better not make any trouble, Quarterhorse," said another townsman.

Jenkins said, "Let the boy have his say."

"—but I know you'll give me a straight answer. What's going to be done here?"

Jenkins was a leathery little man, burnt almost as dark as an Indian. He looked at him, not unkindly, through the spectacles which magnified his blue eyes. "Why, you know, son, there's nothing personal in all this. The land belongs to them that can hold it and use it. It was made to be used. You people've had your chance, Lord knows— Well, no speeches. You see, here on the map, where this here dotted line is? The county is putting through a new road to connect with a new highway the state's going to construct. There'll be a lot of traffic through here, and this Agency ought to make a fine motel.

"And right along *here*—" his blunt finger traced, "—there's going to be the main irrigation canal. There'll be branches all through the Reservation. I reckon we can raise some mighty fine alfalfa. Fatten some mighty fine cattle . . . I always thought, son, you'd be good with stock, if you had some good stock to work with. Not these worthless scrubs. If you want a job—"

One of the men cleared his sinus cavities with an ugly sound, and spat. "Are you out of your mind, Jenk? Here we been workin for years ta git these Indyins outa here, and you tryin ta make um stay . . ."

The Superintendent was a tall, fat, soft man with a loose

smile. He said ingratiatingly, "Mr. Jenkins realizes, as I'm sure you do too, Mr. Waldo, that the policy of the United States government is, and always has been—except for the unfortunate period when John Collier was in charge of the Bureau of Indian Affairs—man may have *meant* well, but Lord! hopeless sentimentalist—well, our policy has always been: Prepare the Indian to join the general community. Get him off the reservation. Turn the tribal lands over to the *individual.* And it's been done with other tribes, and now, finally, it's being done with this one." He beamed.

Newt gritted his teeth. Then he said, "And the result was always the same—as soon as the tribal lands were given to the individual red man they damn quick passed into the hand of the individual white man. That's what happened with other tribes, and now, finally, it's being done with this one. Don't you *know,* Mr. Scott, that we can't adapt ourselves to the system of individual land-ownership? That we just aren't strong enough by ourselves to hold onto real estate? That—"

"Root, hog, er die," said Mr. Waldo.

"Are men *hogs?"* Newt cried.

Waldo said, at large, "*Told* ya he w's a trouble-maker." Then, bringing his long, rough, red face next to Newt's, he said, "Listen, Indyin, you and all y'r stinkin relatives are through. If Jenkins is damnfool enough ta hire ya, that's his look-out. But if he don't, you better stay far, far away, because nobody likes ya, nobody wants ya, and now that the Guvermint in Worshennon is finely come ta their sentces, nobody is goin ta protec ya—you and y'r mangy cows and y'r smutty-nosed sheep and y'r blankets—"

Newt's face showed his feelings, but before he could voice them, Billy Cottonwood broke in. "Mr. Scott," he said, "we sent a telegram to Washington, asking to halt the break-up of the Reservation."

Scott smiled his sucaryl smile. "Well, that's your privilege as a citizen."

Cottonwood spoke on. He mentioned the provisions of the bill passed by Congress, authorizing the Commissioner of Indian Affairs to liquidate, at his discretion, all reservations including less than one hundred residents, and to divide the land among them.

"Mr. Scott, when the Treaty of Juniper Butte was made between the United States and the Tickisalls," Cottonwood said, "there were thousands of us. That treaty was to be kept 'as long as the sun shall rise or the grasses grow.' The Government pledged itself to send us doctors—it didn't, and we died like flies. It pledged to send us seed and cattle; it sent us no seed and we had to eat the few hundred head of stock-yard cast-offs they did send us, to keep from starving. The Government was to keep our land safe for us forever, in a sacred trust—and in every generation they've taken away more and more. Mr. Scott—Mr. Jenkins, Mr. Waldo, and all you other gentlemen—you knew, didn't you, when you were kind enough to loan us money—or rather, to give us credit at the stores, when this drought started—you knew that this bill was up before Congress, didn't you?"

No one answered him. "You knew that it would pass, and that turning our lands over to us wouldn't mean a darned thing, didn't you? That we already owed so much money that our creditors would take all our land? Mr. Scott, how can the Government let this happen to us? It made a treaty with us to keep our lands safe for us 'as long as the sun rises or the grasses grow.' Has the sun stopped rising? Has the grass stopped growing? We believed in you—we kept our part of the treaty. Mr. Scott, won't you wire Washington—won't you other gentlemen do the same? To stop this thing that's being done to us? It's almost a hundred years now since we made treaty, and we've always hoped. Now we've only got till midnight to hope. Unless—?"

But the Superintendent said, No, he couldn't do that. And Jenkins shook his head, and said, sorry; it was really all for the best. Waldo shrugged, produced a packet of legal papers. "I've been deppatized to serve all these," he said. "Soons the land's all passed over ta individj'l ownership—which is 12 P.M. tanight. But if you give me y'r word (whatever that's worth) not ta make no trouble, why, guess it c'n wait till morning. Yo go back ta y'r shacks and I'll be round, come morning. We'll sleep over with Scott f'r tanight."

Sam Quarterhorse said, "We won't make any trouble, no. Not much use in that. But we'll wait right here. It's still possible we'll hear from Washington before midnight."

The Superintendent's house was quite comfortable. Logs (cut by Indian labor from the last of the Reservation's trees) blazed in the big fireplace (built by Indian labor). A wealth of rugs (woven by Indians in the Agency school) decorated walls and floor. The card-game had been on for some time when they heard the first woman start to wail. Waldo looked up nervously. Jenkins glanced at the clock. "Twelve midnight," he said. "Well, that's it. All over but the details. Took almost a hundred years, but it'll be worth it."

Another woman took up the keening. It swelled to a chorus

of heartbreak, then died away. Waldo picked up his cards, then put them down again. An old man's voice had begun a chant. Someone took it up—then another. Drums joined it, and rattles. Scott said, "That was old Fox-head who started that just now. They're singing the death-song. They'll go on till morning."

Waldo swore. Then he laughed. "Let'm," he said. "It's their last morning."

Jenkins woke up first. Waldo stirred to wakefulness as he heard the other dressing. "What time is it?" he asked.

"Don't know," Jenkins said. "But it feels to me like gettin-up time. . . . You hear them go just a while back? No? Don't know how you could miss it. Singing got real loud—seemed like a whole lot of new voices joined in. Then they all got up and moved off. Wonder where they went . . . I'm going to have a look around outside." He switched on his flashlight and left the house. In another minute Waldo joined him, knocking on Scott's door as he passed.

The ashes of the fire still smoldered, making a dull red glow. It was very cold. Jenkins said, "Look here, Waldo—look." Waldo followed the flash-light's beam, said he didn't see anything. "It's the grass . . . it was green last night. It's all dead and brown now. Look at it . . ."

Waldo shivered. "Makes no difference. We'll get it green again. The land's ours now."

Scott joined them, his overcoat hugging his ears. "Why is it so cold?" he asked. "What's happened to the clock? Who was tinkering with the clock? It's past eight by the clock—it ought to be light by now. Where did all the Tickisalls go to? What's happening? There's something in the air—I don't like the feel of it. I'm sorry I ever agreed to work with you, no matter what you paid me—"

Waldo said, roughly, nervously, "Shut up. Some damned Indyin sneaked in and must of fiddled with the clock. Hell with um. Govermint's on *our* side now. Soons it's daylight we'll clear um all out of here f'r good."

Shivering in the bitter cold, uneasy for reasons they only dimly perceived, the three white men huddled together alone in the dark by the dying fire, and waited for the sun to rise.

And waited . . . and waited . . . and waited. . . .

MY BOY FRIEND'S NAME IS JELLO

FASHION, NOTHING BUT FASHION. VIRUS X HAVING IN THE medical zodiac its course half i-run, the physician (I refuse to say "doctor" and, indeed, am tempted to use the more correct "apothecary")—the physician, I say, tells me I have Virus Y. No doubt in the Navy it would still be called Catarrhal Fever. They say that hardly anyone had appendicitis until Edward VII came down with it a few weeks before his coronation, and thus made it fashionable. He (the medical man) is dosing me with injections of some stuff that comes in vials. A few centuries ago he would have used herbal clysters. . . . Where did I read that old remedy for the quinsy ("putrescent sore throat," says my dictionary)? *Take seven weeds from seven meads and seven nails from seven steeds*. Oh dear, how my mind runs on. I must be feverish. An ague, no doubt.

Well, rather an ague than a pox. A pox is something one wishes on editors . . . strange breed, editors. The females all have names like Lulu Ammabelle Smith or Minnie Lundquist Bloom, and the males have little horns growing out of their brows. They must all be Quakers, I suppose, for their letters invariably begin, "Dear Richard Roe" or "Dear John Doe," as if the word *mister* were a Vanity . . . when they write at all, that is; and meanwhile Goodwife Moos calls weekly for the rent. If I ever have a son (than which nothing is more unlikely) who shows the slightest inclination of becoming a writer, I shall instantly prentice him to a fishmonger or a Master Chimney Sweep. Don't write about Sex, the editors say, and don't write about Religion, or about History. If, however, you *do* write about History, be sure to add Religion and Sex. If one sends in a story about a celibate atheist, however, do you think they'll buy it?

In front of the house two little girls are playing one of those clap-handie games. Right hand, left hand, cross hands on bosom, left hand, right hand . . . it makes one dizzy to watch. And singing the while:

My *boy* friend's *name* is *Jel*lo,
He *comes* from *Cincinello*,

With a *pim*ple on his *nose*
And *three* fat toes;
And *that's* the *way* my *sto*ry goes!

There is a pleasing surrealist quality to this which intrigues me. In general I find little girls enchanting. What a shame they grow up to be *big* girls and make our lives as miserable as we allow them, and oft-times more. Silly, nasty-minded critics, trying to make poor Dodgson a monster of abnormality, simply because he loved Alice and was capable of following her into Wonderland. I suppose they would have preferred him to have taken a country curacy and become another Pastor Quiverful. A perfectly normal and perfectly horrible existence, and one which would have left us all still on *this* side of the looking glass.

Whatever was in those vials doesn't seem to be helping me. I suppose old Dover's famous Powders hadn't the slightest fatal effect on the germs, bacteria, or virus (viri?), but at least they gave one a good old sweat (ipecac) and a mild, non-habit-forming jag (opium). But they're old-fashioned now, and so there we go again, round and round, one's train of thought like a Japanese waltzing mouse. I used to know a Japanese who—now, stop that. Distract yourself. Talk to the little girls . . .

Well, that was a pleasant interlude. We discussed (quite gravely, for I never condescend to children) the inconveniences of being sick, the unpleasantness of the heat; we agreed that a good rain would cool things off. Then their attention began to falter, and I lay back again. Miss Thurl may be in soon. Mrs. Moos (perfect name, she lacks only the antlers) said, whilst bringing in the bowl of slops which the medicine man allows me for victuals, said, My Sister Is Coming Along Later And She's Going To Fix You Up Some Nice Flowers. Miss Thurl, I do believe, spends most of her time fixing flowers. Weekends she joins a confraternity of over-grown campfire girls and boys who go on hiking trips, comes back sunburned and sweating and carrying specimen samples of plant and lesser animal life. However, I must say for Miss Thurl that she is quiet. Her brother-in-law, the bull-Moos, would be in here all the time if I suffered it. He puts stupid quotations in other people's mouths. He will talk about the weather and I will not utter a word, then he will say, Well, It's Like You Say, It's Not The Heat But The Humidity.

Thinking of which, I notice a drop in the heat, and I see it is raining. That should cool things off. How pleasant. A pity that it is washing away the marks of the little girls' last game. They played this one on the sidewalk, with chalked-out patterns and bits of stone and broken glass. They chanted and hopped back and forth across the chalkmarks and shoved the bits of stone and glass—or were they potshards—"potsie" from potshard, perhaps? I shall write a monograph, should I ever desire a Ph.D. I will compare the chalkmarks with Toltec emblems and masons' marks and the signs which Hindoo holy men smear on themselves with wood ashes and perfumed cow dung. All this passes for erudition.

I feel terrible, despite the cool rain. Perhaps without it, I should feel worse.

Miss Thurl was just here. A huge bowl of blossoms, arranged on the table across the room. Intricately arranged, I should say; but she put some extra touches to it, humming to herself. Something ever so faintly reminiscent about that tune, and vaguely disturbing. Then she made one of her rare remarks. She said that I needed a wife to take care of me. My blood ran cold. An icy sweat (to quote Catullus, that wretched Priapist), bedewed my limbs. I moaned. Miss Thurl at once departed, murmuring something about a cup of tea. If I weren't so weak I'd knot my bedsheets together and escape. But I am terribly feeble.

It's unmanly to weep. . . .

Back she came, literally poured the tea down my throat. A curious taste it had. Sassafrass? Bergamot? Mandrake root? It is impossible to say how old Miss Thurl is. She wears her hair parted in the center and looped back. Ageless . . . ageless . . .

I thank whatever gods may be that Mr. Ahyellow came in just then. The other boarder (upstairs), a greengrocer, decent fellow, a bit short-tempered. He wished me soon well. He complained he had his own troubles, foot troubles . . . I scarcely listened, just chattered, hoping the Thurl would get her hence. . . . Toes . . . something about his toes. Swollen, three of them, quite painful. A bell tinkled in my brain. I asked him how he spelt his name. A-j-e-l-l-o. Curious, I never thought of that. Now, I wonder what he could have done to offend the little girls? Chased them from in front of his store, perhaps. There is a distinct reddish spot on his nose. By tomorrow he will have an American Beauty of a pimple.

Fortunately he and Miss Thurl went out together. I must think this through. I must remain cool. Aroint thee, thou mist of fever. This much is obvious: There are sorcerers about. Sorcer*esses*, I mean. The little ones made rain. And they laid a minor curse on poor Ajello. The elder one has struck me in the very vitals, however. If I had a cow it would doubtless be dry by this time. Should I struggle? Should I submit? Who knows what lies behind those moss-colored eyes, what thoughts inside the skull covered by those heavy tresses? Life with Mr. and Mr. Moos is—even by itself—too frightful to contemplate. Why doesn't she lay her traps for Ajello? Why should I be selected as the milk-white victim for the Hymeneal sacrifice? Useless to question. Few men have escaped once the female cast the runes upon them. And the allopath has nothing in his little black bag, either, which can cure.

Blessed association of words! Allopath—Homeopath—*homoios,* the like, the same, *pathos,* feeling, suffering—*similia similibus curantur*—

The little girls are playing beneath my window once more, clapping hands and singing. Something about a boy friend named Tony, who eats macaroni, has a great big knife and a pretty little wife, and will always lead a happy life . . . that must be the butcher opposite; he's always kind to the children. . . . Strength, strength! The work of a moment to get two coins from my wallet and throw them down. What little girl could resist picking up a dime which fell in front of her? *"Cross my palm with silver, pretty gentleman!"*—eh? And now to tell them my tale . . .

I feel better already. I don't think I'll see Miss Thurl again for a while. She opened the door, the front door, and when the children had sung the new verse she slammed the door shut quite viciously.

It's too bad about Ajello, but every man for himself.

Listen to them singing away, bless their little hearts! I love little girls. Such sweet, innocent voices.

> My *boy* friend will *soon* be *heal*thy.
> He *shall* be *very wealthy.*
> No *wo*man shall *har*ry
> Or *seek* to *mar*ry;
> *Two* and *two* is *four,* and *one* to *carry!*

It will be pleasant to be wealthy, I hope. I must ask Ajello where Cincinello is.

THE GOLEM

THE GRAY-FACED PERSON CAME ALONG THE STREET WHERE OLD Mr. and Mrs. Gumbeiner lived. It was afternoon, it was autumn, the sun was warm and soothing to their ancient bones. Anyone who attended the movies in the twenties or the early thirties has seen that street a thousand times. Past these bungalows with their half-double roofs Edmund Lowe walked arm-in-arm with Leatrice Joy and Harold Lloyd was chased by Chinamen waving hatchets. Under these squamous palm trees Laurel kicked Hardy and Woolsey beat Wheeler upon the head with codfish. Across these pocket-handkerchief-sized lawns the juveniles of the Our Gang Comedies pursued one another and were pursued by angry fat men in golf knickers. On this same street—or perhaps on some other one of five hundred streets exactly like it.

Mrs. Gumbeiner indicated the gray-faced person to her husband.

"You think maybe he's got something the matter?" she asked. "He walks kind of funny, to me."

"Walks like a *golem*," Mr. Gumbeiner said indifferently.

The old woman was nettled.

"Oh, I don't know," she said. "*I* think he walks like your cousin Mendel.

The old man pursed his mouth angrily and chewed on his pipestem. The gray-faced person turned up the concrete path, walked up the steps to the porch, sat down in a chair. Old Mr. Gumbeiner ignored him. His wife stared at the stranger.

"Man comes in without a hello, goodbye, or howareyou, sits himself down and right away he's at home. . . . The chair is comfortable?" she asked. "Would you like maybe a glass tea?"

She turned to her husband.

"Say something, Gumbeiner!" she demanded. "What are you, made of wood?"

The old man smiled a slow, wicked, triumphant smile.

"Why should *I* say anything?" he asked the air. "Who am I? Nothing, that's who."

The stranger spoke. His voice was harsh and monotonous.

"When you learn who—or, rather, what—I am, the flesh will melt from your bones in terror." He bared porcelain teeth.

"Never mind about my bones!" the old woman cried. "You've got a lot of nerve talking about my bones!"

"You will quake with fear," said the stranger. Old Mrs. Gumbeiner said that she hoped he would live so long. She turned to her husband once again.

"Gumbeiner, when are you going to mow the lawn?"

"All mankind—" the stranger began.

"Shah! I'm talking to my husband. . . . He talks *eppis* kind of funny, Gumbeiner, no?"

"Probably a foreigner," Mr. Gumbeiner said, complacently.

"You think so?" Mrs. Gumbeiner glanced fleetingly at the stranger. "He's got a very bad color in his face, *nebbich.* I suppose he came to California for his health."

"Disease, pain, sorrow, love, grief—all are naught to—"

Mr. Gumbeiner cut in on the stranger's statement.

"Gall bladder," the old man said. "Guinzburg down at the *shule* looked exactly the same before his operation. Two professors they had in for him, and a private nurse day and night."

"I am not a human being!" the stranger said loudly.

"Three thousand seven hundred fifty dollars it cost his son, Guinzburg told me. 'For you, Poppa, nothing is too expensive—only get well,' the son told him."

"I am not a human being!"

"Ai, is that a son for you!" the old woman said, rocking her head. "A heart of gold, pure gold." She looked at the stranger. "All right, all right. I heard you the first time. Gumbeiner! I asked you a question. When are you going to cut the lawn?"

"On Wednesday, *odder* maybe Thursday, comes the Japaneser to the neighborhood. To cut lawns is *his* profession. *My* profession is to be a glazier—retired."

"Between me and all mankind is an inevitable hatred," the stranger said. "When I tell you what I am, the flesh will melt—"

"You said, you said already," Mr. Gumbeiner interrupted.

"In Chicago where the winters were as cold and bitter as the Czar of Russia's heart," the old woman intoned, "you had strength to carry the frames with the glass together day in and day out. But in California with the golden sun to mow the lawn when your wife asks, for this you have no strength. Do I call in the Japaneser to cook for you supper?"

"Thirty years Professor Allardyce spent perfecting his theories. Electronics, neuronics—"

"Listen, how educated he talks," Mr. Gumbeiner said, admiringly. "Maybe he goes to the University here?"

"If he goes to the University, maybe he knows Bud?" his wife suggested.

"Probably they're in the same class and he came to see him about the homework, no?"

"Certainly he must be in the same class. How many classes are there? Five *in ganzen:* Bud showed me on his program card." She counted off on her fingers. "Television Appreciation and Criticism, Small Boat Building, Social Adjustment, The American Dance . . . The American Dance—nu, Gumbeiner—"

"Contemporary Ceramics," her husband said, relishing the syllables. "A fine boy, Bud. A pleasure to have him for a boardner."

"After thirty years spent in these studies," the stranger, who had continued to speak unnoticed, went on, "he turned from the theoretical to the pragmatic. In ten years' time he had made the most titanic discovery in history: he made mankind, *all* mankind, superfluous: he made *me*."

"What did Tillie write in her last letter?" asked the old man.

The old woman shrugged.

"What should she write? The same thing. Sidney was home from the Army, Naomi has a new boy friend—"

"He made ME!"

"Listen, Mr. Whatever-your-name-is," the old woman said; "maybe where you came from is different, but in *this* country you don't interrupt people the while they're talking. . . . Hey. Listen—what do you mean, he *made* you? What kind of talk is that?"

The stranger bared all his teeth again, exposing the too-pink gums.

"In his library, to which I had a more complete access after his sudden and as yet undiscovered death from entirely natural causes, I found a complete collection of stories about androids, from Shelley's *Frankenstein* through Čapek's *R.U.R.* to Asimov's—"

"Frankenstein?" said the old man, with interest. "There used to be Frankenstein who had the soda-*wasser* place on Halstead Street: a Litvack, *nebbich*."

"What are you talking?" Mrs. Gumbeiner demanded. "His name was Franken*thal*, and it wasn't on Halstead, it was on Roosevelt."

"—clearly shown that all mankind has an instinctive antipathy towards androids and there will be an inevitable struggle between them—"

"Of course, of course!" Old Mr. Gumbeiner clicked his

teeth against his pipe. "I am always wrong, you are always right. How could you stand to be married to such a stupid person all this time?"

"I don't know," the old woman said. "Sometimes I wonder, myself. I think it must be his good looks." She began to laugh. Old Mr. Gumbeiner blinked, then began to smile, then took his wife's hand

"Foolish old woman," the stranger said; "why do you laugh? Do you not know I have come to destroy you?"

"What!" old Mr. Gumbeiner shouted. "Close your mouth, you!" He darted from his chair and struck the stranger with the flat of his hand. The stranger's head struck against the porch pillar and bounced back.

"When you talk to my wife, talk respectable, you hear?"

Old Mrs. Gumbeiner, cheeks very pink, pushed her husband back in his chair. Then she leaned forward and examined the stranger's head. She clicked her tongue as she pulled aside a flap of gray, skin-like material.

"Gumbeiner, look! He's all springs and wires inside!"

"I *told* you he was a *golem*, but no, you wouldn't listen," the old man said.

"You said he *walked* like a *golem*."

"How could he walk like a *golem* unless he *was* one?"

"All right, all right. . . . You broke him, so now fix him."

"My grandfather, his light shines from Paradise, told me that when MoHaRaL—Moreynu Ha-Rav Löw—his memory for a blessing, made the *golem* in Prague, three hundred? four hundred years ago? he wrote on his forehead the Holy Name."

Smiling reminiscently, the old woman continued, "And the *golem* cut the rabbi's wood and brought his water and guarded the ghetto."

"And one time only he disobeyed the Rabbi Löw, and Rabbi Löw erased the *Shem Ha-Mephorash* from the *golem's* forehead and the *golem* fell down like a dead one. And they put him up in the attic of the *shule* and he's still there today if the Communisten haven't sent him to Moscow. . . . This is not just a story," he said.

"*Avadda* not!" said the old woman.

"I myself have seen both the *shule and* the rabbi's grave," her husband said, conclusively.

"But I think this must be a different kind *golem*, Gumbeiner. See, on his forehead: nothing written."

"What's the matter, there's a law I can't write something there? Where is that lump clay Bud brought us from his class?"

The old man washed his hands, adjusted his little black skullcap, and slowly and carefully wrote four Hebrew letters on the gray forehead.

"Ezra the Scribe himself couldn't do better," the old woman said, admiringly. "Nothing happens," she observed, looking at the lifeless figure sprawled in the chair.

"Well, after all, am I Rabbi Löw?" her husband asked, deprecatingly. "No," he answered. He leaned over and examined the exposed mechanism. "This spring goes here . . . this wire comes with this one . . ." The figure moved. "But this one goes where? And this one?"

"Let be," said his wife. The figure sat up slowly and rolled its eyes loosely.

"Listen, Reb *Golem*," the old man said, wagging his finger. "Pay attention to what I say—you understand?"

"Understand . . ."

"If you want to stay here, you got to do like Mr. Gumbeiner says."

"Do-like-Mr.-Gumbeiner-says . . ."

"That's the way I like to hear a *golem* talk. Malka, give here the mirror from the pocketbook. Look, you see your face? You see on the forehead, what's written? If you don't do like Mr. Gumbeiner says, he'll wipe out what's written and you'll be no more alive."

"No-more-alive . . ."

"That's right. Now, listen. Under the porch you'll find a lawnmower. Take it. And cut the lawn. Then come back. Go."

"Go . . ." The figure shambled down the stairs. Presently the sound of the lawnmower whirred through the quiet air in the street just like the street where Jackie Cooper shed huge tears on Wallace Beery's shirt and Chester Conklin rolled his eyes at Marie Dressler.

"So what will you write to Tillie?" old Mr. Gumbeiner asked.

"What should I write?" old Mrs. Gumbeiner shrugged. "I'll write that the weather is lovely out here and that we are both, Blessed be the Name, in good health."

The old man nodded his head slowly, and they sat together on the front porch in the warm afternoon sun.

SUMMERLAND

MARY KING SAID—AND I'M SURE IT WAS TRUE—THAT SHE couldn't remember a thing about the séance at Mrs.

Porteous's. Of course no one tried to refresh her memory. Mary is a large woman, with a handsome, ruddy face, and the sound of that heavy body hitting the floor and the sight of her face at that moment—it was gray and loose-mouthed and flaccid—so unnerved me that I am ashamed to say I just sat there, numb. Others scurried around and cried for water or thrust cushions under her head or waved vials of ammoniated lavender in front of her, but I just sat frozen, looking at her, looking at Mrs. Porteous lolling back in the armchair, Charley King's voice still ringing in my ears, and my heart thudding with shock.

I would not have thought, nor would anyone else, at first impression, that the Kings were the séance type. My natural tendency is to associate that sort of thing with wheat germ and vegeburgers and complete syndromes of psychosomatic illnesses, but Charley and his wife were beef-eaters all the way and they shone with health and cheer and never reported a sniffle. Be exceedingly wary of categories, I told myself; despise no man's madness. Their hearty goodwill, if it palled upon me, was certainly better for my mother than another neighbor's whining or gossip would have been. The Kings, who were her best friends, devoted to her about 500% of the time I myself was willing to give. For years I had lived away from home, our interests and activities were too different, there seemed little either of us could do when long silences fell upon us as we sat alone. It was much better to join the Kings.

"Funny thing happened down at the office today—" Charley often began like that. Ordinarily this opening would have shaken me into thoughts of a quick escape. Somehow, though, as Charley told it, his fingers rippling the thick, iron-gray hair, his ruddy face quivering not to release a smile or laugh before the point of the story was revealed—somehow, it *did* seem funny when Charley told it. To me, the Kings were older people, but they were younger than my mother, and I am sure they helped keep her from growing old too fast. It was worth it to me to eat vast helpings of butter-pecan ice cream when the Real Me hungered and slavered for a glass of beer with pretzel sticks on the side.

If tarot cards, Rosicrucian literature, séances, and milder non-contortionistic exercises made an incongruous note in the middle-class, middle-aged atmosphere the Kings trailed with them like "rays of lambent dullness"—why, it was harmless. It was better to lap up pyramidology than lunatic-fringe politics. Rather let Mother join hands on the ouija board than start cruising the Great Circle of quack doctors to find a cure for imaginary backaches. So I ate baked alaska and discussed the I Am and astral projection, and said "Be still, my soul" to inner yearnings for highballs and carnal conversation. After all, it was only once a week. And I never saw any signs that my mother took any of it more seriously than the parchesi game which followed the pistachio or peanut-crunch.

I am an architect. Charley was In The Real Estate Game. A good chance, you might think, for one hand to wash the other, but it hardly ever happened that our commercial paths crossed. Lanais, kidney-shaped swimming pools, picture windows, copper-hooded fireplaces, hi-fi sets in the walls—that was my sort of thing. "Income property"—that was Charley's. And a nice income it was, too. Much better than mine.

How does that go?—Evil communications corrupt good manners?—Charley might have said something of that sort if I'd ever told him what Ed Hokinson told me. Hoke is on the planning commission, so what with this and that, we see each other fairly often. Coincidence's arm didn't stretch too long before Charley King's name came up between us. Idly talking, I repeated to Hoke a typical Charleyism. Charley had been having tenant trouble.

"Of course there are always what you might call the Inescapable Workings of Fate, which all of us are subject to, just as we are to, oh, say, the Law of Supply and Demand," said Charley, getting outside some dessert. "But by and large whatever troubles people of that sort"—meaning the tenants—"think they have, it's due to their own improvidence, for they won't save, and each week or month the rent comes as a fresh surprise. And then you have certain politicians stirring them up and making them think they're badly off when really they're just the victims of Maya, or Illusion." Little flecks of whipped cream were on his ruddy jowels. Mary nodded solemnly, two hundred pounds of well-fed, well-dressed, well-housed approbation.

"Maya," said Hoke. "That what he calls it? Like to come with me and see for yourself? *I* know Charley King," Hoke said. In the end I did go. Interesting, in its own way, what I saw, but not my kind of thing at all. And the next day was the day Charley died. He was interred with much ceremony and expense in a fabulous City of the Dead, which has been too well described by British novelists for me to try. Big, jolly, handsome, life-loving Mr. Charley King. In a way, I missed him. And after that, of course, Mary and my mother were together even more. After that there was even less of the Akashic Documents or Anthroposophism or Vedanta, and more and more of séances.

"*I* know I have no cause to grieve," Mary said. "*I* know that Charley is happy. I just want *him* to *tell* me so. That's not asking too much, is it?"

How should I know? What is "too much"? I never do any asking, myself, or any answering for that matter.

So off they went, my mother and Mrs. Mary King, and—if I couldn't beg off—I. Mrs. Victory's, Mrs. Reverend Ella Maybelle Snyder's, Madame Sophia's, Mother Honeywell's—every spirit-trumpet in the city must have been on time-and-a-half those days. They got little-girl angels and old-lady angels. They got doctors, lawyers, Indian chiefs, and young boy-babies—they must even have gotten Radio Andorra—but they didn't get Charley. There were slate-messages and automatic writings and ectoplasm enough to reach from here to Punxatawney, P. A., but if it reached to Charley he didn't reach back. All the mediums and all their customers had the same line: There is no grief in Summerland, there is no pain in Summerland—Summerland being the choice real estate development Upstairs, at least in the Spiritualist hep-talk. They all *believed* it, but somehow they all wanted to be assured. And after the séance, when all the spooks had gone back to Summerland, *what* a consumption of coffee, cupcakes, and cold cuts.

Some of the places were fancy, you bought "subscription" for the season's performance and discussed parapsychology over canapés and sherry. Mrs. Porteous' place, however, was right out of the 1920's, red velveteen por*teers* on wooden rings, and all. I almost fancied I could feel the ectoplasm when we came in, but it was just a heavy condensation of boiled cabbage steam and hamburger smoke.

Mrs. Porteous looked like a caricature of herself—down-at-hem evening gown, gaudy but clumsy cosmetic job, huge rings on each finger, and, *oh,* that *voice.* Mrs. Porteous was the phoniest-looking, phoniest-sounding, phoniest-*acting* medium I have ever come across. She had a lady-in-waiting: sagging cheeks, jet-black page-boy bob or bangs or whatever you call it, velvet tunic, so on.

"Dear friends," said the gentlewoman, striking a Woolworth gong, "might I have your attention please. I shall now request that there be no further smoking or talking whilst the séance is going on. We guarantee—*nothing*. We shall attempt—*all*. If there is doubt—if there is discord—the spirits may not come. For there is no doubt, no discord, there is no grief nor pain, in Summerland." So on. Let us join our hands . . . let us bow our heads . . . I, of course, peeked. The Duchess was sitting on the starboard side of the incense, next to Mrs. Porteous, who was rolling her eyes and muttering. Then Charley King screamed.

It was Mrs. Porteous' mouth that it came from, it was her chest that heaved, but it was Charley King's voice—I know his voice, don't you think I know his voice? He screamed. My mother's hand jerked away from mine.

"The fire! The fire! Oh, Mary, how it burns, how—!"

Then Mary fell forward from her seat, the lights went on, went off, then on again, everyone scurried around except me—I was frozen to my seat—and Mrs. Porteous—she lay back in her arm chair. Finally I got to my feet and somehow we managed to lift Mary onto a couch. The color came back to her face and she opened her eyes.

"That's all right, dear," my mother said.

"Oh my goodness!" said Mary. "What happened? Did I faint? Isn't that silly. No, no, let me get up; we must start the séance."

Someone tugged at my sleeve. It was the Duchess.

"Who was that?" she asked, looking at me shrewdly. "It was her husband, wasn't it? Oh-yes-it-twas! He was burned to death, wasn't he? And he hasn't yet freed himself from his earthly ties so he can enter Summerland. He must of been a skeptic."

"He didn't burn to death," I said. "He fell and broke his neck. And he wasn't a skeptic."

(Hoke had said to me: "Of course the board was rotten; the whole house was rotten. All his property was like that. It should have been condemned years ago. No repairs, a family in each room, and the rent sky-high—he must have been making a fortune. You saw those rats, didn't you?" Hoke had asked. "Do you know what the death rate is in those buildings?")

The Duchess shook her head. Her face was puzzled.

"Then it couldn't of been her husband," she said. "There is no pain," she pointed out reasonably, "in Summerland."

"No," I said to her. "No, I'm sure there isn't. I know that."

But I knew Charley King. And I know his voice.

KING'S EVIL

When I first saw the copy of *The Memoirs of Dr. Mainauduc, The Mesmerist* (bound in flaking leather, the spine in shreds, and half the title page missing: which is why I was able to buy it cheap), I assumed it to be a work of fiction. There is something extremely Gothick about "Mainauduc The Mesmerist." It sets one in mind at once of Melmoth The Wanderer. No one today would venture to invent such a name for such a person. (Unless, of course, he were writing for television or the movies, in which case he might venture anything.) But the times bring forth the man, and the man bears the name. Consider, for example, "the Jesuit Hell." This is not a theological conception, it was a man, a Jesuit, whose family name was Hell. Father Hell devised a system or theory of healing based on "metallic magnetism"; he passed it on to Franz Anton Mesmer, who almost at once quarreled with him, produced the counter-theory of "animal magnetism." Mesmer begat (so to speak) D'Eslon, D'Eslon begat Mainauduc. Full of enthusiasm, Mainauduc came to England, and settled in, of all places, Bristol. All this, I admit, sounds most improbable. Truth so often does. Who is not familiar with the bewildered cry of the novice writer, "But that's the way it *happened!*"? Not altogether trusting to my own ability to convince the reader that there really *was* such a person as the Jesuit Hell or such a person as Mainauduc the Mesmerist, I refer him to Mackay's *Extraordinary Popular Delusions And The Madness Of Crowds;* but should he (the reader) not be able to credit that this work exists either, then I must throw up my hands. Mackay, in my opinion, was really too hard on "The Magnetisers," as he called them. Himself so great a sceptic, he could have little cause for complaint if other, later, sceptics should not care to believe that any book bearing such a title ever existed. In a way, it would serve him right. . . .

In Bristol, Dr. Mainauduc flourished to the degree that his reputation went on ahead of him to London. In a short time London was coming to him; he cured Dukes of the dropsy and generals of the gout, he magnetized countesses into convulsions and they emerged from them free of the phthysic, while viscountesses left their vapors behind them—or so he says. At any rate he determined upon going to London and setting up practice there. He recounts in detail his plans for setting up something called "the Hygienickal Society . . . for Females of high Position . . . the fee, Fifteen Guineas" at his house in the capital. And he describes, amongst many other cases, one where he cured a long-seated complaint ("pronounced beyond help") entirely by proxy.

It may be that Dr. Mainauduc's success in Bristol was perhaps not quite so dazzling as his memory in later years led him to fancy. He had come up to London, to discuss his setting up practice there, at the invitation of a Mr. Wentworth, "a Bachelor of Physick," who lived in Rosemary Lane; and despite its pretty name, Rosemary Lane was not located in a pretty district. We might consider it a depressed area. And Mr. Wentworth had arranged to meet him, not in his own quarters, but at an inn called the Mulberry Tree, where they were to dine. Mr. Wentworth had made the necessary arrangements, but Mr. Wentworth was late.

"Dr. Mainauduc? To meet Mr. Wentworth? Certainly, sir," the waiter said. "If the Doctor will only please to step in here, Mr. Wentworth will be along presently." And he led him along to a medium-sized room, with paneled walls, and a fire which seemed to beckon pleasantly from the grate, for it was the first of October, and the air was chill. He had scarcely had the time to give his full attention to the flames licking greedily at the greasy black slabs of coal when he noticed that there was someone already in the room. This person came forward from his corner, where he had been engaged in softening the nether end of one candle in the flame of another so that it might hold fast in its sconce and not wobble, with his hand extended.

"Have I, sir," he asked, with the slightest of smiles, and an air of deference and courtesy, "the honor of beholding the author of the great treatise on the magnetical fluid?"

"You are too kind, sir," said Mainauduc, indicating to the waiter with but a flick of his eye that there was no objection taken to the stranger's presence and that the waiter might leave. "I am sensible of the compliment you pay me merely by having heard of my little pamphlet." And he bowed.

"Heard of it, Doctor?" cries the other man, a smallish, slender man, clad in dark garments. He holds up his finger as if to command attention, and begins to speak.

" 'The magnet attracts iron, iron is found everywhere, everything is therefore under the influence of magnetism. It is only a modification of the general principle, which establishes harmony or foments discord. It is the same agent that gives rise to sympathy, antipathy, and the passions.' Have I not the passage right, sir? My name is Blee, sir: James Blee."

"I am enchanted to meet you, Mr. Blee. I commend your memory. However—" he seated himself at right angles to the fire "—you will doubtless recall that the passage you quote is not mine. *I* was quoting from the Spaniard, Balthazar Graciano." He spread his long fingers to the blaze. "Are you a physician, sir?"

Mr. Blee perhaps did not hear the question.

"Then try my memory on this, Doctor," he said. " 'There is a flux and reflux, not only in the sea, but in the atmosphere, which affects in a similar manner all organized bodies through the medium of a subtile and mobile fluid, which pervades the universe, and associates all things together in mutual intercourse and harmony.' Were you . . . dare we hope . . . is it that . . . ?"

Dr. Mainauduc raised his dark brows.

"What is your question, Mr. Blee?"

"Can it be that London is destined to enjoy the great fortune which has hithertofore been Bristol's alone, Dr. Mainauduc? The reluctant tones of my voice must discover to you that I know I have no right to enquire, but . . ."

The mesmerist smiled. "It may be," he began; but at this moment the door was thrown open and two gentlemen entered, one nervously, the other laughing.

"Oh, pray, *pray* forgive me, Dr. Mainauduc—how d'ye do, Mr. Blee?—for my lateness," said the nervous gentleman, taking off his hat so hurriedly his wig came with it. He struggled to replace it, and, at the same time, gestured towards his companion, who rubbed his hands as he looked about the room and laughed. "This is Mr. Farmer, sir; Mr. Farmer—Dr. Mainauduc, Mr. Blee." He smiled faintly. His face was pale.

"Dr. Mainauduc, Mainauduc, very pleased. Mr. Blee, I hope you do well, well, well. Farmer by name, gentleman," the other man said, "and farmer by profession, farmer by profession. What, what?" He then laughed once more at length and proceeded to repeat his remarks all over again. His face was ruddy.

Mr. Blee courteously asked if he had had good crops, and while Mr. Farmer was merrily discussing corn, hay, and wall-fruit with his questioner, Mr. Wentworth drew Dr. Mainauduc to one side, and spoke closely to his ear.

"The fact of the matter is, that I never saw this gentleman in my life before, till just above an hour ago, when he came into the barber's where I was having my hair attended to, and desired to be shaved. 'Tis my belief, sir, that he is some country squire unused to London ways," Mr. Wentworth said; "for when the man was finished, the gentleman said, oh, as blandly as you please, that he had no money. I presume he'd had his pocket picked, for one can see by his clothes that he *is*—"

"Oh, quite so," murmured Dr. Mainauduc.

"Have you not often wondered," Mr. Farmer chattered to

Mr. Blee, "how the people do? How they live? What their lives are like? What they think, really think? Hey, sir? What, what?"

"Oh, frequently, Mr. Farmer!"

Wentworth murmured, "And so I thought best to pay for the barber, and then I really did not know how to get rid of him."

Dr. Mainauduc saw that his fellow-physician was considerably embarrassed at the introduction of two extra men to what was intended for a private meeting. He assured him that he did not mind, and said that, indeed, it was just as well, for they might get a lay opinion on the subject of introducing to London the practice of the Mesmeric therapy. And so they all four sat down to supper. There was beef and brawn and game pie and goose.

"I little thought to have this honor, Doctor," Mr. Blee said, "but, chancing to hear from Mr. Wentworth, of whose professional parts I bear the highest opinion, that *you* were to be here, I felt I must hazard it, and come to see the prophet of the new-found philosophy."

Wentworth, who had treated Blee for an amorous distemper, kept silence, but his principal guest smiled.

"Newly *re*-found philosophy, I should rather term it," Mainauduc said. "What was the laying on of hands but animal magnetism, anciently practiced? And in what other way did Elisha bring to life the dead child, but by conveyance of the magnetical fluid?" Wentworth nodded gravely.

Mr. Farmer, who had been talking with his mouth full, and smiling happily, suddenly threw down his knife. His face fell.

"Suppose—d'ye see, gentlemen—suppose a man makes mistakes—eh?—bad ones, very bad, bad, bad. Terrible losses. What? Now, now, oughtn't he have the chance, the chance, I say, to do better? Better? What, what? Well, so he must see for himself how things go. See for himself. Eh? How things go. Terrible losses. Was it not a thing to break your heart? It broke *my* heart. I never meant it to happen so—"

"*Gaming!*" Wentworth whispered to Mainauduc.

"To what losses do you refer, Mr. Farmer?" Blee asked, in a solicitous tone. "Did I not understand you to say the harvest was *good* this year?"

"The Mesmeric Method—" Wentworth began, rather loudly. Abashed, he lowered his voice. "Dr. Mainauduc is desirous of opening in London an institute for the practice of the Mesmeric Method of healing. In this, it is contemplated, I am to assist him." The faintest shadow of color came and went in his face. "What think you of the scheme, gentlemen? We, that is, he, should like to know."

Blee rose from the table and gave the fire a poke. The gray pyramid collapsed and the coals blazed up again, making the shadows dance. Mr. Farmer laughed.

"Is not this pleasant?" he cried. "I am so very much obliged to you for the pleasure. Pleasure. We dine simply at home. At home—eh?—we dine very simply. But there is such a degree of stiffness. Strain. Stiffness and strain."

Mr. Blee tapped the poker on the iron dogs. "Such an institution, if headed by such a man as Dr. Mainauduc, can not possibly do otherwise than succeed." The two physicians looked at one another, pleased. Their faces quickened.

"You will make a deal of money," Blee told the fire.

Wentworth looked hastily at a darned place on his hose, and crossed his legs. "It is the science, not the money. The money is not of any consequence to us."

"Not of the least consequence," Mainauduc said, easily. His coat and waistcoat were of French flowered silk. Blee turned from the fire.

"Gentlemen," he said in low tones, "pray give me leave to speak openly. The alchymists strove for centuries to make gold; that they succeeded, no one can say with certainty. But magnetism is the new alchymy. It *will* make gold, I *know* it. Already London is a-tremble with the reports of its success. People who would never go so far as Hackney to consult the best physician of the old school ever known, have gone all the way to Bristol to be magnetized by Dr. Mainauduc. You have only to throw open your doors in London, sir, to have your chambers thronged—with the richest . . . and the wealthiest . . ." His voice hissed upon the sybillants. He brought his dark, clever face nearer. "You will need a man of business. May I serve you?"

The two physicians looked at one another. Dr. Mainauduc's lips parted. Mr. Wentworth inclined his head to the side. And, then, as abrupt as the bursting of a bubble, the mood or spell was shattered: Mr. Farmer, seemingly from nowhere, had produced a grubby child, and was patting its head and stroking its cheeks and asking what its name was and if it would like a glass of wine—all in a tone of boisterous good cheer, his eyes popping with joy.

"Now, damme, sir!" cries Blee, jumping to his feet in a rage and overturning the chair. The child begins to weep.

"Oh, pray, don't," Farmer implores. "I love children. Don't fret, poppet."

"Take care, Mr. Farmer," Wentworth warns him. "Do you

not see the child is diseased? See the lesions—it is certainly scrofulous. Have done, Mr. Farmer!"

Then the waiter came, with many apologies, for it was his child, begged their pardon, took the boy away.

"Well, we shall think of your proposal, Mr. Blee." Dr. Mainauduc sat back, languid from food and fire, tired from his journey. "What, Wentworth, was the child with scrofula?"

"Assuredly, sir. Shall I call it back? Perhaps you wish to examine, or to treat it?" But the Doctor waved his hand. "King's Evil, is what the common people call it, you know. Scrofula, I mean to say. Some of them profess to regard it as beyond *medical* aid. They still remember that the monarchs of the former dynasty, as late as Queen Anne, used to 'touch' for it. An interesting ceremony it must have been. The touch of an anointed king, the common people say, is the only cure for it. Now what think you, Doctor, of sympathetical mummy, or capons fed with vipers?"

Dr. Mainauduc, who had been listening with a trace of impatience, cleared his throat. Blee stood once more by the fire.

"You mentioned, sir, my pamphlet, earlier in the evening—my pamphlet entituled, *A Treatise On The Magnetickal Fluid*. Whilst I was in Paris I met the eminent American sage, Mr. Franklin, and I presented him a copy, for it seems to me evident that what he calls the positive and negative of electricity is none other than the intension and remission of which that great giant of natural philosophy, Franz Anton Mesmer, writes. Mr. Blee—Mr. *Blee?*" But that gentleman was staring, his lower lip caught up beneath his teeth, at Mr. Farmer; and Mr. Farmer was weeping.

"Directly you mentioned Franklin, Doctor, he began to shed tears," whispered Wentworth. "Do you know, Doctor, I commence to think that he is an American himself—a Loyalist—and that the 'loss' he spoke of was his property—or perhaps his son—in the Rebellion there. What think *you*, sir?"

"*I* commence to think, sir, that he is a man whom I am shortly to magnetize, for it is plain he is in need of it."

Doctor Mainauduc rose and blew out all but one of the candles. Wentworth's eyes glistened and he stepped nearer, but Blee retreated further into the gloom. Only a dull red glow now came from the fire. Dr. Mainauduc seated himself facing Mr. Farmer, touching him knee to knee. He took his hands in his.

"Attend to me now, sir," Dr. Mainauduc said.

"My head *does* ache," Mr. Farmer murmured.

"It shall presently ache no more. . . . Attend."

He gently placed Farmer's hands so they rested, palms up, on his knees, and slowly began to stroke them with the palms of his own hands. He did this for some time, then drew his hands along Mr. Farmer's arms, leaning forward, until they rested with the fingers touching the neck. Slowly his hands passed up the sides of the man's face, then withdrew till they were opposite his eyes. Again and again he repeated these passes. The candle's light glittered on the single ring he wore, and Wentworth saw the glitter reflected in Mr. Farmer's wide-open eyes. Mr. Farmer was motionless, and the noise of his heavy breathing died away. It seemed to Wentworth, as he watched, that a smoke or vapor, like a thin mist, or the plume from a tobacco-pipe, was exuded from the mesmerist's face and hands.

And as Wentworth watched, he fancied that he saw strange scenes take form for fleeting moments in this miasmic suspiration: a procession of people in heavy robes and men with miters, a phantasm of silent men in violent riot, and noiseless battles on land and sea. Then all vanished, ghosts and mists alike. He heard once more the sound of Mr. Farmer's breathing, and Dr. Mainauduc had lit the candles and the light was reflected on the paneled walls.

Wentworth cleared his throat. Mainauduc looked at him, and there was terror in his eyes.

"We had better leave, you and I," he said, at last. "Do you know who your country squire is, your Loyalist?"

"*I* know," said Blee's voice from the door. He stood there, his sallow skin gone paler than Wentworth's, but a look of determination fixed upon his face. Behind him were two broad-shouldered, shifty-looking men. "We will take charge of Mr. Farmer, if you please."

"No, I think not," Mr. Farmer said. He stood up, an air of dignity upon him. "There has been enough taking charge of Mr. Farmer, and Mr. Farmer has a task to do."

"Oh, sir, you are unwell," Blee said, in a fawning tone, and he sidled forward, followed by his minions. And then, without warning, the room was filled with men: constables with their staves in their hands, soldiers in red coats, Mr. Martinson the magistrate, a tall young man looking very much like Mr. Farmer himself, and others.

"You had better come with us, sir, I think," said the tall young man. Mr. Farmer slumped. The air of dignity fell from him. Then he laughed, vacantly.

"Very well, Fred, very well," he said. "Very well, very well. You think it best, what, what?" He shambled forward, stopped, looked over his shoulder. "These two gentlemen—" he indicated Dr. Mainauduc and Mr. Wentworth, "—treated me with great consideration. They are not to be bothered, d'ye hear?" The magistrate bowed. Mr. Farmer went out slowly, leaning on the arm of the tall young man, and muttering, "Bothered, bothered, bothered . . ."

Let us return to the *Memoirs*.

"On this occasion [Mainauduc writes] the entire Atmosphere was so saturated with the Magnetickal Fluid that there was cured in another part of the House a Child suffering from a Complaint longseated and pronounced beyond help, *viz.*, Scrofula, or King's Evil. There was not a Lesion or Scar or Mark left, and all this without my even having touched him."

As to the identity of Mr. Farmer, Dr. Mainauduc is coy. He says only that he was "a Gentleman of exceedingly high Station, exceedingly afflicted. Had I been allowed to treat him further, a Privilege denied me, he might have been spared the terrible Malady which had already begun its Ravages, and which, save for a few brief periods, never entirely left him."

Thus far, on this subject—*The Memoirs of Dr. Mainauduc, The Mesmerist,* a man of his time—or behind his time, if you prefer; or, considering that mesmerism was the forerunner of hypnotism and that the study of hypnotism led Freud on to psychoanalysis, perhaps a man ahead of his time. Could he, perchance—or could anyone—really have cured "Mr. Farmer?"

It is impossible to say. If certain private papers of Frederick, Duke of York, still sealed to public inspection, could be opened, we might learn what truth there was—if any—to a curious legend concerning his father. Is it really so that he evaded all who surrounded him, and for six hours one day in early October of 1788 wandered unrecognized through London on some strange and unsuccessful quest of his own, in the month when it was finally deemed impossible to doubt any longer that he was mad—that longest-lived and most unfortunate of British Kings, George III?

GREAT IS DIANA

"WHENEVER THE SEXES SEPARATE, AT A PARTY LIKE THIS, I mean, after dinner," Jim Lucas said, "I keep feeling we ought to have walnuts and port and say *'Gempmun, the Queen!'* like in the old English novels."

"Naa, you don't want any *port,"* Don Slezak, who was the host, said, opening the little bar. "What you want—"

Fred Bishop, who had taken a cigar out of his pocket, put it back. "Speaking of the old English," he began. But Don didn't want to speak of the old English.

"I want you to try this," he said. "It's something I invented myself. Doesn't even have a name yet." He produced a bottle and a jug and ice and glasses. Jim looked interested; Fred, resigned. "It's really a very simple little drink," Don observed, pouring. "You take white rum—any good white rum—and cider. But it's got to be *real* cider. None of this pasteurized apple juice that they allow them to sell nowadays as cider. So much of this . . . so much of that. Drink up."

They drank. "Not bad at all. In fact," Fred smacked his lips, "very good. Strange, how fashions in drink change. Rum was It until gin came in; then whisky. Now, in the seventeen hundreds . . ."

Don got up and noisily prepared three more rum-and-ciders. "Ah," he said, quaffing, "it goes down like mother's milk, doesn't it." Jim put his glass down empty with a clatter. Don promptly made more.

"Mother's milk," Jim said. He was reflective. "Talk about fashions in *drink* . . . dextrose, maltose, corn syrup, and what the hell else they put into the babies nowadays. How-come the women aren't born flat-chested, explain me *that,* Mr. Bishop?"

Fred smiled blandly. "Proves there's nothing *to* this evolution nonsense, doesn't it. Particularly after that sordid Piltdown business . . ."

Don Slezak poured himself another. "Got to go a little bit easy on the cider," he said. "Rum, you can get rum anywhere, but real cider . . . That's a *revolting* idea!" he exclaimed, struck by a delayed thought. "Flat-chested. Ugh."

Jim said, defensively, that it would serve the women right. "Dextrose, maltose, corn syrup. No wonder the kids nowadays are going to Hell in a hotrod. They're rotten with chemicals before they can even *walk!"*

"The poor kids." Don choked down a sob. Jim waved his glass.

"Another thing. Besides that, Nature *meant* women to nurse their babies. Nature meant them to have *twins.* 'Sobvious. Or else they'd just have *one.* In the middle. Like a cyclops or something. And how many women do *you* know or do *I* know, who have twins? Precious damn few, let *me* tell you. . . . Oh, Margaret Sanger has a lot to answer for," he said, darkly.

Don smirked. "Spotted the flaw in *that* argument right away. According to *you,* cows should have quadruplets." He began to laugh, then to cough. Jim's face fell. Fred Bishop at once put his cigar back again.

"Curious you should bring that up. The late Alexander Graham Bell passed the latter years of his life developing a breed of sheep which would produce quadruplets. In order for the ewes to be able to nourish these multiple births they had to possess four functioning teats instead of the usual two."

Don squirmed. "I wish you'd pronounce that word as it's spelled," he said. "It sounds so *vul*gar when you rhyme it with *'pits.'* "

Jim crunched a piece of ice, nodded his head slowly. Then he spat out the pieces. "Just occurred to me: Doesn't something like that sometimes occur in women? *'Polyman-'* something? Once knew a woman who was a custom brassiere-maker, and she claimed that—"

Fred waved his arm. "All in good time," he said. "In the seventeen hundreds—"

A dreamy look had come into Don's eyes. "Suppose a fellow was one of these whatdayacallits? a breast-fetichist." He got the latter word out with some difficulty. "Why, he'd go *crazy*—"

"Why don't you mix up another round, Don?" Fred suggested, craftily. "Jim could help you. And I will tell you about the interesting career of Mr. Henry Taylor, who was, in a way, an example of what Aldous Huxley calls the glorious eccentrics who enliven every age by their presence."

Mr. Henry Taylor [Fred continued] was an Englishman, which is a thing glorious enough in itself. He was not, even by our foolish modern standards, too much of an eccentric; which is an argument in favor of free will over heredity. His grandfather, Mr. Fulke Taylor, in unsolicited response to the controversies between the Houses of Hanover and Stuart, had managed to plague both—and the Houses of Parliament as well—with genealogical pamphlets he had written in favor of the claims (which existed only in his own mind) of a distant, distaff branch of the Tudors. He also willed a sum of money to be used in translating the works of Dryden into the Cornish language. The task was duly carried out by a prolific and penniless clergyman named Pendragon, or Pendennis, or Pen-something; it did much to prevent the extinction of the latter's family, but had, alas, no such effect upon the Cornish language.

Trevelyan Taylor, Henry's father, was much taken up—you will recall this was in the seventeen hundreds—with what he called *"These new and wonderful Discoveries"*: meaning the efforts of Robert Bakewell and the brothers Bates in the recently developed science of selective breeding. *"Previously,"* wrote Trevelyan Taylor, *"Animal Husbandry was left entirely to the animals themselves. We shall alter that."*

Other might inbreed, crossbreed, linebreed, and outbreed in the interest of larger udders or leaner bacon; old Trevelyan spent thirty devoted years in the exclusive purpose of developing a strain of white sheep with black tails. There has seldom been a longer experiment in the realm of pure science, but after the old man's death the whole flock (known locally as Taylor's Tails) was sold to an unimaginative and pre-Mendelian drover named Huggins, thus becoming history. And mutton.

The flock, if it produced no profit, at least paid for itself, and its owner had spent little on other things. Henry Taylor, who had enjoyed a comfortable allowance, now found himself with an even more comfortable income. He turned ancestral home and estate over to his younger brother, Laurence (later, first Baron Osterwold), and set forth on his travels. London saw him no more—*"London, where I have passed so much of my youth,"* as he wrote in a letter to his brother, *"in profligate Courses as a Rake and a Deist."* These two terms are, of course, not necessarily synonymous.

Henry Taylor crossed over to the continent with his carriage, his horses, his valet, clothes, commode, dressing case, and toilet articles. No one had yet begun to vulcanize or galvanize or do whatever it is to rubber which is done, but he had a portable, collapsible sailcloth bath—all quite in the Grand Tradition of the English Milord. Throughout all the years that he continued his letters—throughout, at least, all of the European and part of the Asiatic term of his travels —he insisted that his tour was for educational purposes.

"I devote myself," he wrote, *"to the study of those Institutions of which I count myself best qualified to judge. I leave to others the Governance and Politick of Nations, and their Laws and Moral Philosophies. My Inquiries—empirick, all—are directed towards their Food, their Drink, their Tobacco, and their Women.* Especially *their Women! Glorious Creatures, all, of whatsoever Nation. I love them all and I love every Part of them, Tresses, Eyes, Cheeks, Lips, Necks, Napes, Arms, Bosoms . . .*

"Why do Women cloack their lovely Bosoms, Brother?" he demands to know. *"Why conceal their Primest Parts? So much better to reveal them pridefully, as do the Females in the Isles of Spice. . . . I desire you'll send* [he adds] *by next vessel to stop at Leghorn, 6 lbs. fine Rappee Snuff and 4 cases Holland Gin."*

Taylor passed leisurely through France, the Low Countries, various German States, Denmark, Poland, Austria, Venice, Lombardy, Modena, Tuscany, the Papal Dominions, the Kingdom of Naples and the Two Sicilies, and—crossing the Adriatic—entered the Turkish hegemonies in Europe by way of Albania . . . the tobacco was much better than in Italy, but he complained against the eternal sherbets of the Turks, who were, he said, in the manner of not offering strong waters to their guests, *"no better than the Methodies or other dehydrated Sectarians."* He was not overpleased with the Greek practice of putting resin in their wine, and noted that *"they eat much Mutton and little Beef and drink a poor sort of Spirits called Rockee."* He liked their curdled milk, however, and—of course—their women.

"The Men here wear Skirts," Henry Taylor says, *"and the Women wear Pantalones. . . . I have made diligent Inquiry and learned that this unnatural Reversal doth not obtain in* all *Matters domestick, however."* He cites details to support this last statement.

There is a picture of him done at this time by an itinerant Italian painter of miniatures. It shows a well-made man in his thirties, dressed in the English styles of the year of Taylor's departure, with a line of whisker curling down his jaw; clean-shaven chin and upper-lip, and a rather full mouth. He began to learn Turkish and the Romaic, or vernacular Greek, to sit cross-legged and to suck at a hookah, to like the tiny cups of black and syrupy coffee, and—eventually—to dispense with an interpreter. He spoke face to face with the pasha of each district he passed. He rather liked the Turks.

"There is among them none of this Hypocritical Nonsense, as with us, of having One Wife, to whom we are eternally yoked unless we care to display our Horns and our Money to the House of Lords." He reports a conversation he had with *"a Black Eunuch in Adrianople. I asked him quite Boldly if he were not sensible of his Great Loss, and he pointed to an Ass which was grazing nearby and said with a Laugh—"* But I really cannot repeat what he said.

Taylor said he *"admired his Wit, but was not happy at the aptness of his Analogy."*

From the Balkans he went on to Asia Minor, where he made a closer acquaintance of the famous Circassian women —the raising and the sale of whom was seemingly the chief business of their native hills. He pauses in his flow of metaphors to ask a question. *"If I compare the Breasts of the Turkish Women to full Moons, with what shall I compare those glorious Features possessed by the Circassians? I would liken them to the warm Sun, were the Sun Twins."*

"Polymastia!" Jim exclaimed. He smiled happily. Fred blinked, Don said, "Huh?"

"Not *'polymam-'* something, but polymastia: 'Having many breasts.' Just now remembered. Came across it once, in a dictionary."

"Just like that, huh?" Don asked. "Were you considering becoming a latter-day A. G. Bell with the human race instead of sheep?"

"Go on, Fred," Jim said, hastily. "I didn't mean to interrupt."

Taylor's next letter [Fred continued, after a very slight pause] was dated more than a year later, from Jerusalem. He had conceived a desire to visit the more remote regions of Western Asia Minor, eventually heading for the coast, whence he hoped to visit certain of the Grecian islands. As large areas were impassable to his carriage, he was obliged to hire mules. He gives a description, as usual, of the nature of the country and people, but without his usual lively humor. Suddenly, without any connecting phrases, the letter plunges into an incident which had occurred that day in Jerusalem.

"I visited a synagogue of the Polish Jews here, having some business of minor Importance with one of their Melamedins, or Ushers. It is a small room, below Street-level, furnished as well as their Poverty permits of. There was an Inscription of some sort at the Lectern, but they had been burning Candles by it for so long that it was obscured by Soot and Smoke.

"Only the single word Hamatho *was visible, and I confess to you, Dear Brother, that when I saw this word, which means, His Wrath, a Shudder seized me, and I groaned aloud. Alas! How much have I done to merit His Wrath. . . ."*

And then, without further explanation, he reverts to his ramble in Asia Minor. His party had come over the Duz-bel Pass to a miserable Turkish village east of Mt. Koressos, *"a wretched marshy neighborhood where I was loth to stop, fearing the Ague. But some of the Mules required to be shod, and we were preceded at the forge by some Turkishes officers, Yezz Bashy or Bimm Bashi, or like preposterous Rank and Title. So there was no help for it. It promised to take Hours, and I went a-walking."* Henry Taylor soon left the village behind and found himself in wild country. He had no fears for his safety, or of being lost, he explained, because he had pistols and a small horn always about him. By and by he entered a sort of small valley down which a stream rushed, and there, drinking at a pool, he saw a woman.

"She was dark, with black Eyes and Hair, buxom and exceedingly comely. I thought of the Line in the Canticle: I am black but beautiful. Alas! That I did not call to mind those other lines, also of Solomon, about the Strange Woman. And yet it was, I suppose, just as well, for 'Out of the Strong came forth Sweet.'"

On seeing her, he freely confesses, he had no hopes other than for an amorous adventure, and was encouraged by her lack of shyness. He spoke to her in Turkish, but she shook her head. She understood Greek, however, though her accent was strange to him, and she said that her name was Diana. She offered him a drink from her cup, he accepted, and they fell into conversation. *"Although she gave no Details about her Home, and I pressed her for none, I understood that she was without present Family and was in what we should call Reduced Circumstances. For she spoke of Times past, when she had many Maid Servants and much Wealth, and the tears stood in her Eyes. I took her hand and she offered no objections."*

The next lines are written in ink of a different color, as if he had put off writing until another time. Then, *"In short, Brother, I pursued the Way usual to me in those Days, and although she gave me her Lips, I was not content to stop, but was emboldened to thrust my Hand into her Bodice . . . and thus perceived in very short order that she was not a Human Female but an Unnatural Monstrosity. I firmly believe, and was encouraged in my Belief by a worthy Divine of the Eastern Church to whom I revealed the Matter, that this Creature who called herself* Diana *had no Natural Existence, but was a Dæmon, called forth, I first thought, by the Devil himself. . . .*

"I am now convinced that she was a very Type of Lust, sent to test or prove me. That is, to horrify me in that same Sin in which I had so long wallowed, and to turn those Features, in which I had intended to take illicit Delight, into

a Terror and Revulsion. I ran, I am not ashamed to own it, until I fell bleeding and exhausted at the Forge, and was taken by a Fever of which I am long recovering. . . ."

According to the standards of his time there was only one thing for him to do under the circumstances, and he did it. He got religion. There had lately been established in Jerusalem an office of the British and Overseas Society for the Circulation of Uncorrupted Anglican Versions of the Scriptures; Henry Taylor became a colporteur, or agent, of this Society, and was sent among the native Christians of Mesopotamia, Kurdistan, and Persia.

He never knew, because he died before it became known, that the Turkish village where he had his shocking experience was near the site of the ancient city of Ephesus. Its famous Temple of Diana was one of the Seven Wonders of the World and was served by hundreds of priestesses and visited by pilgrims in throngs. But that was before the Apostle Paul came that way and "*Many of those which used curious arts brought their books together and burned them before all men.*" But not every one in Ephesus was so quickly convinced.

A certain "*Demetrius, a silversmith, which made silver shrines for Diana . . . called together the workmen of like occupation, and said . . . that not alone in Ephesus, but almost throughout all Asia, this Paul hath persuaded and turned away much people, saying that they be no gods, which are made with hands: So that not only this our craft is in danger . . . but also that the temple of the great goddess Diana should be despised, and her magnificence be destroyed, whom all Asia and the world worshippeth. And when they heard these sayings, they were full of wrath, and cried out saying, Great is Diana of the Ephesians. And the whole city was filled with confusion. . . .*"

"I am also filled with confusion," Don said. "First we hear about this Limey, Taylor: he tries to grab a feel and gets the screaming meemies. All of a sudden—a Bible class."

Jim clicked his tongue. "That *word*—it's slipped my mind again. Poly—? Ploy—?"

"Patience," Fred pleaded. "Why aren't you more patient?"

The confusion in Ephesus [Fred said] was finally ended by a city official who "*appeased*" the mob by asking, "*What man is there that knoweth not now that the City of t*
Ephesians is a worshipper of the great goddess Dia
of the image which fell down from Jupiter? .
to be quiet, and to do nothing rashly."

Long after Henry Taylor's time, the archeologists uncovered the temple site. Among the many images they found was one which may perhaps be that same one *"which fell down from Jupiter."* It is carven from black meteoric stone, and was obviously intended for reverence in fertility rituals, for the goddess is naked to the waist, and has, not two breasts, but a multitude, a profusion of them, clustering over the front of the upper torso. . . .

"Well, you're not going to make too much out of this story, are you?" Jim asked. "Obviously this condition was hereditary in that district, and your pal, H. Taylor, just happened to meet up with a woman who had it, as well as the name Diana."

"It is certainly a curious coincidence, if nothing more," said Fred.

Don wanted to know what finally became of Henry Taylor. "He convert any of the natives?"

"No. They converted him. He became a priest."

"You mean, *he gave up women?"*

"Oh, no: Celibacy is not incumbent upon priests of the Eastern Church. He married."

"But not one of those babes from the Greater Ephesus area, I'll bet," Don said.

Jim observed, musingly, "It's too bad old Alexander Graham Bell didn't know about this. He needn't have bothered with sheep. Of course, it *takes* longer with people—"

Fred pointed out that Dr. Bell had been an old man at the time.

"He could have set up a foundation. I would have been *glad* to carry on the great work. It wouldn't frighten *me*, like it did Taylor. . . . Say, you wouldn't know, approximately, how *many* this Diana had—?"

"It must sure have taken a lot out of Taylor, all right," Don said. "I bet he was never much good at anything afterwards."

Fred took one last swallow of his last drink. The jug and bottle, he observed, were empty. "Oh, I don't know about t," he said. "In the last letter he wrote to his brother be- latter's death, he says: *'My dear Wife has observed th Birthday by presenting me with my Fifth Child. . . . I preach Sunday next on the lso Shall not Wither" (Psalms) .'"*

I DO NOT HEAR YOU, SIR

BLOODGOOD BIXBEE KNEW NOTHING ABOUT ART, BUT HE knew what he didn't like: What he didn't like, he said—loudly and with much profane redundancy—was Bein Played For A Sucker . . . See?

Milo Anderson saw, all right; he knew he should never have sold Bixbee the unauthenticated Wilson Peale, any more than he should have collected in advance the five per cent of the contract which he knew he could never negotiate. But there were so few people left in the capital whom he could still expect to swindle . . . and he needed the money. He had counted too much on Bixbee's not being able to admit participation in an illegal deal, and it certainly wasn't the moral aspect of not telling the rich lumberman about the cloud on the picture's title which worried him. In fact, nothing about Bixbee had worried him at the time—for who, back in Qualliupp, Washington, would know a Wilson Peale from a citron peel?—all that concerned him had been getting the check to the bank in time. And then to the phone . . .

Checks, checks, telephones, telephones, and . . .

Damn them all, with their greedy open hands and yapping mouths.

Big crooks have littler crooks to bite 'um,
And so on down, ad infinitum.

Wasn't Bloodgood Bixbee a crook, stealing lumber rights and ravishing the forests with a ruthless hand? Sure he was. And then following the classic pattern of trying to set himself up as a man of culture, with Genuine Oil Paintings on his walls. How the *Hell* did he find out, anyway? Was it possible that even Qualliupp had in it someone like Edmond Hart Ransome, from whom Milo had gotten the picture? No, impossible. The whole State of Washington was too new to interest old E.H.R. who seldom concerned himself with anything later than the end of the 1700's.

Anderson ran over in his mind the list of those with whom he had done business. Some one of them—there had to be at least *one*—would be in a mood to help him now, to advance money against future cooperation.

He dialed an unlisted number, tried to swallow. A man's voice, very quiet and cautious: "Yes?"

"Ovlomov?" He must not seem too—

"Who is this?" the voice inquired. A man with whom M
Ovlomov had done business? Didn't he know that M
Ovlomov had returned only that day to his homeland?
should follow the newspapers—No, no—he, the one spea
ing, was not interested in Ovlomov's contacts. Nor would
be of any use to call again: the number was being disco
tinued: Ovlomov was indiscreet.

So that way—the way of being a tenth-rate spy pretendi
to be a third-rate one—was out, and he was no closer
being clear of his snarl of checks and phone calls: peo
he was blackmailing (but only able to get small sums fro
people who were blackmailing *him* (and getting large sum
For a while he had had an easy stretch, living at old R
some's place.

The lease was up in a few days—another problem.

It wasn't as if the painting wasn't his, Ransome had
it to him, it was clear enough in his will. That was
devilish part of it—before simply stating "and all the rest
my property now located in my apartment," the old
had "left" him, had specifically named, every single art
Milo had stolen from him. He had *known.* "And this beq
I make for a reason well known to my secretary, the
Milo Anderson." Rubbing it in. *Always* rubbing it in. "
horses and slow women, eh, Mr. Anderson?" That sor
thing.

Perhaps it would have been better not to have med
with the old man's medicine bottles—but it was *so* ea
and so soon after the doctor had called; no trouble
a death certificate . . . *All the rest of my property* . . .
reason well-known to the said Milo Anderson.

But little enough property was left in the apartme
now.

By now everything was coming all at once. Bloo
Bixbee wanting his money back and raving raw hea
bloody bones if he didn't get it. Big Patsy the book
wanting the markers to be made good, wanting it right
not threatening but promising. And Mrs. Pritchard, her
like half-melted margarine: "Carried you on the books
time, Milo—been good to you—we all've been good t
Now we have to get the money because the Syndicat
over the books tomorrow, and you know what *that*
Milo."

And he knew, oh, he *knew* all right. Even bef
phone rang and the voice—an ordinary coarse un
unviolent sort of voice, saying its say as the cabbie

ask Where To or the laundryman announce the bill—Anderson: Get it ready, get the money ready, we'll pick it up (by now the voice a bit bored with so many routine calls) as soon after midnight as we get around there. . . .

Milo Anderson's eye ran hopelessly around the apartment. Over the mantelpiece (or over where the marble had been before he'd sold it) was the faded place where the alleged Wilson Peale had hung before going to take its place over the silent hi-fi set in the Bloodgood Bixbee place in Qualliupp (who'd bother with hi-fi when the TV offered such quality fare?). The cabinet of old coins had stood over there—the Pine Tree shillings, the "York" pieces, half-reales, the dismes: all sold by now, and sold well, but the money long ago (it seemed long ago) spent . . . Big Patsy, Mrs. Pritchard, and all the others . . . Edward Hart Ransome's place had been stuffed with the treasures of the late 1700's, but almost everything had been sold or pawned by now except for a few pieces of essential furniture. These had been already priced and would bring only a fraction of what was needed.

Milo Anderson was not more fearful than most men, perhaps he was a degree less fearful. But there were too many things piling up just now. Everybody was putting the screws on him and there was nobody he could squeeze in turn—not *now*—not *tonight* . . . Like a hungry man who opens and reopens icebox and pantry: there must be *some* food left, only let me look once more: Milo roamed the shadowy apartment, looking and peering and hoping and fearing, something to sell, something overlooked, *something* . . .

With sweat cold on his back and with kneecaps articulating far from firmly he pawed among the discards the dealers had left. Bellows, wool-carders, trivets ("Three fr a quarter on the Boston Post Road," the dealer said.), apple-corers and nutmeg graters, new model spinningwheels . . . and *this* damned thing. Whatever *it* was. The dealer had simply laughed. Milo was about to kick it. He groaned, sighed heavily, listlessly began to examine it.

Basic design was a cabinet, a smallish box, done—he peered closer—in curly cherrywood, a favorite wood of the period. It stood on four legs and on *one* side was a little wheel and on the *other* side, just sticking out, was a curved copper or brass . . . funnel, was it? He twisted the metal horn, it moved under pressure. He turned the wheel. Nothing happened, and this was, of course, wrong: for no Colonial craftsman would have spent time making a device which didn't *do* anything. He spun the wheel again, and a bell tinkled inside.

Well, yes—a box had to have an inside. Why hadn't he looked inside? People (he pushed a stubborn peg) were always hiding money inside of . . . There. The panel slid open easily enough. The bell tinkled again, a tiny silver bell on a silver loop in an upper corner. A small black horn (calf? bison?) hung on a thong. Copper wires led from the small end of the horn, and parchment, like a tiny drumhead, covered the wide end. Wedged firmly behind a glass panel were two glass jars lined with metal foil.

The thing to do was to get a hammer and—the bell rang a third time. Death, he thought, was waiting, and here *he* was, playing with an antique toy. He seized the horn, was about to tear it loose, then he put it to his ear instead. At once he dropped it and jumped.

"Your conversant, Sir?" That was what the horn had said in his ear. Or was it, "You're conversant . . . ?" What was the apparatus supposed to be, a music box with vox humana, a primitive phonograph, a . . . No, if it resembled any piece of equipment he was familiar with, it was the telephone. Without stopping to rationalize his action in turning eagerly to anything which could divert him from his trouble, he thought, Let's see: Buffalo horn to ear, speak into . . . mm . . . copper tube (funnel, trumpet) on outside. Feeling a bit foolish, he said—what else *could* he say but: "Hello?"

The odd voice in his ear repeated what it had said before. Milo asked, "Conversant with *what?*"

"With *whom,* Sir," the voice corrected him; and then, as he remained baffled and silent: "I do not hear you, Sir. Pray consult the compendium, Sir, for the cypher of the conversant desired. . . . Servant, Sir."

"Hello? Hello? Hey!" He even whistled shrilly, but there was no reply.

Putting the horn down he began pressing and poking around the box, and dislodged something from a narrow space under the shelf where the odd jars were. It was a small thin leatherbound book. He opened it. Obviously laid paper, linen-rag, age-yellowed and "foxed": brown-flecked . . . names, numbers . . . turn to the front . . .

**THE COMPENDIUM OF THE
NAMES, RESIDENCES, &
CYPHERS OF THE
HONORABLE & WORTHY
PATRONS OF THE
MAGNETICKAL INTELLI-
GENCE ENGINE.**

Assuming—and a crazy-mad assumption it was, but here the thing stood in front of him—assuming that the telephone, or some long-forgotten precursor of it, *had* been invented in those days . . . But how could it still be working? Or was this some quirk of a few other off-beat antiquarians like old Ransome, to have their own odd-ball Bell System? Or was he simply out of his senses and imagining it all? Oh, well. He turned the page.

EXORDIUM. *The Artificers of this Device have spared neither Pains nor Oeconomy to obtain the primest Materials and Workmanship, the Cabinetmaking being that of Mr. D. Phyfe, the Leyden-jars and other Magnetick Parts are the Manufactory of Dr. B. Franklin, Mr. P. Revere has fabrickated the Copper and Brass, and Mr. Meyer Meyers the Pewter and Silver.*

SUBMONITION. *The Cypher of each Patron is listed Alphabetickally. Spin the Wheel and on perceiving the Tintinnabulation of the Bell, Inform the Engineer of the Cypher of the Conversant desired.* CAVEAT. *It is absolutely inhibited to tamper with the Leyden-jars.*

Still dubious, but certainly curious, so much so that he even forgot his own danger, Anderson looked through the book. Almost automatically his finger stopped at *Washington, Geo., Gent. Planter, Mt. Vernon.* He spun the wheel. The bell tinkled. He put the small horn to his ear.

"Your conversant, Sir?"

This time he was prepared. He cleared his throat and said, "Patriot 1-7-7-0."

"Your servant, Sir." Somewhere away another little bell began to tinkle.

"Say—Engineer?" Milo ventured.

"Servant, Sir."

"Um . . . what's your name?"

"There are no names, Sir."

Trrrinnggg . . . trrrinnggg . . .

"Well, uh, what *time* are you in—or where *are* you?"

"There is neither time nor place, Sir. And it is not permitted to hold non-pertinent discourse whilst the engine is in use, Sir." Trrrinnggg . . .

Suddenly the parchment crackled and a deep voice boomed from the horn: "Ah heah you, Seh!" Milo swallowed.

"Mr. *Wash*ington?" Surely not yet General in 1770.

"Yes, Seh—*and* no thanks to you, Seh! What do you mean by it, you damned horse-leecher? Sellin me these *con*founded artifized denticles—! Why, a wind-broken, bog-spavined *stal*lion couldn't get 'em comftable in his mouth!"

The false teeth were heard clacking and grinding. The Patriot's voice rose. "Haven't ett a decent piece of butcher's meat in *days!* Live on syllabub and sugar-tiddy! Plague take your flimsy British crafts—give me honest Colonial works, say I!" The outraged voice rang in Milo's ear, then died away.

Mistaken for a quack dentist! Perhaps the only crime he never had committed. Milo wanted to call back, found he'd forgotten the number—the "cypher," rather—but the place where it had been was blank. He shivered. The engineer's voice responded to his signal. "What is George Washington's cypher?" Milo demanded.

"That intelligence is not available, Sir. Pray consult—"

"But it's no longer *in* the compendium!"

"Cyphers not in the compendium do not exist. . . . Your servant, Sir."

Well, so much for the Father of His Country. Anderson had discovered a hitherto-overlooked cause of the American Revolution, but a lot of good it did him. Once again, he realized his position. There was no one he could turn to—not in the present, anyway. Not knowing what else *to* do, he turned once more to the past. Spun the wheel, opened the little book.

"Your conversant, Sir?"

"Printinghouse 1-7-7-1. . . ." Trrrinnggg . . . The voice was brisk, still retaining after all the years a trace of the Boston twang.

"We must all hang together or we shall surely hang separately. . . . What's your need, neighbor? The colonies should and will unite, but meanwhile the day's work goes on."

"Benjamin Franklin I presume?"

"That same, my friend. Job-printing? Nice new line of chapbooks for your pleasure and instruction? Latest number of Poor Richard's Almanack? Bay Psalm Book? Biblical Concordance? Hey?"

"No, no . . ."

The voice dropped a notch, became confidential. "Just on hand by the last vessel to arrive in port, a French novel in three volumes . . . no? Make you a special price for *Fanny Hill!*"

"Dr. Franklin"—Milo grew anxious— "I need your help. I appreciate—I appeal to you—a Fellow American—" he stumbled.

The voice grew wary, then a trifle amused. "Nay, nay, I'm too old a tomcod to be taken with such bait as that. None of your Tory tricks. If you're working for Sir William Johnson, now, tell him—"

"But—"

"Tell him I'm a loyal subject of the King until he proves otherwise. I do but propose a continental union against French Lewis, the Dons, and the savage Enjians—though if Providence doesn't take most of these off our hands by rum and pox—"

Milo cried, "My life's in terrible danger!"

"Sell you a nice ephemeris—you can cast your horoscope and thus see the hazards you must needs discountenance. . . . Stove? Sell you a Franklin st—"

Of course, the cypher had vanished from the book and from his memory. It was plain he was allowed but one call to each name. And time was running short: it grew close to midnight and he could expect to hear from the Syndicate about the money he owed Mrs. Pritchard—if Bloodgood Bixbee and his friends, or Big Patsy and *his* friends didn't arrive first.

Well, no help from the Continentals: Try the Tories. Try the line he'd first used to approach Ovlomov: spin the wheel and hear the bell ring. ". . . Sir?"

"Slaughter 1-7-7-7. . . . Hello?"

"I hear you, Sir." Cold, this voice, and smooth as an adder's skin.

"Sir Henry Hamilton? I'm a loyal subject of the King and I have information to sell. . . ." He held his face close to the brazen mouthpiece. By now he had no slightest doubt but that it was all real: he would connive, he would—

"Oh, demn the loyal subjects of the King. I buy no information; I buy *hair,* Sir! *That's* how I make rebels into loyal subjects of the King, Sir! I buy their sculps! Have you some'at to sell, fellow? I pay top prices to encourage the trade—for the sculps of male Yenkees, two-pun-ten—female Yenkees, two-pun-even—infant Yenkees and disaffected Injians, ten shillin."

"Help me—help me get through to where you are—Sir Henry—I'll do—"

The Tory agent's voice grew cautionary. "Though, mind," he said; "mind they be well-cured, for if there's one thing I can*not* abide, d'ye hear, Sir," he said with fastidious distaste, "it's a mouldy stinking sculp. *Fah!*"

"*You* can find out how, some way, there must be a way I can come over—"

The voice grew fainter. *"Hair;* not the whole head: just the *haiiirrr . . ."*

It died away altogether and while Milo watched the name faded from the page.

One after the other he called them up. And one after the other, though they did not know who he really was, they knew at once that he was a rogue and a scoundrel. He could not make them understand, could not find out how to get from his time and place to theirs. Voices traveled it, why not bodies? Desperately he riffled the pages of his compendium. Another name leaped at him. *This* man would not repulse him. He spun the wheel.

"Your conversant, Sir?"

"Tammany 1-7-8-9. And hurry!"

". . . Servant, Sir." Trrrinnggg . . .

A babble of voices . . . laughter . . . the sound of a fiddler . . .

Milo's voice trembled. "Colonel Aaron Burr?"

The colonel's voice was soft as cream. "That same, Sir."

Lay the cards on the table. "Colonel Burr, I'm a thief, a swindler, a blackmailer, and a traitor."

The colonel chuckled. "Ecawd, but withal an honest knave. . . . Nay, babe, nay, my poppet, don't jump so when I—"

"I need your help. I need it *now!"*

"Ah, not tonight, me lad. Burr might sell his soul for gold, but he'd not move outside the door even to *save* his soul when a pretty wench is on his knee— Why so flushed, my sweet tapstress? Bodice tight? Let me loose it. . . . Nay, don't slap my fingers. You know you love me. . . ."

Was there a single name left in the book? (Only a few minutes to midnight.) Yes. One.

"Your conversant, Sir?" Milo licked dry lips. "West Point 1-7-8-0." This time no silver bell tinkled. Slowly and with abrupt bursts, as if blown by gusts of wind, he heard the sound of a ruffle of drums. . . . A puff of yellow choking sulfurous smoke billowed from the coppery horn. Milo ducked his head.

"I hear you, Sir." The voice was infinitely weary, infinitely bitter.

Milo croaked, "General Benedict Arnold?" And he told the whole story. There was a silence, but he sensed the listener was still there. And finally—

"I *can* help you. Matter *can* pass the barrier of time and place. For the sake of my wounded leg at Saratoga, shattered and bloodied in the service of my native land, I will do my native land this last service." Milo babbled thanks. The bitter, weary voice spoke on. "For my treasons I received money, commissions for myself and sons, a pension for my wife. Dust, all dust and ashes . . . I ask in my will that I be buried in my Continental uniform—"

"But *me*, you said you'd help *me*—" And the clock hands almost—

"I shall do for you what I should have done for myself. My old trade, in Hartford-town, ere I turned to war, I learned—But it's too late now. I should have done it that night at West Point, before I wrote to poor André—" One of the Leyden jars shattered with a sharp crack, splitting the glass panel. He reeled from a blast of heat. Amid the dust and shards he saw a small round box.

"No!" he cried, pulling back. The clock began softly to strike the hour. An automobile drove up below, heavy feet tramped the hallway, stopped outside his door.

Without further hesitation he opened the box, thrust something into his mouth. He trembled, fell forward, grasping the wheel. The bell tinkled once. The pillbox lay to one side. "Ben.dT Arnold, Hartford," the label said. "Licensed Apotheckary."

Fists beat at the door, feet kicked it, rough voices called out.

The bell tinkled once more in the cabinet.

"Your conversant, Sir?" a voice asked faintly.

It repeated the question.

"I do not hear you, Sir," it said, at length.

"I do not hear you. . . ."

AUTHOR, AUTHOR

RODNEY STIRRUP HAD ALWAYS TAKEN CARE (TAKEN *damned good* care! he often emphasized) not to get married; several former morganatic lady friends, however, frequently testified that the famous writer was Not A Very Nice Person. Perhaps even they might have felt sorry for him if they could have been with him that day at Boatwright Brothers, the publishers. And thereafter.

But then again, perhaps they might not.

Rodney stared at J. B. across the vast, glossy desk.

"With one hand you cut my throat," he protested; "And with the other hand you stab me in the back!"

A slightly pained look passed across Jeremy Boatwright's pink and widespread face, hesitated, and decided to stay. "Come now, Rodney . . . these professional phrases. . . . Really, there are no other choices left to us, owing, ah, to Conditions In The Trade."

Stirrup confounded conditions in the trade. "You reduce my royalties—I call that cutting my throat. And you demand a larger share in the secondary rights: reprints, paperbacks, television—I call that stabbing me in the back. If this continues I won't be able to keep my car. It is bad enough," he said, bitterly, "that I am confined to London in the winter. I *always* went to the South of France, the West Indies—or, at *least*, to Torquay. Next winter I shall not only shiver and cough in the damp, but I won't even be able to drive away for a week end. I'll have to go by train or bus—if you are good enough to leave me my fare. . . . You aren't giving up *your* car, are you?" he asked.

J. B. leaned his well-tailored elbows on the desk, bent forward. "Confidentially, old man, it's my wife's money that pays for it." Stirrup asked if it weren't true that Mrs. Boatwright's income was derived in large part from her stock in the publishing firm. J. B.'s face went stiff. "Let's leave Mrs. Boatwright out of this, shall we?" he proposed.

"But—"

"Why don't you mix yourself a drink? Sobriety always makes you surly."

Stirrup said he supposed he might as well. "It's my books that are paying for your booze," he observed gloomily.

"Look here—" The publisher flung out his plump hand. "You seem to think this is a special plot to defraud our writers, don't you?" Rodney shrugged. "Oh, my dear fellow!" Boatwright's voice was pained, pleading. "Do let me explain it to you. It is true that Rodney Stirrup, whom I have known since the days when he was still Ebenezer Quimby—" the writer shuddered—"is one of the world's top-ranking writers of the classical detection story. But what good's it do a man to be one of the world's top-ranking designers of carriage whips if no one is buying carriages? Have you *seen* the paperbacks coming out these days? Sex and slaughter." He tittered.

Stirrup angrily put down his drink. He suspected, strongly, that the bottle he'd poured it from was not the one proffered to better-selling writers. "I can show you—you should have read them yourself, dammit—my latest reviews."

Jeremy Boatwright shrugged away the latest reviews. "The reviewer gets his copies free; *our* only concern is with copies *sold*. Now, in the past, old man—" he made a church roof of his well-manicured fingers—"your books sold chiefly, and sold admittedly very well, to the American circulating libraries. Now, alas, the libraries are dying. Hundreds of them—thousands—are already dead. Dreadful pit-y. The people who used to take your books out now stay home and watch television instead. Eh?" He glanced, none too subtly, at his watch.

"Then why don't you sell more of my things to television? Eh?"

Boatwright said, Oh, but they *tried*. "Sometimes we succeed. But in order to equalize our losses, we—Boatwright Brothers—simply have to take a larger slice of your television and other secondary earnings. It's as simple as that."

Stirrup suggested that there was a simpler way: that Boatwright Brothers move to cheaper quarters, cut down on their plushy overhead and pass the savings on to their writers. J. B. smiled indulgently. "Oh, my dear fellow, how I wish we could. You've no idea how this place *bores* me—to say nothing of what dining out does to my poor liver. But we're not so lucky as you. A writer can pig it if he wants to, but we publishers, well, we simply are obliged to maintain the façade."

And, with a sigh, he changed the subject; began to explain to Stirrup why it was difficult nowadays to sell his writings. "You hit upon a good formula. A *very* good formula. But it's outmoded now. Almost all your stories begin the same way: a traveler's car breaks down on a lonely road across the moors, about dusk. Just over the hill is a large mansion, to which he is directed by a passing rustic. Correct? Well, large mansions are out of date. No one can afford them. The rustics are all home watching television and reading their newspapers. And another thing: your books have too many butlers in them, and too many noblemen. In actuality, butlers are dying off. (Mine died not long ago and we're having no luck in finding a replacement; they've all gone into the insurance business.) Things have *changed*, dear boy, and your books have failed to change with them. In effect, you are writing ghost stories." He smiled moistly. "Must you go quite so soon?" he asked, as Stirrup continued to sit.

Stirrup put down the empty glass and began to draw on his gloves. "Yes—unless you are planning to invite me to luncheon."

Boatwright said, "I'd love to. Unfortunately I have a prior engagement with Marie-Noëmi Valerien and her mother. You know, the fifteen-year-old French girl who wrote *Bon Soir, Jeunesse.* I understand she's finished another, and her publishers have treated her simply vilely, so— Where are you off to?"

"Out of town. Some old friends have a place in the country." The publisher inquired if they lived in a large mansion. "As a matter of fact," the writer said, not meeting his eye, "the big house is closed for the time being, and they are living in what used to be the gatekeeper's cottage. Very cosy little place," he added bitterly, remembering Nice, Cannes, Antibes. . . . "They raise poultry."

The publisher, Stirrup reflected, had no need to raise poultry at *his* country place—which was in the same county as his friends' rundown acreage. The Mill Race (a name, unknown to the local Typographical Society, bestowed by its current proprietor in fancied honor of an all but vanished ruin by an all but dried-up stream) was both well furnished and well kept. Once a year Stirrup was invited down for the long week end; no oftener. He felt no twinge at hearing of the demise of Boatwright's butler, Bloor, a large, pear-shaped man with prominent and red-rimmed eyes who had always treated him with insultingly cold politeness—a treatment he repaid by never tipping the man.

Jeremy Boatwright magnanimously walked Stirrup to the door. "Have a *pleasant* week end, old man. Perhaps taste will change; in the meanwhile, though, perhaps *you'll* consider changing. A psychological thriller about a couple who live in the gatekeeper's cottage and raise poultry—eh?"

Rodney Stirrup (he was a withered, short man, with a rufous nose) did think about it, and as a result he lost his way. There are many people who dislike to ask directions, and Stirrup was one of them. He was certain that if he continued to circle around he would find the needed landmarks and then be able to recognize the way from there. It grew late, then later, and he was willing to inquire, but there was no one in sight to ask.

And finally, just at dusk, his engine gave a reproachful cough and ceased to function. He had passed no cars and no people on this lonely side road, but still he couldn't leave his car standing in the middle of it. The car was small and light; steering and pushing, he got it off to the side.

"Damned devil wagon!" he said. Wasn't there a rule about lighting a red lantern and leaving it as a warning? Well, too bad; he had none. He looked around in the failing light, and almost—despite his vexation—almost smiled.

" 'A traveler's car breaks down on a lonely road about dusk. Just over a hill is a large mansion,' " he quoted. "Damn Boatwright anyway. 'Ghost stories!' " He sighed, thrust his hands into his pockets and started walking. Ahead of him was a slight rise in the road. "If only there were someone I could ask directions of," he fretted. "Even 'a passing rustic.' "

A man in a smock came plodding slowly over the rise. In that first moment of relief mingled with surprise, Stirrup wondered if the thought had really preceded the sight. Or if—

"I say, can you tell me where I can find a telephone?" he called out, walking quickly toward the figure, who had halted, open-mouthed, on seeing him. The rustic slowly hook his head.

"Televown?" he repeated, scratching his chin. "Nay, marster, ee wown't voind näo devil's devoice loike that erebäouts."

Stirrup's annoyance at the answer was mixed with surprise at the yokel's costume and dialect. When had he last heard and seen anything like it? Or not heard and seen—read? If anyone had asked him, and found him in an honest mood, he should have said that such speech and garb had been nothing but literary conventions since the Education Acts had done their work. Why, he himself hadn't dared employ it since before the first World War. And the fellow didn't seem that old.

"Surely there must be a house somewhere along here." Reaching the top of the rise, he looked about. "There! That one!" About a quarter mile off, set back in grounds quickly being cloaked in coming night, was a large mansion.

The man in the smock seemed to shiver. "That gurt äouze? Ow, zur, daon't ee troy they'm. Ghowsties and bowgles. . . ." His voice died away into a mumble, and when Stirrup turned to him again, he was gone. Some village idiot, perhaps, unschooled because unschoolable. Well, it didn't matter. The house—

At first glance the house had seemed a mere dark huddle, but now there were lights. He made his way quickly ahead. A footman answered his knock. Self-consciously, Stirrup spoke the words he had so often written. "I'm afraid my car has broken down. May I use your telephone?" The footman asked—of course—if he might take his hat and coat. Feeling very odd, Stirrup let him. Then another man appeared. He was stout and tall and silver-haired.

"Had a breakdown? Too bad." Voices sounded and glasses clinked in the room he had left. It was warm. "My name is Blenkinsop," he said.

"Mine is Stirrup—Rodney Stirrup." Would Mr. Blenkinsop recognize— Evidently Mr. Blenkinsop did. He stared, his eyes wide.

"Rod-ney *Stir*rup?" he cried. *"The writer?"* His voice was like thunder.

Another man appeared. He was thin, with small white side whiskers—lamb chop rather than mutton chop. "My dear Blenkinsop, pray modulate your voice," he said. "Richards is telling a capital story. And whom have we here?"

"This gentleman, my dear Arbuthnot," said Blenkinsop in clear and even tones, "is Mr. Rodney Stirrup. The wri-ter. He's come *here!*"

"No!"

"Yes!"

"Oh, ho-ho-ho!" Mr. Arbuthnot laughed.

"Ah, ha-ha-ha!" Mr. Blenkinsop laughed.

Stirrup, first puzzled, grew annoyed. Young men, the kind who wear fuzzy beards and duffle coats, read *avant-garde* publications and live in attics where they entertain amoral young women, might understandably be moved to laugh at a writer of the Classical Detective Story. But there seemed no excuse at all for men older than himself, contemporaries of Hall Caine and Mrs. Belloc Lowndes and other all but forgotten literary figures, to laugh.

The two men stopped and looked at him, then at each other.

"I fear we must seem very boorish to you," Mr. Arbuthnot said. He looked very much like Gladstone, a picture of whom had hung in the home of Malachi Quimby, the Radical cobbler, Stirrup's long dead father. Something of the awe felt for his father had transferred itself to the Grand Old Man; and even now a remnant of it was left for Mr. Arbuthnot. "Pray accept my apologies," Mr. Arbuthnot said.

"Oh, don't mention it."

"The fact is," explained Blenkinsop, "that we are all of us very great followers of your books, Mr. Stirrup. It is the coincidence of meeting our favorite author, via a fortuitous accident, which provoked our untimely risability. Do excuse us."

Stirrup said that it was pleasant to realize he was not forgotten.

"Oh, not here," said Arbuthnot. "Never. Pray come and meet our friends."

"Do," urged Blenkinsop, leading the way. "Oh, no, indeed, we've not forgotten you. We have a little celebration tonight. We often do. . . . Right through this door, Mr. Stirrup."

The room to which they led him contained perhaps a dozen men, all distinguished in mien, all well on in years. They looked up as Stirrup entered. Glasses were in their hands, and cigars. Several of them were still chuckling, presumably at the "capital" story told by Richards, whichever one he was. A tall and heavy man, with a nose like the Duke of Wellington's, sipped from his glass and smacked his lips.

"Excellent, my dear Richards," he said.

"I thought you'd like it, Peebles," Richards said. He was a red-faced, husky-voiced, many-chinned man. "Whom have we here, Arbuthnot, Blenkinsop?"

Arbuthnot smiled on the right side of his face. Blenkinsop rubbed his hands. "This gentleman has had the ill chance to suffer a breakdown of his motorcar. I am sure—quite sure—that we shall endeavor to welcome him in a fitting manner. He is no ordinary guest. He is a well-known author."

There was a stir of interest. "He writes thrillers." Another stir. "He is none other than—" a dramatic pause—*"Mr. Rodney Stirrup!"*

The reaction was immense.

Three men jumped to their feet, one dropped a lit cigar, one snapped the stem of his wine glass, another crashed his fist into his palm.

"I told Mr. Stirrup—" Blenkinsop lifted his voice; the hum subsided—"that few writers, if any, have received the attention which we have given to the works through which his name became famous. We followed his tales of crime and detection very carefully here, I told him."

Peebles said, "You told him no more than the truth, Mr. Blenkinsop. Do us the honor, sir, of taking a glass of wine. This is a great occasion, indeed, Mr. Stirrup." He poured, proferred.

Stirrup drank. It was a good wine. He said so. The company smiled.

"We have kept a good cellar here, Mr. Stirrup," said Peebles. "It has been well attended to." Stirrup said that they must have a good butler, then. A good butler was hard to find, he said. Between the men there passed a look, a sort of spark. Mr. Peebles carefully put down his glass. It was empty. "How curious you should mention butlers," he said.

Stirrup said that it was not so curious, that he was, in a

way, very fond of butlers, that he had put them to good use in his books. Then he turned, surprised. A noise very like a growl had come from a corner of the room where stood a little man with a red face and bristly white hair.

"Ye-e-es," said Mr. Peebles, in an odd tone of voice. "It is generally conceded, is it not, that you, Mr. Stirrup, were the very first man to employ a butler as the one who stands revealed, at story's end, as the murderer? That it is you who coined the phrase which so rapidly became a household word wherever the English tongue is spoken? I refer, of course, to: *'The butler did it.'*?"

Rather proudly, rather fondly, Stirrup nodded. "You are [illegible]."

"And in novel after novel, though the victims varied and the criminal methods changed, the murderer was almost invariably—a butler. Until finally you were paid the supreme compliment one writer can pay another—that of imitation. A line of thrillers long enough to reach from here to London—to say nothing of short stories, stage plays, music hall acts, movie and television dramas—each with a murderous butler, poured forth upon the world, Mr. Stirrup—beginning, if I am not mistaken, with Padraic, the butler of Ballydooly House, in *Murder By The Bogs.*"

Stirrup was pleased. "Ah, do you remember Padraic? Dear me. Yes, that was my very first detective novel. Couldn't do it today, of course. Irish butlers are dreadfully passé, obsolete. De Valera and Irish Land Reform have extinguished the species, so to speak."

The red-faced little man dashed from his corner, seized a poker, and brandished it in Stirrup's face. "The truth is not in ye!" he shouted. "Ye lie, ye scribbling Sassenach!" Stirrup could not have said with any degree of accuracy if the brogue was that of Ulster, or Munster, or Leinster, or Connaught—the four provinces of Northern Ireland—but he recognized as being of sound British workmanship the heavy iron in the speaker's hand.

In a rather quavering tone, Stirrup demanded, "What is the meaning of this?"

"Allow me to introduce you," Peebles said, "to O'Donnell, for fifty years butler to Count Daniel Donavan of Castle Donavan. O'Donnell, put that away."

Still growling, O'Donnell obeyed. Stirrup, regaining his aplomb, said: *"Count?* Surely not. The peerage of Ireland, like other British peerages, contains countesses, but no counts. The husband of a countess is an earl."

"The count's toitle, sor," said O'Donnell, looking at him

with an eye as cold and gray as Galway Bay in winter, "is a Papal toitle. Oi trust ye've no objections?"

Stirrup hastily said he had none, then retreated to the other side of a table. The man whose wine glass had snapped in his hand finished wiping port from his fingers with a monogrammed handkerchief, then spoke in mellowed, measured tones.

"We must, of course," he said, "make due allowances for Celtic—I do not say, West British—exuberance; but the matter now before us is too serious to permit any element of disorder to enter." There was a general murmur of agreement. "Gentlemen, I move that the doors be locked. Those in favor will signify by saying "Aye." The ayes have it."

He locked the doors and pocketed the key. "Thank you, Mr. Piggot," said Peebles.

"Mr. Arbuthnot," Stirrup said, loudly, "since I am here in response to your invitation, it is from you that I must demand an explanation for these actions."

Arbuthnot smiled his slant smile again. Peebles said, "All in good time. By the way," he inquired, "I trust you have no objections if I refer to you henceforth as the Accused? Protocol, you know, protocol."

Stirrup said that he objected very much. "Most vehemently. Of what am I accused?" he asked plaintively.

Peebles flung out his arm and pointed at him. "You are accused, sir," he cried, "of having for over thirty years pursued an infamous campaign of literary slander designed to bring into contempt and disrepute a profession the most ancient and honorable, dating back to Biblical days and specifically mentioned—I refer to Pharoah's chief butler—in the Book of Deuteronomy."

Knuckles were rapped on tables and the room rang with murmurs of, "Hear, hear!" and, "Oh, well said, sir!"

"Pardon me, Mr. Peebles," said Blenkinsop. "The Book of Genesis."

"Genesis? H'm, dear me, yes. You are correct. Thank you."

"Not at all, not at all. Deuteronomy is very much like Genesis."

Stirrup interrupted this feast of love. "I insist upon being informed what all this has to do with you, or with any of you except O'Donnell."

Peebles peered at him with narrowed, heavy-lidded eyes. "Are you under the impression, Mr.—is Accused under the impression that our esteemed colleague, Mr. Phelim O'Donnell, is the only butler here?"

Stirrup licked dry lips with a dry tongue. "Why, ah, yes,"

he stammered. "Isn't he? Is there another?" A growl went round the circle, which drew in closer.

"No, sir, he is *not. I* was a butler. *We were all of us butlers!*"

A hoarse scream broke from Stirrup's mouth. He lunged for the open windows, but was tripped up by the watchful Piggot.

Peebles frowned. "Mr. Blenkinsop," he said, "will you be good enough to close the windows? Thank you. I must now warn the Accused against any further such outbursts. Yes, Accused, we were all of us, every one of us, members of that proud profession which you were the first to touch with the dusty brush of scorn. Now you must prepare to pay. Somehow, Mr. Stirrup, you have pushed aside what my former lady—the justly-famed Mme. Victoria Algernonovna Grabledsky, the theosophical authoress—used to call 'The Veil of Isis.' This room wherein you now stand is none other than the Great Pantry of the Butlers' Valhalla. Hence—"

"May it please the court," said Piggot, interrupting. "We find the Accused guilty as charged, and move to proceed with sentencing."

"Help!" Stirrup cried, struggling in O'Donnell's iron grasp. *"He-e-e-l-l-p!"*

Peebles said that would do him no good, that there was no one to help him. Then he looked around the room, rather helplessly. "Dear me," he said, a petulant note in his voice; "whatever shall I use for a black cap while I pronounce sentence?"

A silence fell, broken by Richards. "In what manner shall sentence be carried out?" he asked.

Piggot, his face bright, spoke up. "I must confess, Mr. Peebles, to a fondness for the sashweight attached by a thin steel wire to the works of a grandfather's clock," said Piggot; "as utilized (in the Accused's novel of detection, *Murder In The Fens*) by Murgatroyd, the butler at Fen House—who was, of course, really Sir Ethelred's scapegrace cousin, Percy, disguised by a wig and false paunch. I recall that when I was in the service of Lord Alfred Strathmorgan, his lordship read that meretricious work and thereafter was wont to prod me quite painfully in my abdominal region, and to inquire, with what I considered a misplaced jocularity, *if my paunch were real!* Yes, I favor the sashweight and the thin steel wire."

Peebles nodded, judiciously. "Your suggestion, Mr. Piggot, while by no means devoid of merit, has a—shall I say—a certain degree of violence, which I should regret having to utilize so long as an alternative—"

"I would like to ask the opinion of the gentlemen here assembled," said Blenkinsop, "as to what they would think of a swift-acting, exotic Indonesian poison which, being of vegetative origin, leaves no trace; to be introduced via a hollowed corkscrew into a bottle of Mouton Rothschild '12? Needless to say, I refer to the Accused's trashy novel *The Vintage Vengeance.* In that book the profligate Sir Athelny met his end at the hands of the butler, Bludsoe, whose old father's long-established wine and spirits business was ruined when the avaricious Sir Athelny cornered the world's supply of corks—thus occasioning the elder Bludsoe's death by apoplexy. The late Clemantina, Dowager Duchess of Sodor and Skye, who was quite fond of her glass of wine, used frequently to tease me by inquiring if I had opened her bottle with a corkscrew of similar design and purpose; and I am not loath to confess that this habit of Her Grace's annoyed me exceedingly."

"The court can well sympathize with you in that, Mr. Blenkinsop." The Great Pantry hummed with a murmur of accord.

Blenkinsop swallowed his chagrin at this memory, nodded his thanks for the court's sympathy, and then said smoothly, "Of course we could not *force* the Accused to drink without rather a messy scene, but I have hopes he would feel enough sense of *noblesse oblige* to quaff the fatal beverage Socraticlike, so to speak."

Stirrup wiped his mouth with his free hand. "While I should be delighted, under ordinary circumstances," he said, "to drink a bottle of Mouton Rothschild '12 I must inquire if you have on hand such an item as a swift-acting, exotic Indonesian poison, which, being of vegetative origin, leaves no trace? Frankly, I have neglected to bring mine."

A mutter of disappointment was followed by a further consultation of the assembled butlers, but no sooner had they begun when a shot rang out, there was a shattering of glass, and O'Donnell fell forward. Richards turned him over; there was a bullet hole in the exact center of his forehead. Everyone's eyes left Stirrup; his captor's grip perceptably loosened. Stirrup broke away, snatched up the poker, smashed the window and, jumping forward onto the terrace, ran for his life.

He reached the road just in time to see the headlights of an automobile moving away. *"Help!"* he shouted. *"Help! Help!"*

The car went into reverse, came back to him. Two men emerged.

"Oh, a stranger," said the driver. He was a man with long gray hair, clad neatly, if unconventionally, in golf knickers, deerstalking cap, and smoking jacket.

"The most fantastic thing—" Stirrup gasped. "My life was threatened by the inhabitants of that house back there!"

The other man cried, "Ah, the scoundrels!" He wore a greasy regimental dinner jacket and a soft, squashed hat; he shook a clenched fist toward the house and slashed the air with his cane. Deep-set eyes blazed in a gaunt face. Then, abruptly, his expression changed to an ingratiating smile. "It is at a time like this, sir," he said to Stirrup, "that I am sure you must ask yourself, 'Are my loved ones adequately protected in case of mishap, misadventure, or untoward occurrences affecting me?' Now, the Great South British Assurance Company, of which I happen to be an agent, has a policy—"

"Stop that, you fool!" said the driver. "Can't you ever remember all that's over with now?" He took a revolver from his pocket, and Stirrup—suddenly recalling the bullet in O'Donnell's head—trembled. But as the other man's face creased with disappointment and petulance, the driver said to Stirrup, "Pray do not be alarmed, sir. But in the matter of butlers one simply *must* be prepared with strong measures. *They* stop at nothing. Fancy threatening an innocent, inoffensive gentleman such as you! My motto, when confronted with butlers, is: 'St. George and no quarter'!"

A trifle nervously, Stirrup said, "If you could drive me to the nearest town—"

"All in good season, sir" the man answered, waving his weapon carelessly. "I was once tried for shooting my butler; did you know that? I am not ashamed; in fact, I glory in the deed. It was during the grouse season in Scotland. I'd caught the swine pilfering my cigars. I gave him a fair run before bringing him down, then claimed it was an accident." He chuckled richly. "Jury returned a verdict of Not Proven. You should've seen the face of the Procurator-Fiscal!"

"*I* was never even indicted," the man in the dirty regimentals and crushed hat observed, with no small amount of smugness. "When I discovered that *my* butler had been selling the wine to the local pub, I chased him with hounds through the Great Park. Would have caught him, too, only the cowardly blighter broke his neck falling from a tree which he had climbed in trying to escape. 'Death by misadventure' was all the coroner could say. Hah! But then these damnation taxes obliged me to sell the Great Park, and reduced me to a low insurance broker. *Me!*" He ground his teeth.

Scarcely knowing if he should believe these wild tales, Stirrup said, "You have all my sympathy. Now, my book, *The Vintage Vengeance*—to give you only a single example—brought me in twenty-one hundred pounds clear of taxes the year it was written; whereas last year—"

The driver of the car turned from his revolver. His brows, which were twisted into horny curves of hair at the ends, went up—up—up. "*You* wrote *The Vintage Vengeance? You* are that fellow Rodney Stirrup?"

Stirrup drew himself erect. It was recognition such as this which almost made up for treacherous publishers, ungrateful mistresses, and a declining public. "I am. Did you read it? Did you like it?"

"Read it? We read it twen-ty-sev-en times! We were particularly interested in the character of Sir Athelny Aylemore, the unfortunate victim: an excellently-delineated portrait of a great gentleman. But you will recall that Sir Athelny was a baronet. Now, baronets possess the only hereditary degree of knighthood, and hence should be accorded an infinite degree of respect. And yet we feel your book failed to show a correct amount of respect."

The other man scowled and cut at the air with his cane. "Not at all a correct amount of respect," he said.

"The butlers," Stirrup began, trying to shift the conversation.

Again the driver ground his teeth. "I'm prepared for *them!* See here—a cartridge clip with silver bullets. My gunsmith, Motherthwaite's of Bond Street, wriggled like an eel when I ordered them, and a similar set for shotguns, but in the end he had them made up for me. Lucky for him. Hah!" He snorted, aimed at an imaginary and refractory gunsmith, went *Poom!*, and—with an air wickedly self-pleased—blew imaginary smoke from the muzzle.

Stirrup gave a nervous swallow, then said, with a half-convulsive giggle, "My word, but there's a lot of superstition in this part of the country! That yokel in the smock—"

The driver rubbed the muzzle of his revolver against his smoking jacket. "Yokel in a smock? Why, that's Daft Alfie. He drowned in the mill pond about the time of the Maori War—or was it the Matabele? But they couldn't prove suicide, so he ended up in the churchyard instead of at the crossroads. So Daft Alf's been walking again, has he? Hah!"

His friend came forward, turned his feverishly-bright eyes

on Stirrup. "Now, in *our* case," he said, "there was no doubt at all. Prior to crashing our car into the ferro-concrete abutment, we left in triplicate a note explaining that it was an act of protest against the Welfare State which had, through usurpatous taxation, reduced us to penury."

"And furthermore had made the people so improvident that they no longer even desired to purchase the insurance policies which we were obliged to sell. And we *insisted* upon crossroads burial as a further gesture of defiance. But the wretched authorities said it would be a violation of both the Inhumation and Highways Acts. *So*—"

Stirrup felt the numbness creeping up his legs. "Then you are—then you were—"

The man with the revolver said, "Forgive my boorishness. Yes: I, my dear fellow, was Sir Sholto Shadwell, of Shadwell-upon-Stour; and this was Sir Peregrine de Pall of Pall Mall, Hants., my partner in the insurance agency to which these degenerate times had driven us. We were well known. The venal press often said of us that in our frequent pranks and japes we resembled characters from the novels of Rodney Stirrup more than we did real people. They used to call us—"

"They used to call us 'The Batty Baronets,' " said Sir Peregrine; "though I can't think why!"

Their laughter rang out loud and mirthlessly as Sir Sholto snapped the safety catch off on his revolver and Sir Peregrine slid away the casing from his sword cane.

"It grows so damn tedious back at the Baronets' Valhalla," one of them muttered sulkily, as they closed in.

Rodney Stirrup, suppressing the instinct which rose in every cell of him to flee shrieking down the lonely road across the moors, raised his hand and eyebrows.

"One moment, gentlemen—or should I not rather phrase it, 'Sirs Baronet'?"

"*Hem*. You should, yes." Sir Sholto let his revolver sink a trifle. Sir Peregrine, prodding a turf with the point of the sword, nodded portentously.

Straining very hard, Stirrup managed to produce the lineaments of gratified desire in the form of a thankful smile. "I am *so* glad to have that point cleared up. Burke's Peerage was of no help at all, you know."

"None whatsoever. Certainly not. *Burke's*, pah!" Sir Peregrine spitted the turf. A trifle uncertainly, he asked, "You had some, ah, special reason—"

Never since that frenzied but glorious week at Monte in the year '27, when deadlines of novels from three publishers were pressing upon him, had Rodney Stirrup improvised so rapidly. "A very, very special reason. I *had* intended, in my next novel, due to appear on Boatwright's spring list, to urge the election of a certain number of baronets to the House of Lords, in a manner similar to that of representative Scottish peers. Such a proposal could not fail to be of benefit. ("Certainly not!" said Sir Sholto) But then the question arises, how is such a one to be addressed? 'The honorable member' obviously won't do. ("Won't do at all!" said Sir Peregrine) What, then? You, with that erudition which has always characterized your rank—" the two hereditary knights coughed modestly and fiddled their weapons with a certain measure of embarrassment— "have supplied the answer: 'Sir Baronet.' " Stirrup allowed the smile to vanish, an easy task, and sighed.

"Mphh. I notice your use of the past pluperfect. *'Had* intended.' Eh?"

With a horrible start Stirrup noticed, just beyond the headlights' brightness, the silent approach of a company of men. Temper obviously in no way improved by the hole in his forehead, O'Donnell scowled hideously.

Speaking very rapidly, Stirrup said in a loud voice, "I am not to blame. The reading public little realize the small extent to which writers are their own masters. My own attitude in regard to baronets and, ah, butlers, was of no importance at all. *It was my publisher!* He laughs at butlers. Despises baronets. I give you my word. Indeed, I would freely admit how richly I deserve the punishment an ignoble government has failed to mete out to me for the slanders I have written—but I really could not help it. I was bound hand and foot by contracts. How many times have I stood there with tears in my eyes. 'Another bad butler,' demanded Boatwright. 'Another silly baronet,' Boatwright insisted. What could I do?"

There was a long silence. Then Peebles stepped forward. "It was very wrong of you, sir," he said. "But your weakness is not altogether beyond exculpation."

"Not altogether, no," conceded Sir Sholto, twisting a lock of his long, gray hair. "The second Sir Sholto, outraged by the filthy treatment accorded the proferred manuscript of his experiences in the Peninsular Wars, was in the habit of toasting Napoleon for having once shot a publisher."

"And quite properly, Sir Sholto," said Peebles. "*And* quite rightly."

"Never would've been allowed if the Duke of Cumberland hadn't been cozened out of the crown by Salic Law," said Sir Peregrine, moodily.

Peebles stiffened. "While it is true that a mere valet has not the status of a butler, and equally true that His Royal Highness (later King Ernest of Hanover) was absolved of guilt for having caused the death of his personal gentleman—"

"Who was a foreigner anyway," Stirrup put in; "taking bread from the mouths of honest British men, and doubtless richly deserved his fate. . . ."

Butlers and baronets, once the matter was put in this light, nodded judiciously.

"Therefore," said Peebles, "I propose a joint convocation of both Houses, as it were, to deal with the case of the Infamous Publisher Boatwright."

"Bugger the bastard with a rusty sword, you mean? And then splatter his tripes with a silver bullet or two?"

Peebles said that that was the precise tenor of his meaning, and he much admired Sir Sholto's vigorous way of phrasing it.

"Mr. Boatwright is at his country place not far from here at this very moment," Rodney Stirrup quickly pointed out. "The Mill Race, Little Chitterlings, near Guilford." He held his breath.

Then, *"Fiat justicia!"* exclaimed Peebles.

And, "St. George, no quarter, and perish publishers!" cried the baronets.

There was a diffident cough, and a large, pear-shaped man with prominent and red-rimmed eyes stepped forward. He looked at Stirrup and Stirrup felt his hair follicles retreat.

"If I may take the liberty, gentlemen," he said, with an air both diffident and determined.

"Hullo, hullo, what's this?" Peebles queried. "A newcomer to our ranks. Pray, silence, gentlemen: a maiden speech."

"It is not without misgivings that I feel obliged to pause *en route* to the Butlers' Valhalla and raise a rather unpleasant matter," said the newcomer. "I am Bloor, late butler to Jeremy Boatwright. Not being conversant with the latter's business affairs, I can neither confirm nor deny Mr. Stirrup's charges. However, I feel it my duty to point out that while Mr. Stirrup was for many years an annual week end guest at The Mill Race (Little Chitterlings, near Guilford), *he invariably failed to tip the butler on taking his departure!"*

There was a chorus of sharp, hissing, indrawn breaths. Lips were curled, eyebrows raised.

"Not the thing, not the thing at all," said Sir Peregrine. "Shoot butlers, yes, certainly. But—fail to tip them on leaving? Not done, simply not done."

"A loathsome offense," said Arbuthnot.

"Despicable," Peebles declared.

Stirrup, trembling, cried, "It was the fault of my publisher in not allowing me a proper share of royalties." But this was ill received.

"Won't do, won't do at all." Sir Sholto shook his head. "Can't scrape out of it that way a second time. If one's income obliges one to dine on fish and chips in a garret, then *dine* on fish and chips in a garret—dressing for dinner first, I need hardly add. But unless one is prepared to tip the butler, one simply does not accept week end invitations. By gad," he said furiously, "a chap who would do that would shoot foxes!"

"Afoot," said Sir Peregrine.

Bloor said it was not that he wished to be vindictive. It was purely out of duty to his profession that he now made public the offense which had rankled—nay, festered—so long in his bosom.

"I see nothing else for it," said Peebles, heavily, "but that Mr. Rodney Stirrup must occupy the lesser guest room at Butlers' Valhalla until his unspeakable dereliction be atoned for."

("Man's a rank outsider," huffed Sir Sholto. "And to think I was about to ask him to shoot with us when the were grouse season starts!")

The lesser guest room! In a sudden flash of dim, but all-sufficient, light, Stirrup saw what his fate must be. Henceforth his life was one long week end. His room would be the one farthest from the bath, his mattress irrevocably lumpy. The shaving water would always be cold, the breakfast invariably already eaten no matter how early he arose. His portion at meals would be the gristle; his wine (chocked with leas), the worst of the off-vintage years. The cigar box was forever to be empty, and the whisky locked away . . .

His spirits broke. He quailed.

For a brief moment he sought comfort in the fate awaiting Boatwright. Then despair closed in again, and the most dreadful thought occurred to him. Sir Sholto Shadwell's silver bullets: ghosts, werewolves (and were grouse) vampires, ghouls—yes. But would they work, he wondered, dispairingly, *could* they really work, on a creature infinitely more evil and ungodly? Was there anything of any nature in any world at all which could kill a publisher?

DAGON

Then the Lords of the Philistines gathered together to rejoice before Dagon their god, and behold, the image of Dagon was fallen upon its face to the ground, with both his face and his hands broken off, and only the fishy part of Dagon was left to him. . . .

THE OLD CHINAMAN, HALF MAGICIAN, HALF BEGGAR, WHO made the bowl of goldfish vanish and appear again, this old man made me think of the Aztecs and the wheel. Or gunpowder. Gunpowder appeared in Western Europe and Western Europe conquered the world with it. Gunpowder had long ago been known in China and the Chinese made firecrackers with it. (They have since learned better.) When I was free, I heard men say more than once that the American Indians did not know the use of the wheel until Europeans introduced it. But I have seen a toy, pre-conquest, fashioned from clay, which showed that the Aztecs knew the use of the wheel. They made toys of it. Firecrackers. Vanishing goldfish.

Noise.

Light and darkness.

The bright lotos blossoms in the dark mire. Lotos. Plural, lotoi? loti? That is a coincidence. On October 12, 1900, Pierre Loti left at Taku the French naval vessel which had brought him to China and proceeded to Peking. Part of the city was still smoking, Boxers and their victims were still lying in the ruins. On October 12, 1945, *I* left the American naval vessel which had brought me and my fellow officers to China, and proceeded to Peking—Peiping, as they called it then. I was not alone; the whole regiment came. The people turned out and hailed and glorified us. China, our friend and partner in the late great struggle. The traffic in women, narcotics, stolen goods, female children? Merely the nation's peculiar institutions. Great is China, for there I was made manifest. Peking, or Peiping, is a very old establishment and is always being captured by somebody or other. The Tatars called it Khan-baluc, or king city: here are more coincidences: that is the same translation as Tsargrad, the Russian name for Constantinople. It is about 500 years that this outer city was taken by the Turks. Istanbul they call it now; the Jews called it Koshta and the Norse called it Micklegarth, the Great City. There is something inescapably droll about the word *Micklegarth.*

Old, old, old . . . crumbling temples, closed-off palaces, abandoned *yamens,* broken walls; places where the gilding and paint had worn off and the tiles had been stripped away and the tiny glass panes hung loosely in the frames—if they hung there at all—and strips of paper fluttered raggedly and the steps and doorsills were worn and slippery and heaps of rubble lay here and there, often in the middle of the alley doing service as a street. Mud-colored walls with plaster crumbling off them reached a few feet over a man's head and lined these alleys so that if a gate were closed all that could be seen was the rooftop of a one-story building or the upper lineage of a tree. If a gate were open a tall screen directly in front of it blocked the view, except for tiny glimpses of flatstone-paved courtyards and plants in huge glazed pots. Rich and poor and in between and shabby genteel lived side by side. There was no way of knowing if the old man in dun-colored rags who squatted by a piece of matting spread with tiny paper squares holding tinier heaps of tea or groups of four peanuts or ten watermelon seeds was as poor as he and his trade seemed, or had heaps of silver taels buried underneath the fourth tile from the corner near the stove. Things were seldom what they seemed. People feared to tempt powers spiritual or temporal or illegal by displays of well being, and the brick screens in front of (or behind, depending on whether one were coming in or going out) the doors blocked both the gaze of the curious and the path of demons. Demons can travel only in straight lines; it is the sons of men whose ways are devious.

Through these backways and byways I used to roam each day. I had certain hopes and expectations, based on romantic tales read in adolescence, and was determined that the Cathayans should not disappoint me. When these alleys led into commercial streets, as they did sooner or later, I sought what I sought there as well. It is not too difficult to gain a command of spoken Mandarin, which is the dialect of Peking. The throaty sound which distinguishes, for example, between *lee-dza,* peaches, and *lee'dza,* chestnuts, I soon mastered. The more southerly dialects have eleven or nineteen or some such fantastic number of inflections, but Pekingese has only four. Moreover, in the south it is hot and steamy and the women have flat noses.

In one of my wanderings I came to the ponds where the carp had been raised for the imperial table in days gone by. Strange it was to realize that some of the great fish slowly passing up and down among the lily pads must have been fed from the bejeweled hands of Old Buddha herself—and that others, in all likelihood (huge they were, and vast), not only outdated the Dowager but may well have seen—like some strange, billowing shadow above the water sky—Ch'ien Lung the Great, he who deigned to "accept tribute" from Catherine of Russia, scattering rice cake like manna.

I mused upon the mystery of fish, their strange and mindless beauty, how—innocently evil—they prey upon each other, devouring the weaker and smaller without rage or shout or change of countenance. There, in the realm of water, which is also earth and air to them, the great fish passed up and down, growing old without aging and attaining eternal growth without the softness of obesity. It was a world without morality, a world without choices, of eating and spawning and growing great. I envied the great fish and (in other, smaller ponds) the lesser fish, darting and flashing and sparkling gold.

They speak of "the beast in man," and of "the law of the jungle." Might they not (so I reflected, strolling underneath a sky of clouds as blue and as white as the tiles and marble of the Altar of Heaven), might they not better speak of "the fish in man"? And of "the law of the sea"? The sea, from which they say we came?

Sometimes, but only out of sociability, I accompanied the other officers to the singsong houses. A man is a fool who cannot accommodate himself to his fellows enough to avoid discomfort. But my own tastes did not run to spilled beer and puddles of inferior tea and drink-thickened voices telling tales of prowess. Nor to grinning lackeys in dirty robes or short sessions in rabbit-warren rooms with bodies which moved and made sounds and asked for money but showed no other signs of sentient life. I did not enjoy, afterward, the inevitable hoot and clamor for hot water which passed down the chain of command and echoed over the omnipresent rattle of noise, shooway . . . ooway . . . way . . . ayyyyyyeeeee!

Once, but once only, we visited the last of the imperial barber eunuchs, who had attended to the toilet of the Dowager's unfortunate nephew. A tall old man, this castrate, living alone with his poverty, he did for us what he would for any others who came with a few coins and a monstrous curiosity.

I mingled, also, officially and otherwise, with the European colony, none of whom had seen Europe for years, many of whom had been born in China. Such jolly Germans! Such cultured Italians! Such pleasant-spoken, *çi-devant* Vichy Frenchmen! How well dressed and well kept their women were, how anxious, even eager, to please, to prove their devotion to the now victorious cause—and to the young and potent and reasonably personable officers who represent it.

After many an afternoon so well spent I would arise and take a rickshaw to one of the city gates to be there at the sunset closing, and would observe how, when half the massy portal was swung shut, the traffic would increase and thicken and the sound of cries come from far down the road which led outside the city and a swollen stream pour and rush faster and faster—men and women on foot and clutching bundles, and carriers with sedan chairs, and families leading heavy-laden oxcarts and horses, children with hairlike manes, trotting women swollen in pregnancy, old women staggering on tiny, bound feet, infants clinging to their bent backs. Only the caravans did not increase their pace at this time. Slow, severe, and solemn, wooly, double-humped, padfooted, blunt, their long necks shaking strings of huge blue beads and bronze bells crudely cast at some distant forge in the Gobi or at the shore of Lop Nor, the camels came. By their sides were skull-capped Turkomen, or Buryat Mongols with their hair in thick queues.

My eyes scanned every face and every form in all this, but I did not find what I looked for.

Then I would go and eat, while the gates swung shut and the loungers dispersed, murmuring and muttering of the *Bah Loo,* the said-to-be-approaching-slowly-but-steadily-and-as-yet-undefeated-*Bah Loo,* the Eighth Route, Communist Army; and the air grew dark and cold.

Once I was called to attend at the levee of a publisher of three great magazines. He landed at the airfield at ten in the morning and was conveyed at once to the Grand Hotel des Wagon-Lits, where he received in audience the foreign diplomatic corps, the mayor and provincial governor, the Nationalist and American generals, the press, and such minorlings as were thought to merit the honor. He and they then dined and afterward must have talked for all of two hours. After that he was conveyed to the airport and flew back to the States, where he then spoke with his usual authority of the problems facing China, and published these words in all three of his great magazines. Afterward I was free to go about my usual tasks.

That afternoon I chose to visit some of the temples—not the well-frequented ones such as those of Heaven, Agriculture, Confucius, and the Lamas, but the ones not on the tourist lists, not remarkable for historical monuments, not preserved (in a manner of speaking) by any of the governments which had held Peking since the days of "the great" Dr. Sun. In these places the progress of decay had gone on absolutely unchecked and the monks had long ago sold everything they could and the last fleck of paint had peeled from the idols. Here the clergy earned corn meal (rice in North China was a delicacy, not a staple) by renting out the courtyards for monthly fairs and charging stud fees for the services of the Pekingese dogs. Worshipers were few and elderly. Such, I imagine, must have been the temples in the last days of Rome, while the Vandal and Goth equivalents of the Eighth Route Army made plans to occupy the city at their leisure.

These ancients were pleased to see me and brought bowls of thin tea and offered to sell me dog-eared copies of pornographic works, poorly illustrated, which I declined; but left them some dirty notes of what was grandly called the Federal Reserve Bank of North China. What, I wondered, would these withered priests do when the barbarians came down at last? What, indeed, but destruction, could be predicted for the whole time-wormed culture of the city, when Alaric and Attila bestirred themselves and broke camp in far-off Yennan?

Later, outside, in the street, there was an altercation between a huge and pockmarked rickshaw "boy" and a Marine. I stepped up to restore order—could not have avoided it, since the crowd had already seen me—and met the Man In Black.

I do not mean a foreign priest.

The coolie was cuffed and sent on his way by the Man In Black, and the Marine told to go elsewhere by me. The Man In Black seemed quite happy at my having come along—the incident could have gotten out of hand—and he stuck to me and walked with me and spoke to me loudly in poor English, but I suffered it because of the Face he would gain by having been seen with me. Of course I knew what he was, and he must have known that I knew. I did not relish the idea of yet another pot of thin tea, but he all but elbowed me into his home.

Where my search ended.

The Civil Police in Peking were nothing, nothing at all. The Japanese Army had not left much for them to do, nor did the Chinese Nationalist Army nor the U.S. Forces, M. & S. P. As for suppressing indigenous crime, why one had heard of the thieves' guilds; their market was held daily in the polo grounds at Hatamen Street in the heart of the city. So the Peking police force had not much of anything to do but direct traffic and cuff recalcitrant rickshaw coolies and collect the pittance which inflation made nothing of.

Black is not a good color for uniforms, nor does it go well with a sallow skin.

She was not sallow.

I drank cup after cup of that vile, unsugared tea, just to see her pour it.

Her nose was not flat.

When he asked her to go and borrow money to buy some cakes, not knowing I could understand, I managed to slip him money beneath the table: he was startled and embarrassed and this was well. After that, the advantage was even more mine.

She caught my glance and the color deepened in her cheeks. She went for the cakes.

He told me his account of woes, how his father (a street mountebank of some sort) had starved himself for years in order to buy him an appointment on the police force and how it had come to nothing at all, salary worth nothing, *cumshaw* little more. How he admired the Americans—which was more than I did myself. Gradually, with many diversions, circumlocutions, and euphemisms, he inquired about the chances of our doing some business.

Of course, I agreed.

She returned.

I stayed long; she lit the peanut-oil lamps and made a small fire in the stove of briquets fashioned from coal dust and, I should judge, by a faint but definite odor—dung.

After that I came often, we made plans, I named sums of money which caused his mouth to open, a sight to sell dentifrice, indeed. Then, when his impatience was become irritating, I told him the whole thing was off. Military vigilance had been redoubled at the warehouses, and so on. I made a convincing story. He almost wept. He had debts, he had borrowed money (on his hopes) to pay them.

No one could have been more sympathetic than I.

I convinced him that I wished only to help him.

Then, over several dinner tables, I told him that I was planning to take a concubine shortly. My schedule, naturally, would leave less time for these pleasant conversations and equally pleasant dinners. The woman was not selected yet, but this should not take long.

Finally, the suggestion came from *him,* as I had hoped it would, and I let him convince me. This was the only amusing part of the conversation.

I suppose he must have convinced *her.*

I paid him well enough.

There was the apartment to furnish, and other expenses, clothes for her and what have you. Expenses. So I was obliged to do some business after all. But not, of course, with *him*. The sulfa deal was dull enough, even at the price I got per tablet, but the thought of having sold the blood plasma as an elixir for aging Chinese vitality (masculine) was droll beyond words.

So my life began, my real life, for which the rest had been mere waiting and anticipation, and I feel the same was true of her. What had she known of living? He had bought her as I had bought her, but my teeth were not decayed, nor did I have to borrow money if I wanted cakes for tea.

In the end he became importunate and it was necessary to take steps to dispense with him. Each state has the sovereign right, indeed, the duty, to protect its own existence; thus, if bishops plot against the Red governments or policemen against the Kuomintang government, the results are inevitable.

He had plotted against *me*.

The curious thing is that she seemed genuinely sorry to hear he'd been shot, and as she seemed more beautiful in sorrow, I encouraged her. When she seemed disinclined to regard this as the right moment for love, I humbled her. In the end she came to accept this, as she came to accept everything I did, as proper, simply because it was I who had done it.

I.

She was a world which I had created, and behold, it was very good.

My fellow officers continued, some of them, their joint excursions to the stews of Ch'ien Men. Others engaged in equally absurd projects, sponsoring impecunious students at the Protestant university, or underwriting the care of orphans at the local convent schools. I even accompanied my immediate superior to tea one afternoon and gravely heard the Anglican bishop discuss the moral regeneration of mankind, after which he told some capital stories which he had read in *Punch* several generations ago. With equal gravity I made a contribution to the old man's worthy cause of the moment.

Afterward she and I went out in my jeep and had the chief lama show us the image of a djinn said to be the superior of rhinoceros horn in the amorous pharmacopea, if one only indulged him in a rather high-priced votive lamp which burned butter. The old Tibetan, in his sales talk, pointed out to us the "Passion Buddha's" four arms, with two of which he held the female figure, while feeding her with the other two; but neither this nor the third thing he was doing interested me as much as his head. It was a bull's head, huge, brutal, insensate, glaring. . . .

If I am to be a god, I will be such a god as this, I thought; part man and part . . . bull? No. But what? Part man and—

I took her home, that she might worship *me*.

Afterward, she burned the brass butter lamps before me, and the sticks of incense.

I believe it was the following day that we saw the old Chinamen. We were dining in a White Russian restaurant, and from the unusual excellence of the food and the way the others looked at me I could sense that awareness of my true Nature and its approaching epiphany was beginning to be felt.

The persimmons of Peking are not like the American persimmons, they are larger and flattened at each end. In order for the flavor to be at its best, the fruits must have begun to rot. The top is removed and cream is put on, heavy cream which has begun to turn sour. This is food fit for a god, and I was the only one present who was eating it. The Russians thought that persimmons were only for the Chinese, and the Chinese did not eat cream. There was an American at the next table, in the guise of an interfering angel, talking about famine relief. The fool did not realize that famine is itself a relief, better even than war, more selective in weeding out the unfit and reducing the surfeit of people from which swarming areas such as China and India are always suffering. I smiled as I heard him, and savored the contrast between the sweet and the sour on my spoon, and I heard her draw in her breath and I looked down. There was the old Chinaman, in his smutty robe and with some object wrapped in grimed cloth next to him as he squatted on the floor. I heard her murmur something to him in Chinese. She greeted him, called him *lau-yay*—old master, or sir—and something else which I knew I knew but could not place. The air was thick with cigarette smoke and cheap scent. The fool at the next table threw the old man some money and gestured him to begin.

His appearance was like that of any beggar, a wrinkled face, two or three brown teeth showing when he smiled in that fawning way. He unwrapped his bundle and it was an empty chinaware bowl and two wooden wands. He covered the bowl with cloth again, rapped it with the wands, uncovered it, and there was a goldfish swimming. He covered, he rapped and rapped and whisked away the cloth and the bowl was gone. I darted my foot out to the place where it had been, but there was nothing there.

The American at the next table spread out a newspaper on the floor, the old man rolled his sleeves up his withered, scrannel, pallid-sallow arms; he spread the cloth, struck it with his sticks, and then removed it, showing a much larger bowl, with goldfish, on top of the newspaper. So it had not come from some recess in the floor, nor from his sleeve. I did not like to see anyone else exercising power. I spoke roughly to the old man, and he giggled nervously and gathered his things together. The fools opposite began to protest; I looked at them and their voices died away. I looked at *her*, to see if she would still presume to call him *old master;* but she was my creation and she laughed aloud at him, and this pleased me.

My powers increased. With drops of ink I could kill and I could make alive. The agents of the men of Yennan came to Me at night and I wrote things for them and they left offerings of money on the table.

Infinitely adaptive, I, polymorphous, porphyrogenitive, creating iniquity, transgression, and sin.

But sometimes at night, when they had left and we had gone to bed and I pretended to sleep as others do, sometimes there was a noise of a faint rattling and I saw something in the room turning and flashing, like a flash of gold, and the shadows loomed like the shadow of an old man. And once it came to me—the meaning of the Chinese words she had used once. They meant *father-in-law*, but I could not remember when she had used them, though distantly I knew she had no more husband. I awoke her and made her worship me and I was infinitely godlike.

When was this? Long ago, perhaps. It seems that I do not remember so well as formerly. There is so little to remember of present life. I have withdrawn from the world. I do not really know where I now am. There is a wall of some sort; it extends everywhere I turn, it is white, often I press my lips against it. I have lips. I do not know if I have hands and feet, but I do not need them.

The light, too, has an odd quality here. Sometimes I seem to be in a small place and at other times it seems larger. And in between these times something passes overhead and all goes dark and there is a noise like the beating of heavy staves and then it is as if I am nothing . . . noplace. But then all is as before and there is light once more and I can move freely through the light, up and down; I can turn, and when I turn swiftly I can see a flashing of gold, of something gold, and this pleases and diverts me.

But when I am still I cannot see it at all.

THE MONTAVARDE CAMERA

MR. AZEL'S SHOP WAS SET IN BETWEEN A GLAZIER'S establishment and a woolen draper's; three short steps led down to it. The shopfront was narrow; a stranger hurrying by would not even notice it, for the grimy brick walling of the glazier's was part of a separate building, and extended farther out.

Three short steps down, and there was a little areaway before the door, and it was always clean, somehow. The slattern wind blew bits of straw and paper scraps in circles up and down the street, leaving its discarded playthings scattered all about, but not in the areaway in front of the shop door. Just above the height of a man's eye there was a rod fastened to the inside of the door, and from it descended, in neat folds, a red velveteen curtain. The shop's window, to the door's left, was veiled in the same way. In old-fashioned lettering the gold-leaf figures of the street number stood alone on the glass pane.

There were no slot for letters, no name or sign, nothing displayed on door or window. The shop was a blank, it made no impression on the eye, conveyed no message to brain. If a few of the many people scurrying by noticed it at all, it was only to assume it was empty.

No cats took advantage of this quiet backwater to doze in the sun, although at least two of them always reclined under the projecting window of the draper. On this particular day the pair were jolted out of their calm by the running feet of Mr. Lucius Collins, who was chasing his hat. It was a high-crowned bowler, a neat and altogether proper hat, and as he chased it indignantly Mr. Collins puffed and breathed through his mouth—a small, full, red-lipped mouth, grazed on either side by a pair of well-trimmed, sandy, mutton chop whiskers.

Outrageous! Mr. Collins thought, his stout little legs pumping furiously. *Humiliating!* And no one to be blamed for it, either, not even the Government, or the Boers, or Mrs. Collins, she of the sniffles and rabbity face. *Shameful!* The gold seals on his watchchain jingled and clashed together and beat against the stomach it confined, and the wind carried the hat at a rapid clip along the street.

Just as the wind had passed the draper's, it abruptly

abandoned the object of its game, and the forsaken bowler fell with a thud in front of the next shop. It rolled down the first, the second, and the third step, and leaned wearily against the door.

Mr. Collins trotted awkwardly down the steps and knelt down to seize the hat. His head remained where it was, as did his hands and knees. About a foot of uncurtained glass extended from the lower border of the red velveteen to the wooden doorframe, and through this Mr. Lucius Collins looked. It almost seemed that he gaped.

Inside the shop, looking down at Mr. Collins' round and red face, was a small, slender gentleman, who leaned against a showcase as if he were (the thought flitted through Mr. Collins' mind) posing for his photograph. The mild amusement evident on his thin features brought to Mr. Collins anew the realization that his position was, at best, undignified. He took up his hat, arose, brushed the errant bowler with his sleeve, dusted his knees, and entered the shop. Somewhere in the back a bell tinkled as he did so.

A red rug covered the floor and muffled his footsteps. The place was small, but well furnished, in the solid style more fashionable in past days. Nothing was shabby or worn, yet nothing was new. A gas jet with mantle projected from a paneled wall whose dark wood had the gleam of much polishing, but the burner was not lit, although the shop was rather dark. Several chairs upholstered in leather were set at intervals around the shop. There were no counter, and no shelves, and only the one showcase. *It* was empty, and only a well-brushed Ascot top hat rested on it.

Mr. Collins did not wish the slender little gentleman to receive the impression that he, Lucius, made a practice of squatting down and peering beneath curtained shop windows.

"Are you the proprietor?" he asked. The gentleman, still smiling, said that he was. It was a dry smile, and its owner was a dry-looking person. His was a long nose set in a long face. His chin was cleft.

The gentleman's slender legs were clad in rather baggy trousers, but it was obvious that they were the aftermath of the period when baggy trousers were the fashion, and were not the result of any carelessness in attire. The cloth was of a design halfway between plaid and checkered, and a pair of sharply pointed and very glossy shoes were on his small feet. A gray waistcoat, crossed by a light gold watchchain, a rather short frock coat, and a wing collar with a black cravat completed his dress. No particular period was stamped on his clothes, but one felt that in his prime—whenever that had been—this slender little gentleman had been a dandy, in a dry, smiling sort of way.

From his nose to his chin two deep lines were etched, and there were laughter wrinkles about the corners of his eyes. His hair was brown and rather sparse, cut in the conventional fashion. Its only unusual feature was that the little gentleman had on his forehead, after the manner of the late Lord Beaconsfield, a ringlet of the type commonly known as a "spit curl." And his nicely appointed little shop contained, as far as Mr. Collins could see, absolutely no merchandise at all.

"The wind, you know, it—ah, blew my hat off and carried it away. Dropped it at your door, so to speak."

Mr. Collins spoke awkwardly, aware that the man seemed still to be somewhat amused, and believed that this was due to his own precipitate entry. In order to cover his embarrassment and justify his continued presence inside, he asked in a rush, "What is it exactly that you sell here?" and waved his arm at the unstocked room.

"What is it you wish to buy?" the man asked.

Mr. Collins flushed again, and gaped again, and fumbled about for an answer.

"Why, what I meant was: in what line *are* you? You have nothing displayed whatsoever, you know. Not a thing. How is one to know what sort of stock you have, if you don't put it about where it can be seen?" As he spoke, Mr. Collins felt his self-possession returning, and went on with increased confidence to say: "Now, just for example, my own particular avocation is photography. But if you have nothing displayed to show you sell anything in that line, I daresay I would pass by here every day and never think to stop in."

The proprietor's smile increased slightly, and his eyebrows arched up to his curl.

"But it so happens that I, too, am interested in photography, and although I have no display or sign to beguile you, in you came. I do not care for advertising. It is, I think, vulgar. My equipment is not for your tuppeny-tintype customer, nor will I pander to his tastes."

"Your equipment?" Mr. Collins again surveyed the place. "Where is it?" A most unusual studio—if studio it was—or shop, he thought; but he was impressed by what he considered a commendable attitude on the part of the slender gentlemen—a standard so elevated that he refused to lower it by the most universally accepted customs of commerce.

The proprietor pointed to the most shadowy corner of the shop. There, in the semidarkness between the showcase and the wall, a large camera of archaic design stood upon a tripod. Mr. Collins approached it with interest, and began to examine it in the failing light.

Made out of some unfamiliar type of hardwood, with its lens piece gleaming a richer gold than ordinary brass, the old camera was in every respect a museum piece; yet, despite its age, it seemed to be in good working order. Mr. Collins ran his hand over the smooth surface; as he did so, he felt a rough spot on the back. It was evidently someone's name, he discovered, burned or carved into the wood, but now impossible to read in the thickening dusk. He turned to the proprietor.

"It is rather dark back here."

"Of course. I beg your pardon; I was forgetting. It is something remarkable, isn't it? There is no such workmanship nowadays. Years of effort that took, you know." As he spoke, he lit the jet and turned up the gas. The soft, yellow light of the flame filled the shop, hissing quietly to itself. More and more shops now had electric lights; this one, certainly, never would.

Mr. Collins reverently bowed his head and peered at the writing. In a flourishing old-fashioned script, someone long ago had engraved the name of *Gaston Montavarde.* Mr. Collins looked up in amazement.

"Montavarde's camera? Here?"

"Here, before you. Montavarde worked five years on his experimental models before he made the one you see now. At that time he was still—so the books tell you—the pupil of Daguerre. But to those who knew him, the pupil far excelled the master; just as Daguerre himself had far excelled Niepce. If Montavarde had not died just as he was nearing mastery of the technique he sought, his work would be world famous. As it is, appreciation of Montavarde's style and importance is largely confined to the few—of whom I count myself one. You, sir, I am pleased to note, are one of the others. One of the few others." Here the slender gentleman gave a slight bow. Mr. Collins was extremely flattered, not so much by the bow—all shopkeepers bowed—but by the implied compliment to his knowledge.

In point of fact, he knew very little of Montavarde, his life, or his work. Who does? He was familiar, as are all students of early photography, with Montavarde's study of a street scene in Paris during the 1848 Revolution. *Barricades in the Morning*, which shows a ruined embattlement and the still bodies of its defenders, is perhaps the first war photograph ever taken; it is usually, and wrongly, called a Daguerrotype. Perhaps not more than six or eight, altogether, of

Montavarde's pictures are known to the general public, and all are famous for that peculiar luminous quality that seems to come from some unknown source within the scene. Collins was also aware that several more Montavardes in the possession of collectors of the esoteric and erotic could not be published or displayed. One of the most famous of these is the so-called *La Messe Noire*.

The renegade priest of Lyons, Du Val, who was in the habit of conducting the Black Mass of the Demonolaters, used for some years as his "altar" the naked body of the famous courtesan, La Manchette. It was this scene that Montavarde was reputed to have photographed. Like many popular women of her type, La Manchette might have eventually retired to grow roses and live to a great age, had she not been murdered by one of her numerous lovers. Montavarde's photographs of the guillotine (*The Widow*) before and after the execution, had been banned by the French censor under Louis Napoleon as a matter of public policy.

All this is a digression, of course. These asides are mentioned because they were known to Mr. Lucius Collins, and largely explained his awe and reverence on seeing the—presumably—same camera which had photographed these scenes.

"How did you get this?" he asked, not troubling to suppress or conceal his eagerness.

"For more than thirty years," explained the proprietor, "it was the property of a North American. He came to London, met with financial reverses and pawned his equipment. He did not know, one assumes, that it was *the* Montavarde camera. Nor did he redeem. I had little or no competition at the auction. Later I heard he had gone back to America, or done away with himself, some said; but no matter: the camera was a *bon marché*. I never expected to see it again. I sold it soon after, but the payments were not kept up, and so here it is."

On hearing that the camera could be purchased, Mr. Collins began to treat for its sale (though he knew he could really not afford to buy) and would not take no for an answer. In short, an agreement was drawn up, whereby he was to pay a certain sum down, and something each month for eight months.

"Shall I make out the check in pounds or in guineas?" he asked.

"Guineas, of course. I do not consider myself a tradesman." The slender gentleman smiled and fingered his watch-chain as Mr. Collins drew out his check book.

"What name am I to write, sir? I do not—"

"My name, sir, is Azel. The initials, A. A. Ah, just so. Can you manage the camera by yourself? Then I bid you a good evening, Mr. Collins. You have made a rare acquisition, indeed. Allow me to open the door."

Mr. Collins brought his purchase home in a four-wheeler, and spent the rest of the evening dusting and polishing. Mrs. Collins, a wispy, weedy little figure, who wore her hair in what she imagined was the manner of the Princess of Wales —Mrs. Collins had a cold, as usual. She agreed that the camera *was* in excellent condition, but, with a snuffle, she pointed out that he had spent far too much money on it. In her younger days, as one of the Misses Wilkins, she had done quite a good bit of amateur photography herself, but she had given it up because it cost far too much money.

She repeated her remarks some evenings later when her brother, the Reverend Wycliffe Wilkins, made his weekly call.

"Mind you," said Mr. Collins to his brother-in-law, "I don't know just what process the inventor used in developing his plates, but I did the best I could, and I don't think it's half bad. See here. This is the only thing I've done so far. One of those old Tudor houses in Great Cumberland Street. They say it was one of the old plague houses. Pity it's got to be torn down to make way for that new road. I thought I'd beat the wreckers to it."

"Very neatly done, I'm sure," said his brother-in-law. "I don't know much about photography myself. But evidently you haven't heard about this particular house. No? Happened yesterday. My cook was out marketing, and just as she came up to the corner, the house collapsed in a pile of dust. Shoddy worksmanship somewhere; I mean, the house couldn't have been more than three hundred years old. Of course, there was no one in it, but still, it gave the cook quite a turn. I suppose there's no harm in your having this camera, but, as for me, considering its associations, I wouldn't have it in the house. Naked women, indeed!—saving your presence, Mary."

"Oh, come now," said Mr. Collins. "Montavarde was an artist."

"Many artists have been pious, decent people, Lucius. There can be no compromise between good and evil." Mrs. Collins snuffled her agreement. Mr. Collins pursed his little mouth and said no more until his good humor was restored by the maid's coming in with the tea tray.

"I suppose, then, Wycliffe, you wouldn't think of letting me take your picture."

"Well, I don't know why ever not," Mrs. Collins protested.

"After the amount of money Lucius spent on the camera, we ought to make *some* use out of it, I think. Lucius will take your likeness whenever it's convenient. He has a great deal of free time. Raspberry jam or gooseberry, Wycliffe?"

Mr. Collins photographed his brother-in-law in the vicarage garden—alone, and then with his curate, the Reverend Osias Gomm. Both clerical gentlemen were very active in the temperance movement, and this added a note of irony to the tragic events of the following day. It was the carriage of Stout, the brewer; there was no doubt about that. The horses had shied at a scrap of paper. The witnesses (six of them) had described seeing the two clergymen start across the street, deep in conversation. They described how the carriage came flying around the corner.

"They never knew wot 'it 'em," the witnesses agreed. Mrs. Collins said that was the only thing that comforted her. She said nothing, of course, about the estate (three thousand pounds in six percent bonds), but she did mention the picture.

"How bright it is, Lucius," she said. "Almost shining."

After the funeral she felt free to talk about the financial affairs of her late brother, and until the estate was close to being settled, Mr. Collins had no time for photography. He did keep up the monthly payments on the camera, however, although he found them rather a drain. After all, it had not been *his* income which had just been increased by 180 pounds per annum.

It was almost November before Mrs. Collins would consent to have a fire laid. The inheritance of her brother's share of their patrimony had not changed her habits for what her husband, if no one else, would have considered the better. Although he still transferred the same amount each quarter from his personal account to the household funds, there was less and less to show for it each week. Meat appeared on the table less often, and it was much more likely to be a piece of the neck than a cut off the joint. The tea grew dustier and the pieces of butter shrank in size, and more than once Mr. Collins had asked for another bit of cake at tea and been told (truthfully, as he learned by prowling around the kitchen later at night) that there wasn't another bit of cake in the house. (Perhaps it was his going to sleep on an empty —and hence, nervous, stomach—that caused the odd dreams which began about this time: confused scenes he could never remember, come daylight, and a voice—flat, resonant—repeating over and over, *"The life is in the light . . . the life in the light."*)

He had, of course, protested, and it had, of course, done him no good at all. Mrs. Collins, with a snuffle, spoke of increased prices, the unsteady condition of World Affairs, and the necessity of Setting Something Aside For the Future, because, she said, who knows?

So, at any rate, here it was November, and a nice sea-coal fire in the grate, with Mr. Collins sitting by it in his favorite chair, reading the newspaper (there had formerly been two, but Mrs. Collins had stopped one of them in the interests of domestic economy). There were a number of interesting bits in the paper that evening, and occasionally Mr. Collins would read one of them aloud. Mrs. Collins was unraveling some wool with an eye toward reknitting it.

"Dear me!" said Mr. Collins.

"What is that, Lucius?"

" 'Unusual Pronouncement By the Bishop of Lyons.' " He looked over at his wife. "Shall I read it to you?"

"Do."

His Grace the Bishop of Lyons had found it necessary to warn all the faithful against a most horrible series of crimes that had recently been perpetrated in the City and See of Lyons. It was a sign of the infamy and decadence of the age that not once but six times in the course of the past year, consecrated wafers had been stolen from churches and rectories in the City and See of Lyons. The purpose of these thefts could only indicate one thing, and it behooved all of the faithful, and so forth. There was little doubt (wrote the Paris correspondent of Mr. Collins' newspaper) that the bishop referred to the curious ceremony generally called the Black Mass, which, it would appear, was still being performed in parts of France; and not merely, as might be assumed, among the more uneducated elements of the population.

"Dear me!" said Mr. Collins.

"Ah, those French!" said Mrs. Collins. "Wasn't it Lyons—wasn't that the place that this unpleasant person came from? The camera man?"

"Montavarde?" Mr. Collins looked up in surprise. "Perhaps. I don't know. What makes you think so?"

"Didn't poor Wycliffe say so on that last night he was here?"

"Did he? I don't remember."

"He must have. Else how could I know?"

This was a question which required no answer; but it aroused other questions in Mr. Collins' mind. That night he had the dream again, and he recalled it very clearly on awakening. There was a woman, a foreign woman . . . though how he knew she was foreign, he could not say. It was not her voice, for she never spoke, only gestured: horrid, wanton gestures, too! Nor was it in her clothes, for she wore none. And she had something in her hand, about the size of a florin, curiously marked, and she offered it to him. When he went to take it, she snatched it back, laughing, and thrust it into her red, red mouth. And all the while the voice—inflectionless, echoing—repeated over and again, *"The light is in the life . . . the light is in the life.* It seemed, somehow, a familiar voice.

The next day found him at his bookdealer's, the establishment of little Mr. Pettigew, the well-known antiquary, known among younger and envious members of the trade as "the well-known antiquity." There, under pretense of browsing, Mr. Collins read as much as he could on demonolatry in general, and the Black Mass in particular. It was most interesting, but, as the books all dated from the previous century, there was no mention of either Duval or Montavarde. Mr. Collins tipped his hat to the bookdealer (it was the same bowler) and left the shop.

He bought an *Illustrated London News* at a tobacconist's, got a seat on top of the omnibus, and prepared to enjoy the ride home. It was a bright day despite the time of year, one of the brightest Guy Fawkes' Days that Mr. Collins could remember.

The *Illustrated,* he noted, was showing more and more photographs as time went on, and fewer drawings. Progress, progress, thought Mr. Collins, looking with approval and affection at a picture of the Duke of York and his sons, the little princes, all in Highland costume. Then he turned the page, and saw something which almost caused him to drop the paper. It was a picture of a dreadnought, but it was the style and not the subject that fixed his attention to the page.

"The above photograph," read the caption, "of the ill-fated American battleship, the *U.S.S. Maine,* was taken shortly before it left on its last voyage for Havana. Those familiar with photography will be at once attracted by the peculiar luminosity of the photograph, which is reminiscent of the work of the Frenchman, Montavarde. The *Maine* was built at—" Mr. Collins read no further. He began to think, began to follow a train of thought alien to his mind. Shying away from any wild and outrageous fantasies, Mr. Collins began to enumerate as best he could all the photographs known to him to have been taken by the Montavarde camera.

Barricades in the Morning proved nothing, and neither did

The Widow; no living person appeared in either. On the other hand, consider the matter of La Manchette, the subject of Montavarde's picture *La Messe Noire*; consider the old house in Great Cumberland Street, and the Reverends Wilkins and Gomm. Consider also the battleship *Maine.*

After considering all this, Mr. Collins found himself at his stop. He went directly home, took the camera in his arms, and descended with it to the basement.

Was there some quality in the camera which absorbed the life of its subjects? Some means whereby that life was transmuted into light, a light impressed upon the photograph, leaving the subjects to die?

Mr. Collins took an ax and began to destroy the camera. The wood was intensely hard, and he removed his coat before falling to work again. Try as he might, Mr. Collins could not dent the camera, box, brass or lens. He stopped at last, sweat pouring down his face, and heard his wife's voice calling to him. What*ever* was he doing?

"I'm breaking up a box for kindling wood," he shouted back. And then, even as she warned him not to use too much wood, that the wood had to last them another fortnight, that wood had gone up—even as she chattered away, Mr. Collins had another idea. He carried the camera up to the fire and thrust it in. He heaped on the coals, he threw in kerosene at the cost of his eyebrows, and he plied the bellows.

Half an hour's effort saw the camera not only unconsumed, but unscorched. He finally removed it from the fire in despair, and stood there, hot and disheveled, not knowing what to do. All doubts that he had felt earlier were now removed. Previously he had been uncertain as to the significance of Montavarde's presence with his dreadful camera at the Rites of Lucifer, at the foul ritual conducted by the renegade priest Duval. It was *not* merely as a spectator that the cameraman had attended these blasphemous parodies. The spitting on the crucifix, the receiving of the witch mar, the signing of the compact with his own blood, the ceremonial stabbing of the stolen Host while awaiting the awful moment when the priest or priestess of the unholy sect declared manifest in his or her own body the presence of the Evil One—surely Montavarde had *done* all these things, and not just seen them.

Mr. Collins felt that he needed some air. He put on his hat and coat and went down to the street. The breeze cooled his hot face and calmed his thoughts. Several children came down the street toward him, lighting firecrackers and tossing them into the air.

"Remember, remember, the 5th of November
Was gunpowder, treason, and plot"

the children began to chant as they came up to him. They were wheeling a tatterdemalion old bath chair, and in it was a scarecrow of a Guy Fawkes, clad in old clothes; just as Mr. Collins had done as a boy.

"I see no reason why gunpowder treason
Should ever be forgot"

ended the traditional phrases, and then the outstretched, expectant grimy paws, and a general cry of "Remember the Guy, sir! Remember the Guy!" Mr. Collins distributed some money to the eager group, even though he could see that his wife, who had come down and was now looking out of the first floor window, was shaking her head at him and pursing her lips, pantomiming that he wasn't to give them a farthing. He looked away and glanced at the Guy.

Its torn trousers were of a plaid design, its scuffed shoes were sharply pointed. A greasy gray waistcoat, a ragged sort of frock coat, a drooping and dirty wing collar, and a battered Ascot top hat completed its dress. The costume seemed unpleasantly familiar to Mr. Collins, but he could not quite place it. Just then a gust of wind blew off the old topper and revealed the Guy's head. It was made of one of those carven coconuts that visitors from southern countries sometimes bring back, and its carven features were a horrible parody of the face of the slender gentleman who had sold the camera.

The children went on their way while Mr. Collins remained standing, his mind a maze of strange thoughts, and Mrs. Collins frowned down at him from the window. She seemed to be busy with something; her hands moved. It seemed to him that an age passed as he stood there, hand in pocket, thinking of the long-dead Montavarde. (How did he die? "Untimely" was the word invariably used) who had purchased, at a price unknown and scarcely to be guessed at, unsurpassable skill in building and using his camera. What should one do? One might place the camera in a large sack, or encase it in concrete, and throw it in the Thames.

Or one might keep it hidden in a safe place that one knew of.

He turned to his house and looked up at Mrs. Collins, there at the window. (What *had* she been busied with?) It seemed to him that she had never looked so much like a rabbit before, and it also occurred to him how much he disliked rabbits and always had, since he was a boy. That, after all, was not so very long ago. He was still a comparatively young man. Many attractive women might still find him attractive too.

Should he submit, like some vegetable, while his wife nibbled, nibbled away at him forever? No. The way had been shown him; he had fought, but that sort of victory was plainly not to be his. So be it; he would follow the way which had been open to him since the moment he took the camera. And he would use it again, this time with full knowledge.

He started up the steps, and had just reached the top one when a searing pain stabbed him in the chest, and the sun went out. His hat fell off as he dropped. It rolled down the first, the second, and the third step. Mrs. Collins began to scream. It occurred to him, even in that moment of dark agony, how singularly unconvincing those screams sounded.

For some reason the end did not come at once.

"I'm not completely satisfied with that likeness I took of you just before you were stricken," Mrs. Collins said. "Of course, it *was* the first time I had used a camera since we were married. And the picture, even while you look at it, seems to be growing brighter."

Logically, Mr. Collins thought; for at the same time he was growing weaker. Well, it did not matter.

"Your affairs *are* in order, aren't they, Lucius?" Her eyes, as she gazed at him, were bright, birdlike. A bird, of course, is not human. He made no reply. "Yes, to be sure they are. I made certain. Except for this unpleasant Mr. Azel asking me for money he claims is still owing on the camera. Well, I shan't pay it. I have all I can do to keep myself. But I mean to show him. He can have his old camera back, and much good may it do him. I took my mother's ring and I scratched the nasty lens up completely with the diamond."

Her voice was growing weaker now. "It's a tradition in our family, you know. It's an old diamond, an heirloom; it has been in our family ever so long, and they say that it was once set in a jeweled monstrance that stood upon the high altar at Canterbury before the days of good King Harry.

"*That* will teach that Mr. A. A. Azel a good lesson."

THE WOMAN WHO THOUGHT SHE COULD READ

ABOUT A HUNDRED YEARS AGO A MAN NAMED VANDERHORN built the little house. He built it one and a half stories high, with attached and detached sheds snuggling around it as usual; and he covered it with clapboards cut at his own mill—he had a small sawmill down at the creek, Mr. Vanderhorn did. After that he lived in the little house with his daughter and her husband (being a widower man) and one day he died there. So the daughter and son-in-law, a Mr. Hooten or Wooten or whatever it was, they came into his money which he made out of musket stocks for the Civil War, and they built a big new house next to the old one, only further back from the street. This Mr. Wooten or Hooten or something like that, *he* didn't have any sons, either; and *his* son-in-law turned the sawmill into a buggy factory. Well, you know what happened to *that* business! Finally, a man named Carmichael, who made milk wagons and baggage carts and piewagons, he bought the whole Vandehorn estate. He fixed up the big house and put in apartments, and finally he sold it to my father and went out of business. Moved away somewhere.

I was just a little boy when we moved in. My sister was a lot older. The *old* Vandenhorn house wasn't part of the property any more. A lady named Mrs. Grummick was living there and Mr. Carmichael had sold her all the property the width of her house from the street on back to the next lot which faced the street behind ours. I heard my father say it was one of the narrowest lots in the city, and it was separated from ours by a picket fence. In the front of the old house was an old weeping willow tree and a big lilac bush like a small tree. In back were a truck garden and a few flowerbeds. Mrs. Grummick's house was so near to our property that I could look right into her window, and one day I did, and she was sorting beans.

Mrs. Grummick looked out and smiled at me. She had one of those broad faces with high cheekbones, and when she smiled her little bright black eyes almost disappeared.

"Liddle boy, hello!" she said. I said Hello and went right on staring, and she went right on sorting her beans. On her head was a kerchief (you have to remember that this was before they became fashionable) and there was a tiny gold earring in each plump earlobe. The beans were in two crocks on the table and in a pile in front of her. She was moving them around and sorting them into little groups. There were more crocks on the shelves, and glass jars, and bundles of herbs and strings of onions and peppers and bunches of garlic all hanging around the room. I looked through the room and out the window facing the street and there was a sign in front of the little house, hanging on a sort of one-armed gallows. *Anastasia Grummick, Midwife,* it said.

"What's a midwife?" I asked her.

"Me," she said. And she went on pushing the beans around, lining them up in rows, taking some from one place and putting them in another.

"Have you got any children, Mrs. Grimmick?"

"One. I god one boy. *Big* boy." She laughed.

"Where is he?"

"I think he come home today. I *know* he come home today." Her head bobbed.

"How do you know?"

"I know because I know. He come home and I make a bean soup for him. You want go errand for me?"

"All right." She stood up and pulled a little change purse out of her apron pocket, and counted out some money and handed it to me out of the window.

"Tell butcher Mrs. Grummick want him to cut some meat for a bean soup. He knows. Mr. Schloutz. And you ged iche-cream comb with nickel, for you."

I started to go, but she gave me another nickel. "Ged *two* iche-cream combs. I ead one, too." She laughed. "One, too. One, two, three—Oh, Englisht languish!" Then she went back to the table, put part of the beans back in the crocks, and swept the rest of them into her apron. I got the meat for her and ate my French vanilla and then went off to play.

A few hours later a taxicab stopped in front of the little gray house and a man got out of it. A big fellow. Of course, to a kid, all grown-ups are real big, but he was *very* big—tremendous, he was, across, but not so tall. Mrs. Grummick came to the door.

"Eddie!" she said. And they hugged and kissed, so I decided this was her son, even before he called her "Mom."

"Mom," he said, "do I smell bean soup?"

"Just for you I make it," she said.

He laughed. "You knew I was coming, huh? You been reading them old beans again, Mom?" And they went into the house together.

I went home, thinking. My mother was doing something over the washtub with a ball of bluing. "Mama," I said, "can a person read beans?"

"Did you take your milk of magnesia?" my mother asked. Just as if I hadn't spoken. "Did you?"

I decided to bluff it out. "Uh-huh," I said.

"Oh *no* you didn't. Get me a spoon."

"Well, why do you ask if you ain't going to believe me?"

"Open up," she ordered. "More. Swallow it. Take the rest. All of it. If you could see your face! Suppose it froze and stayed like that? Go and wash the spoon off."

Next morning Eddie was down in the far end of the garden with a hoe. He had his shirt off. Talk about shoulders! Talk about arms! Talk about a chest! My mother was out in front of our house, which made her near Eddie's mother out in back of hers. Of course my mother had to know everybody's business.

"That your son, Mrs. Grummick?"

"My son, yes."

"What does he do for a living?"

"Rachel."

"No, I mean your *son* . . . what does he do. . . ."

"He rachel. All over country. I show you."

She showed us a picture of a man in trunks with a hood over his head. "The Masked Marvel! Wrestling's Greatest Mystery!" The shoulders, arms, and chest—they could only have been Eddie's. There were other pictures of him in bulging poses, with names like, oh, The Slav Slayer, Chief Thunderwing, Young Kehoe, and so on. Every month Eddie Grummick sent his mother another photograph. It was the only kind of letter he sent because she didn't know how to read English. Or any other language, for that matter.

Back in the vegetable patch Eddie started singing a very popular song at that time, called "I Faw Down And Go *Boom!*"

It was a hot summer that year, a long hot summer, and September was just as hot as July. One shimmering, blazing day Mrs. Grummick called my father over. He had his shirt off and was sitting under our tree in his BVD top. We were drinking lemonade.

"When I was a kid," he said, "we used to make lemonade with brown sugar and sell it in the streets. We used to call out

'Brown lemonade
Mixed in the shade
Stirred by an old maid.'

"People used to think that was pretty funny."

Mrs. Grummick called out: "Hoo-hoo! Mister! Hoo-hoo!"

"Guess she wants *me*," my father said. He went across the lawn. "Yes ma'am. . . ." he was saying. "Yes ma'am."

She asked, "You buy coal yed, mister?"

"*Coal?* Why, no-o-o . . . not *yet*. Looks like a pretty mild winter ahead, wouldn't you say?"

She pressed her lips together, closed her eyes and shook her head. "No! Bedder you buy soon coal. Lots coal. Comes very soon bad wedder. Bad!"

My father scratched his head. "Why, you sound pretty certain, Mrs. Grummick, but—uh—"

"I *know*, mister. If I say id, if I tell you, I *know*."

Then I piped up and asked, "Did you read it in the beans, Mrs. Grummick?"

"Hey!" She looked at me, surprised. "How you know, liddle boy?"

My father said, "You mean you can tell a bad winter is coming from the *beans*?"

"Yes true. I know. I read id."

"*Well*, now, that's very interesting. Where I come from, used to be a man—a weather prophet, they called him—*he* used to predict the weather by studying skunk stripes. Said his grandfather'd learned it from the Indians. How wide this year, how wide last year. Never failed. So you use beans?"

So I pushed my oar in and I said, "I guess you don't have the kind of beans that the man gave Jack for the cow and he planted them and they were all different colors. Well, a beanstalk grew way way up and he climbed—"

Father said, "Now don't bother Mrs. Grummick, sonny," but she leaned over the fence and picked me up and set me down on her side of it.

"You, liddle boy, come in house and tell me. You, mister: buy coal."

Mrs. Grummick gave me a glass of milk from the nanny goat who lived in one of the sheds, and a piece of gingerbread, and I told her the story of Jack and the beanstalk. Here's a funny thing—she believed it. I'm sure she did. It wasn't even what the kids call Making Believe, it was just a pure and simple belief. Then she told *me* a story. This happened on the other side, in some backwoods section of Europe where she came from. In this place they used to teach the boys to read, but not the girls. They figured, what did they need it for? So one day there was this little girl, her brothers were all off in school and she was left at home sorting beans. She was supposed to pick out all the bad beans and the worms, and when she thought about it and about everything, she began to cry.

Suddenly the little girl looked up and there was this old woman. She asked the kid how come she was crying. Because all the boys can learn to read, but not me. Is *that* all? the old lady asked.

Don't cry, she said. *I'll* teach you how to read, only not in books, the old lady said. Let the *men* read books, books are new things, people could read before there were books. Books tell you what *was*, but you'll be able to tell you what's *going* to be. And this old lady taught the little girl how to read the beans instead of the books. And I kind of have a notion that Mrs. Grummick said something about how they once used to read *bones*, but maybe it was just her accent and she meant beans. . . .

And you know, it's a funny thing, but, now, if you look at dried beans, you'll notice how each one is maybe a little different shape or maybe the wrinkles are a little different. But I was thinking that, after all, an "A" is an "A" even if it's big or small or twisted or. . . .

But that was the story Mrs. Grummick told me. So it isn't remarkable, if she could believe *that* story, she could easily believe the Jack and the Beanstalk one. But the funny thing was, all that hot weather just vanished one day suddenly, and from October until almost April we had what you might call an ironbound winter. Terrible blizzards one right after another. The rivers were frozen and the canals were frozen and even the railroads weren't running and the roads were blocked more than they were open. And coal? Why, you just couldn't *get* coal. People were freezing to death right and left. But Mrs. Grummick's little house was always warm and it smelled real nice with all those herbs and dried flowers and stuff hanging around in it.

A few years later my sister got married. And after that, in the summertime, she and her husband Jim used to come back and visit with us. Jim and I used to play ball and we had a fine time—they didn't have any children, so they made much of me. I'll always remember those happy summers.

Well, you know, each summer, a few of the churches used to get together and charter a boat and run an excursion. All the young couples used to go, but my sister always made some excuse. See, she was always afraid of the water. This particular summer the same thing happened, but her friends urged her to come. My brother-in-law, he didn't care one way or the other. And then, with all the joking, someone said, Let's ask Mrs. Grummick to read it in the beans for us. It had gotten known, you see. Everybody laughed, and more for the fun of it than anything else, I suppose, they went over and spoke to her. She said that Sister and Jim could come inside, but there wasn't room for anybody else. So we watched through the window.

Mrs. Grummick spread her beans on the table and began to shove them around here and there with her fingers. Some she put to one side and the rest she little by little lined up in rows. Then she took from one row and added to another row and changed some around from one spot to another. And meanwhile, mind you, she was muttering to herself, for all the world like one of these old people who reads by putting his finger on each word and mumbling it. And what was the answer?

"Don't go by the water."

And that was all. Well, like I say, my sister was just looking for any excuse at all, and Jim didn't care. So the day of the excursion they went off on a picnic by car. I'd like to have gone, but I guess they sort of wanted to be by themselves a bit and Jim gave me a quarter and I went to the movies and bought ice-cream and soda.

I came out and the first thing I saw was a boy my own age, by the name of Bill Baumgardner, running down the street crying. His shirt was out and his nose was running and he kept up an awful grinding kind of howl. I called to him but he paid no attention. I still don't know where he was running from or where to and I guess maybe he didn't know either. Because he'd been told, by some old fool who should've known better, that the excursion boat had caught on fire, with his parents on it. The news swept through town and almost everybody with folks on the boat was soon in as bad a state as poor Billy.

First they said everybody was burned or drowned or trampled. Later on it turned out to be not that bad—but it was bad enough.

Oh, my folks were shook up, sure enough, but it's easier to be calm when you know it's not your own flesh and blood. I recall hearing the church clock striking six and my mother saying, "I'll never laugh at Mrs. Grummick again as long as I live." Well, she never did.

Almost everyone who had people on the boat went up the

river to where it had finally been run ashore, or else they waited by the police station for news. There was a deaf lady on our street, I guess her daughter got tired of its being so dull at home and she'd lied to her mother, told her she was going riding in the country with a friend. So when the policeman came and told her—shouted at her they'd pulled out the girl's body, she didn't know what he was talking about. And when she finally understood she began to scream and scream and scream.

The policeman came over toward us and my mother said, "I'd better get over there," and she started out. He was just a young policeman and his face was pale. He held up his hand and shook his head. Mother stopped and he came over. I could hear how hard he was breathing. Then he mentioned Jim's name.

"Oh, no," my mother said, very quickly. "They didn't *go* on the boat." He started to say something and she interrupted him and said, "But I tell you, they didn't *go*" and she looked around, kind of frantically, as if wishing someone would come and send the policeman away.

But no one did. We had to hear him out. It was Sister and Jim, all right. A big truck had gotten out of control ("—but they didn't go on the boat," my mother kept repeating, kind of stupidly. "They had this warning and so—") and smashed into their car. It fell off the road into the canal. The police were called right away and they came and pulled it out ("Oh, *oh!* Then they're all *right!*" my mother cried. *Then* she was willing to understand.) But they weren't all right. They'd been drowned.

So we forgot about the deaf neighbor lady because my mother, poor thing, *she* got hysterical. My father and the policeman helped her inside and after a while she just lay there on the couch, kind of moaning. The door opened and in tiptoed Mrs. Grummick. She had her lower lip tucked in under her teeth and her eyes were wide and she was kind of rocking her head from side to side. In each hand she held a little bottle—smelling salts, maybe, and some kind of cordial. I was glad to see her and I think my father was. I *know* the policeman was, because he blew out his cheeks, nodded very quickly to my father, and went away.

Mother said, in a weak, thin voice: "They didn't go on the boat. They didn't go because they had a warning. That's why—" Then she saw Mrs. Grummick. The color came back to her face and she just leaped off the couch and tried to hit Mrs. Grummick, and she yelled at her in a hoarse voice I'd never heard and called her names—the kind of names I was just beginning to find out what they meant. I was, I think, more shocked and stunned to hear my mother use them than I was at the news that Sister and Jim were dead.

Well, my father threw his arms around her and kept her from reaching Mrs. Grummick and I remember I grabbed hold of one hand and how it tried to get away from me.

"You *knew!*" my mother shouted, struggling, her hair coming loose. "*You* knew! You read it there, you witch! And you didn't tell! You didn't tell! She'd be alive now if she'd gone on the boat. They weren't all killed, on the boat— But you didn't say a *word!*"

Mrs. Grummick's mouth opened and she started to speak. She was so mixed up, I guess, that she spoke in her own language, and my mother screamed at her.

My father turned his head around and said, "You'd better get out."

Mrs. Grummick made a funny kind of noise in her throat. Then she said, "But, Lady—mister—no—I tell you only what I see—I read there, *'Don't go by the water.'* I only can say what I see in front of me, only what I read. Nothing else. Maybe it mean one thing or maybe another. I only can read it. Please, lady—"

But we knew we'd lost them, and it was because of her.

"They ask *me*," Mrs. Grummick said. "They *ask* me to read."

My mother kind of collapsed, sobbing. Father said, "Just get out of here. Just turn around and get out."

I heard a kid's voice saying, high, and kind of trembling, "We don't want you here, you old witch! *We hate you!*"

Well, it was *my* voice. And then her shoulders sagged and she looked for the first time like a real old woman. She turned around and shuffled away. At the door she stopped and half faced us. "I read no more," she said. "I never read more. Better not to know at all." And she went out.

Not long after the funeral we woke up one morning and the little house was empty. We never heard where the Grummicks went and it's only now that I begin to wonder about it and to think of it once again.